"You look like a woman who's just accomplished a miracle."

"Thank you, Ben." Ellie shifted slightly in her seat, disturbing the infant nestled against her neck. The baby frowned in her sleep.

Ben dropped to his haunches so that his face was level with Ellie's. She smiled at the man who had brought her child safely into the world. Who had probably saved *her* life, as well. "I don't believe you've been officially introduced. Ben MacAllister meet Merry Christine Lawrence."

Ben repeated the baby's name, emphasizing the vowel sound.

"Yes. Merry. M-e-r-r-y," Ellie said, spelling it out. "I know it's going to cause confusion. Everyone will assume her name is Mary, but—"

"She's a Christmas baby. She deserves a special name." Ben reached out and touched Merry's cheek.

"Yes, she is special. Thank you, Ben MacAllister, from both of us, for what you did last night."

"You're welcome, Ellie Lawrence. And Merry Christine." Ben put his arms around mother and child.

Ellie leaned into his embrace. "Merry Christmas, Ben," she said, and placed her daughter in his arms.

ABOUT THE AUTHOR

Marisa Carroll is the pen name of sisters Carol Wagner and Marian Scharf. This talented duo has written twelve Superromance novels, five Harlequin American Romance titles and has contributed to the continuing series, TYLER. They wrote two books for the original series, and completed two more for the return-to-Tyler series, entitled HOMETOWN REUNION. The authors have been RITA Award finalists, and their Vietnam trilogy won the *Romantic Times* award for best miniseries.

Be sure to look for Marisa Carroll's next Superromance novel, *Megan*, the third title in Harlequin Superromance's upcoming trilogy, SISTERS. This exciting three-author miniseries begins in April 1997, with *Amy* by Peg Sutherland, followed by *Lisa* by Ellen James and finally, Marisa Carroll's *Megan*.

Books by Marisa Carroll

HARLEQUIN SUPERROMANCE

515—ONE TO ONE
529—KEEPING CHRISTMAS
598—WEDDING INVITATION
635—MARRY ME TONIGHT
655—PEACEKEEPER

HOMETOWN REUNION

UNEXPECTED SON
MISSION: CHILDREN

Marisa Carroll

THE MAN WHO SAVED CHRISTMAS

Harlequin Books

TORONTO • NEW YORK • LONDON
AMSTERDAM • PARIS • SYDNEY • HAMBURG
STOCKHOLM • ATHENS • TOKYO • MILAN
MADRID • WARSAW • BUDAPEST • AUCKLAND

ISBN 0-373-70718-5

THE MAN WHO SAVED CHRISTMAS

Copyright © 1996 by Carol I. Wagner and Marian F. Scharf.

This edition published by arrangement with Harlequin Books S.A.

® and TM are trademarks of the publisher. Trademarks indicated with
® are registered in the United States Patent and Trademark Office, the
Canadian Trade Marks Office and in other countries.

Printed in U.S.A.

THE MAN WHO
SAVED CHRISTMAS

PROLOGUE

THE SIGN ON THE GATE said the cemetery closed at sundown. Matt Westrick shivered and turned up the collar of his coat and shoved his hands into the pockets. He glanced at the western sky. The sun had disappeared. The horizon was streaked with a dozen shades of purple and orange and dark blue, the colors of a nasty bruise. The air was cold and damp as it always was at this time of year in central Ohio. He shivered again and stuffed his hands deeper into his pockets.

Somewhere in the distance, someone was burning a pile of leaves. The smoke made Matt think of football games and foxy cheerleaders at pep rallies, and little kids going trick-or-treating. Except that when he'd been a kid out on Halloween, he'd ended up in trouble, more often than not. Until he met Eric Baden. Eric wasn't like anyone Matt had known before.

He knew what he wanted in life. He had plans and goals. He was popular and friendly, and for some reason he liked Matt, the foster kid with the bad attitude. They had become friends, better than friends. Eric was like the brother Matt had never had. Eric had a home, a mom and dad who loved each other, who didn't drink or do drugs, who cared about where their son went and what he was doing. All the things Matt secretly wished could be his.

Maybe it was jealousy that made Matt dare Eric to take his mother's minivan for a joyride. Jealousy and the need to show Matt's old gang that he was still cool. And that Eric was an okay guy.

But it had all gone terribly wrong and Eric had died. And Matt, with no future and no place to go, was still alive.

Matt looked at the sign and the locked gate once more. It would be dark in another fifteen minutes. If he was still a kid, he'd be afraid of being in a cemetery at night this close to Halloween. But he wasn't a kid. He hadn't been a kid for a long time. Maybe never.

He ought to be heading back to the group home or he'd get another demerit for being out after curfew, but he wasn't prepared to leave just yet. He reached out and shook the heavy gate that barred his entrance. "Damn it, Eric. I'm sorry, man." He laid his forehead against the cold, unyielding iron fence. *He'd screwed up again.*

It had taken him all day to get up the courage to come here. Actually, it had taken him a hell of a lot longer than that. Seven months since Eric had died. *Since Eric had been killed.* And not once had he been able to set foot inside this place, say goodbye to his friend, promise to make things right. He wasn't going to turn back now, not even if he got caught trespassing and thrown back into Juvenile Hall detention. Not even if he went to damned *effing* jail. He had to try to get inside. He owed Eric that much.

Eric had been his best friend. His only friend. He was going to find Eric's grave. He was going to stand there and swear that he would get even with the cop who had killed him.

Except, he couldn't even get inside the cemetery. Matt blinked back weak, hateful tears. He scraped at his eyes with his fist, then pounded the fence again in rage and frustration. Seven months ago he wouldn't have thought twice about hurtling over it, as easily as he'd hurtled over opposing linebackers on the football field. But that was then. This was now.

He stopped pounding on the unyielding fence and pounded the brace on his leg instead. He hated the thing. He hated what had happened to his life. Most of all he hated the cop who had chased down their car that March night. And if it was the last thing he did he was going to find State Trooper Ben MacAllister and make him pay.

CHAPTER ONE

THERE WAS A HINT of wood smoke in the air. It came to him on an eddy of cold wind off Lake Superior, subtle but more insistent than the smells of pine and wet earth and the musty aroma of dead leaves he'd crushed underfoot. Ben MacAllister set his jaw and tried to concentrate on where he put his feet, the drumming of elusive grouse and the lengthening pine shadows along the edge of the overgrown apple orchard he hunted. Anything but the smoke. He hated the smell of smoke.

A dog barked someplace ahead of him. Riley, the English setter Ben's cousin Eldor had given him, came bounding out of the woods trailing far behind the brace of grouse he'd flushed. The khaki-colored, chicken-size birds erupted from the underbrush at eye level, well out of range of Ben's gun.

"Oh, hell." Ben lowered the shotgun from his shoulder and hunkered down, out of the wind. "There goes supper. C'mon, fella," he called. "Let's call it a day." It would be dark soon. There was almost no twilight this far north so late in the year.

Riley trotted over, red tongue lolling, tail proudly erect, totally pleased with himself. He looked around expectantly, then back over his shoulder in the direction the birds had flown. He cocked his head and regarded Ben as if to ask why he hadn't done his part.

"Come here, boy." Ben tried to smile, but the cold had stiffened his facial muscles and made it difficult. "I didn't get a shot off in time. Sorry, buddy."

Riley accepted his apology graciously. He was one of the prettiest setters Ben had ever seen, a loving, friendly animal. But Riley was a lousy hunting dog, and an embarrassment to his former owner. Ben suspected that was why cousin Eldor had given him the half-grown pup when he arrived in North Star five months ago. The old man was a softie beneath his crusty exterior and obviously thought Ben and the pup would be good for each other. And they were. Ben's crack marksmanship on the firing range was a thing of the past. He was almost as bad a bird hunter as Riley was a bird dog. They were a perfect match. A busted-up, burned-out cop and a gun-shy dog loose in the north woods.

"And damned near lost in the north woods," Ben said aloud. He rose, using the butt of his gun for leverage, aware of the lengthening shadows in the deserted orchard as he got his bearings. "C'mon, Riley, we'd better head back to the truck, or we might end up spending the night under a tree."

He had a pretty good idea of where he was, about five miles southwest of North Star, Michigan, another mile or two more than that from the decommissioned lighthouse he'd called home for the last five months. But he'd left the truck over a mile back on the old logging road, and it was going to be a long, cold walk.

By the time they were halfway to the truck, Ben knew something was wrong. The scent on the wind was more than just someone burning brush around their deer camp. Riley obviously sensed trouble, too. He whined and yipped and kept running back to Ben to urge him to hurry. But Ben lagged behind the excited animal, partly because the half-frozen ruts of the logging road were hard going. And partly because of the smell of smoke. It was much stronger now, thicker, visible in the gray twilight.

A hundred yards from the truck he heard the screams, faint but unmistakable, children's voices crying out in fear. His heart slammed against his ribs. He quickened his pace until he was almost running.

He rounded a bend in the road, and his truck came into view. So did the source of the smoke. The rickety, two-story farmhouse across the county road was ablaze. Smoke—black and oily—poured from the upstairs windows. Flames danced on the shingles and ringed the narrow brick chimney. Ben reached his truck, shoved open the door and heaved his shotgun onto the seat. He slammed the door and started running. Time was critical. He'd make it quicker on foot.

The house was occupied. He was certain of that. This morning when he'd driven up, he'd seen an old sedan parked in the weedy yard, and children's bright, plastic toys lying here and there in the snow. It was late afternoon now, which meant the kids who owned those toys would be home from school.

He crossed the road and headed up the driveway as a woman with flyaway brown hair, not too tall, a little on the plump side, wearing a long, baggy sweater and jeans, reeled out of the front door, smoke billowing around her. She was clutching a howling, hissing kitten in one arm and what appeared to be a red metal toolbox in the other. A small pathetic pile of belongings was already outside, a rocking chair, a portable TV set, a lamp and end table and a few books and picture frames. It was obvious that this wasn't her first trip inside the burning house. But Ben intended to see that it was her last.

The woman sank onto the frozen grass by the front wheel of the car, coughing. Two children, a boy and girl, knelt beside her. The little girl, no more than six or seven, Ben guessed, had the same fine, flyaway brown hair and wide-spaced eyes as her mother. She scooped the yowling kitten into her arms, holding it so tightly the yowling stopped abruptly as the feline struggled for breath.

The boy, older, dark-haired and square-jawed, wrapped both arms around the woman's shoulders and buried his face in her neck. The woman pushed aside the toolbox to hold him close, hushing the little girl as she raised one arm to pull her onto her lap, loosening the child's stranglehold on the struggling kitten as she cuddled her close.

Ben took in the details of the scene with a practiced eye as he covered the last few yards to where the small family huddled on the ground. "Is anyone still inside the house?" he called. His voice was harsh and raspy from the cold. He was dressed in hunting clothes and an orange safety vest, with a camouflage-patterned ski mask over his face. He probably looked like some kind of tree monster. Both children and the woman looked up at him with round staring eyes.

"I said, is there anyone still inside the house? Mrs.—" He tore the ski mask off, forgetting for a moment that what lay beneath was even more frightening. He winced as the heat from the fire assaulted the still-sensitive scar tissue on his cheek and temple. The woman's eyes were glued to his face. It didn't take much imagination to guess what he looked like in the lurid light of her burning home. "C'mon, lady, answer me."

"My name's Ellie. Ellie Lawrence. We're all safe, thank God." She bit down hard on her lower lip. "There's no one else inside."

"Spock!" The boy raised his head from his mother's shoulder. "Spock's still inside." He pulled away but the woman held on tight to his arm.

"It's too late, Timmy," she whispered. "We can't go back for Spock." She looked at Ben as though she hoped he would contradict her words.

Ben kept his mouth shut.

"You found Muffin for Carly. Spock's our dog. Mom, we have to save her," the boy begged.

He broke loose from her grip and whirled away. Ben reached out and grabbed his arm. "Whoa, son."

"Let me go. I have to try and get my dog."

Ellie Lawrence struggled to stand, using the door handle of the car to help her rise.

Ben took a step forward. "Are you all right?" he demanded. "Are you hurt?"

"I'm fine," she insisted, waving off his outstretched hand, brushing tears from her cheeks. "It was the smoke. It was so thick... I had no idea it would be like that... It was awful—" She coughed again, her hand on her stomach.

She wasn't overweight as he'd thought when he first caught sight of her. Now that she was standing, he could see very plainly what the baggy pink sweater had hidden before.

Ellie Lawrence was pregnant. Very pregnant.

Automatically, he reached out a hand and steadied her. A pregnant woman suffering from smoke inhalation. It could be a dangerous situation.

"Let me go get my dog!" Ben dropped his hand from Ellie's arm. It was all he could do to hold on to the boy.

"Timothy! Please," Ellie said. She was almost crying now, too.

"I've got to try and get Spock out." Timmy's voice had risen to a scream.

"You can't go back in there," Ben told the hysterical boy sternly. "The roof's going to cave in any minute."

"Spock's tied up on the back porch," the woman replied. "She'll never get loose on her own." She looked at her burning home, then back to Ben. "But if you watch over the children, maybe I could get to her."

Ben couldn't let go of the struggling boy. He held the woman with the force of his gaze, the authority of his words, marveling at her courage—and her foolishness. "No one's going back into that house."

New tears filled Ellie Lawrence's big, dark eyes, spilled onto her sooty cheeks. She held out her hands to her son. "I'm sorry, Timmy. The fire started so quickly... It was the woodstove, I think. Or the chimney? I don't know. I was upstairs working. When I came down, there was already smoke everywhere. I barely had time to dial 911. I tried to save what I could, but there wasn't any time."

"Spock!" Timmy struggled mightily, tears streaming down his face. "We've gotta save my dog." A faint, frantic barking came from the back of the burning house.

"Oh, God. She's still alive," the woman said. She stared in horror at the flames now coming from every door and window.

The heat was intense. The little girl, crying with silent hiccuping sobs, bundled her protesting kitten inside her coat and tried to shield her face with her forearm.

Ben swallowed hard and turned his head away. Her gesture was instinctive. So was his. He'd done exactly the same thing that night seven months ago when his world, literally, blew up in his face.

"Watch the children for me," the woman said. "I... I've got to try and get to her."

Riley was barking and yelping, running back and forth along the edge of the driveway.

"Oh, hell," Ben said, thrusting the boy at his mother. She gathered the youngster into her arms. He couldn't let the dog burn to death, even though the last thing he wanted to do was face that fire. "Stay put," he ordered. "I'll see what I can do."

The woman nodded. "She's right inside the back door. Tied to a spigot. Please hurry. But . . . be careful."

Ben gritted his teeth and started up the driveway at a run. In the distance, he could hear the wail of a siren. The North Star volunteer fire department was on the way. Too bad there wouldn't be anything left to save.

A moment later, he reached the back of the house. It was still intact. That was one small point in his favor. The steadily rising wind off Lake Superior was pushing the flames forward, carrying most of the smoke away. It was probably the only reason the dog was still alive.

He figured he had about fifteen or twenty seconds of leeway inside the house—if he didn't create a back draft when he opened the door. Gingerly, he reached out and touched the knob. It was cool to the touch. The fire hadn't reached the back porch.

"Riley. Stay," he called over his shoulder. Then only to himself and his own demons, "Here I go."

As he'd done once before, Ben ignored every fire-safety rule he'd ever learned as he eased open the door, waited for a handful of heartbeats, then let it bang back on its hinges. Smoke poured from beneath a second door leading into the kitchen, the last barrier for the greedy flames to devour. The old porch had one small window on the far wall, but it was black as pitch, impossible to see through. "Here, Spock," he hollered, hoping the dog was friendly enough, or desperate enough to come to a stranger.

He needn't have worried. Before the words were out of his mouth, a black-and-white cannonball of fur launched itself at his chest. Ben fell back on the buckled linoleum floor, yanking at the chain that secured the dog to the spigot. "C'mon, dog." The chain didn't budge.

Spock wasn't barking any longer, just whimpering in fear. She was a fairly big dog, a Border collie, by the size and shape of her. It would take a stout chain to hold her. And that's what the woman had used. There was no way he was going to bust it loose without a hell of a lot more time than they had.

"Damnation," he said through clenched teeth. Ben began to work the animal's worn leather collar over its head. The back wall of the porch was beginning to steam, red-hot cinders were dropping from the ceiling, stinging his wrist and the backs of his hands, singeing her fur, making Spock more frantic to escape.

They weren't going to make it. He shut down his thoughts, held his clamoring memories at bay, persisted on sheer will alone. "Hold on, dog," he said tightly. "Spock! Sit! What the hell kind of name is Spock for a female dog, anyway?" He coughed, gagged, ducked his head to avoid the smoke. It was very bad now. Much worse than only a few seconds before. "Hold on or you'll get us both fried." With one last tug, he worked the dog free, grabbed her by the scruff of the neck before she had a chance to bolt and dived out the doorway, landing hard on his left side. He rolled through the remains of a scraggly flower bed and scrambled to his feet, the dog in his arms, and started running.

He made it about ten yards from the house before the entire structure folded in on itself with a rush of wind and heat and burning embers that picked him up off his feet and slammed him against the side of a small dilapidated shed. His head spun, the breath rushed out of his lungs with a whoosh. But he was still alive. Just as he'd been that terrible night that changed his life forever.

"Damn it all to hell," he said to no one in particular.

Ben sat up gingerly, still clutching the shivering Spock, and shook his head to clear the cobwebs. Pain arced along his nerve endings and radiated down his arm. A stinger, he decided, just like he used to get playing football in college. Not serious, but painful. The early-November darkness had retreated into the woods, hiding from the firelight. Now it halted, gathered itself and came rushing back. Ben closed his eyes and let the darkness take him.

"HEY, mister. Wake up. Are you okay? Let go of Spock. You're squishing her."

Ben opened his eyes, then shut them again. The earth was still spinning and the dancing red and blue lights of the North Star emergency vehicles pulling into the yard didn't help matters.

"Did you hear me, mister?" The kid sounded scared to death, tugging at the whining dog Ben clutched in his arms. He'd only had the wind knocked out of him. He knew he ought to reassure the boy, but he couldn't. Not yet.

"Mom! Come here. I think he's dead!"

"Dead?" It was the little girl talking. Ben slitted open one eye. She was standing over him, clinging to her mother's leg, crying, her words punctuated by hiccuping sobs.

Ben opened both eyes. He managed to focus on the boy's white face without losing the contents of his stomach. "I'm not dead. I just look that way."

"Are you sure you're okay?" Ellie Lawrence's pretty, soot-streaked face came into focus as she dropped to her knees beside him.

"He's squashing Spock," Tim whimpered. "Make him let go." He *was* still holding on to the dog. Ben loosened his grip and Spock lunged into Tim's arms, knocking the boy off balance, licking the kid's hands and face, mercifully silencing him.

"Are you okay?" Ellie reached out and touched his forehead with the tips of her fingers. "Should I call the paramedics?" She wasn't wearing gloves and her hands were cold. Her fingers trembled. From reaction to the fire, he wondered fleetingly, or the ugliness of his scars?

"I'm fine." Ben closed his eyes again. He didn't want to see the concern in her eyes. Or the pity. Pity was the worst.

"MR. MACALLISTER. Ben." Ellie shook him gently. He'd said he wasn't hurt, but she couldn't be sure. People said and did strange things when they'd been injured. Or had swallowed too much smoke.

"I think Timmy's right. He's dead," Carly whispered. "That's what Grandma Patty looked like when she died. I saw her." Ellie patted Carly's shoulder. She knew how hard their paternal grandmother's death last spring had been on the children.

"Hey, mister. Wake up! Don't be dead," Carly whispered. She was standing beside Ellie, holding the now-quiescent Muffin.

"It's okay," Ellie assured her daughter. "He's not dead. I think he just had the wind knocked out of him."

God, she'd never realized the smoke would be so bad. So thick and strangling. He could have died, this scarred stranger who'd come out of the trees and the twilight to save them, and it would have been her fault.

"You should never have gone back into that house after Spock," she said more sharply than she'd intended, when Ben MacAllister opened his eyes again.

"Now you tell me." He rolled over onto one elbow, coughing the smoke out of his lungs. "How do you know who I am?" he demanded when he'd regained his breath.

"I... I've seen you around North Star. And your dog. He's one of Eldor's setters, obviously. And... your nose."

"What?"

"Your nose." Of course, it wasn't only his dominant beak of a nose. It was the scars on the left side of his face, distinctive in their pattern. His left hand was scarred, too. *Burn scars.* Ellie shivered. *What kind of courage did the man possess to go into a burning building to save an animal when he'd been injured in some other fire?*

"I don't think anyone has ever recognized me because of my nose."

"You have the MacAllister nose," she said numbly, feeling her own delayed panic threaten to overwhelm her. He started coughing again and Ellie waved to attract the attention of the paramedics. "Don't talk," she urged.

Ben pulled himself upright and his lips tightened in pain.

"Stay still," Ellie ordered. She reached out and put a restraining hand on his shoulder, felt the resistance of bone and muscle even through the thick layers of insulated clothing he wore.

"I'm okay," he said in a tone that could only be described as a growl. Ellie withdrew her hand and sat back on her heels. He obviously didn't like to be touched. "The fire department and paramedics are here. Don't you want them to contact your husband for you?"

"I don't have a husband," she said. His face didn't change expression, but his gaze flickered to her swollen stomach. "I'm divorced." This wasn't the time or place to go into details. Anyway, if he wanted to know why she was pregnant and not married, he could ask just about anyone in North Star. Like most small towns, it was a hard place to keep secrets. "Thank you for saving our dog," she said, to change the subject. "It was a brave thing to do. You risked your life for her. I'm in your debt."

"No—" Ben broke off his reply, obviously distracted by the sound of firemen shouting orders in the background.

Ellie turned her head to watch. Spray from the hoses splattered the early-November snow to her right. Water streamed onto the burning ruin, sending great, billowing clouds of steam into the indigo sky. *Only an hour ago, the rented farmhouse had been her home. What was she going to do? Where were they going to live? How was she going to earn a living?*

"Oh, God, my Santas," she said, fighting back a new wave of panic. "They're gone. All of them."

"What? Santas?" Ben asked.

Timmy took one arm from around Spock and placed it around his mother's shoulders. "It's all right, Mom. You can make more Santas."

"It'll be all right, Mommy." Carly sniffed, patting her hand.

Ellie just shook her head, then laid her cheek against Tim's dark hair. He smelled of smoke and singed dog hair. "Not in time," she said, desperation rising like bile in her throat. "Not in time."

"Santas?" Ben repeated.

"My mom carves Santas," Carly said, sticking her snub little nose into the air. "Wonderful Santas. All kinds and sizes and shapes. I help. I help wrap them. And now they're all burned up." She started to cry again. Ellie began stroking her between the shoulder blades.

She tried not to think about the two hundred hand-carved Santa figures, no two alike, boxed and ready to ship to a distributor in Minneapolis, all destroyed.

Instead, she tried to concentrate on how thankful she was that they were all safe and unharmed. She had to put the destroyed Santas out of her mind or she would burst into tears. She couldn't do that to the children. She had to be strong. For all three of them—no, all four of them. She touched her stomach, felt the baby move strongly beneath her fingertips, and closed her eyes in a quick reverent prayer of thanksgiving.

"Hey." Ben's strong, hard fingers closed on her arm. "Are you sure *you're* okay?"

She looked into his storm-gray eyes and her pulse rate slowed and steadied a bit. "I'm fine." He stood up, then helped her to her feet.

"Ben? Is that you, boy?" Ellie recognized the foghorn bass voice of Eldor MacAllister, the proprietor of North Star's only restaurant, the Jack Pine Bar and Grill. She looked over her shoulder to find the rotund little man and his wife approaching, trailed by his two best friends, Baldwin Carmichael, North Star's mayor and postmaster, and Lars Larson, the retired lake-freighter captain, who owned the hardware and general store. They were both as tall and thin as Eldor was short and fat. "What the devil are you doing here?" Eldor demanded of his younger cousin.

Ben's steadying gaze left her face. Ellie felt the world begin to spin in slow circles around her, and fought off a sudden wave of vertigo. "He saved Spock's life," Ellie said.

"You went into a burning building after a dog?" the old man demanded, his prominent MacAllister nose quivering with outrage.

"Not exactly," Ben equivocated.

"My God, boy. What possessed—"

"Hush, Eldor." Martha MacAllister's voice, rough and raspy from a lifetime of smoking two packs of cigarettes a day, overrode Eldor's. "You can ask a bunch of damned fool questions later. We need to get Ellie and her kids checked out. And you too, Benjamin. Then you can tell us how the hell you turned up here."

Almost immediately, they were surrounded by fire fighters and paramedics from the North Star emergency squad. Voices were raised above the sounds of water pumps and straining engines and shouting men.

Ellie and the kids were hustled away to the ambulance to be checked over. She lost track of Ben MacAllister as she fielded questions and tried to make her voice heard. As she let herself be led away from the ruins of her home, she assured everybody that she was fine, the kids and pets were fine.

The baby was fine.

But when she looked over her shoulder to determine if Ben MacAllister, with his scarred face and dark, compelling gray eyes, was fine, she discovered he was gone. He'd disappeared back into the shadows of birch and pine from which he had come.

CHAPTER TWO

ELLIE FOLDED the clean but faded pink nightgown—
a donation from a neighbor—and laid it in the drawer
beside the small pile of new socks and panties Martha
MacAllister, who most of the citizens of North Star
referred to as Mrs. Eldor, had purchased for Carly in
Sault Ste. Marie that morning. In the drawer beneath
were T-shirts, athletic socks and briefs for Tim. There
wasn't enough drawer space in the tiny motel room
where they'd been living for the three days since the
fire, so her own new underthings were in a sack in a
corner.

"Charity is all well and good," that formidable
matron had announced when she arrived on the motel doorstep with two bulging shopping bags. Ellie had
known Martha MacAllister most of her life, and she
had long ago ceased to be frightened by the strident
voice and overbearing manner. "It does good for the
soul of the giver and the receiver. Or, so I've been
told," she'd continued, eyeing the used clothing on
one of the two double beds with some skepticism.
"But I don't think the Almighty meant that we should
wear someone else's castoff underwear. I would have
brought you the fancy-smancy stuff Mr. MacAllister
bought me out of the mail-order catalog for our an-

niversary. It's too damned cold around here to wear that kind of fluff, I told him, but he wouldn't listen. Insisted on spending good money on it, anyway. Said I could wear it on that Caribbean cruise he's been wanting to take all these years..." She snorted like a war-horse. "Of course, even in your condition those bikinis would fall down around your ankles." She thrust the bags into Ellie's hands. "Here."

"I can't take this," Ellie protested, her throat tightening. She hated taking charity from her friends and neighbors, even though she had no other choice. "I...I haven't got enough money to pay you for all this."

"No payment necessary," Mrs. Eldor barked. "I won't hear tell of it. It's a gift."

"I can't," Ellie repeated helplessly.

"A loan then. I'll hunt up the receipt when I get the chance. You can pay me back when you're able."

Ellie had the sinking feeling she'd never see that receipt but she didn't say so. Instead, she swallowed her pride and followed Mrs. Eldor's advice, accepting with good grace. "I hope you get to use your anniversary gift on a Caribbean cruise soon."

Mrs. Eldor waved the statement aside. "Mr. MacAllister is a romantic fool," she asserted, but there was a curious softness in her eyes. "Well, I've got to be going. It's Farley's day off." Farley Tall Trees was the cook at the Jack Pine. "He's gone to the casino to play the slot machines. I have to round something up for the lunch crowd." She went off muttering about reservation casinos turning the place into a north woods Las Vegas and about how much she hated to cook.

Ellie watched the sturdy, short-legged figure disappear into the truck. She hugged the sacks to her distended belly, for a moment imagining Mrs. Eldor encased in a black lace bra and French-cut bikini panties. A reluctant smile turned up the corners of her mouth and kept the tears at bay. At least for a little while.

That had been an hour ago, another hour alone with her dreary thoughts. Her parents had wired money from Florida for new coats, boots and shoes for the children and herself. She knew it was a sacrifice—they were living on a fixed income, and her father's heart medication was expensive. She resolved not to ask for anything more.

She had money for food and necessities—at least for a few days. The North Star community emergency fund was paying for the motel room. Friends and neighbors had donated clothing and household items, even a crib and high chair for when the baby came. Ellie was grateful for their generosity and friendship, but desperation still stalked the edges of her thoughts and invaded her dreams like a hungry wolf.

Her parents had sold their fishing camp on a small lake a few miles outside North Star three years before and moved south. Her older brother and sister and their families lived far away, as did her ex-husband, Lonny's, brothers. Ellie had stayed on in North Star even after her divorce because she knew her mother-in-law would miss the children terribly, and because North Star was her home. She didn't want to live anywhere else. She'd grown up in this wildly beautiful land on the southern shore of Lake Superior and it was where she wanted to raise her own children.

But North Star was a small town and good jobs were few and far between. She'd only just begun to make a name for herself with her carvings. Even before the fire she'd known she would have to find a job soon after the baby was born to help support them. But the fire had destroyed more than their rented home. It had destroyed her inventory, her nest egg, and now she could no longer afford to stay home until the baby was born.

She need to find a job and a place to live. And soon.

She picked up a small carving of a half-formed Santa with a sack of pinecones and holly slung over his shoulder and the rough outline of a fawn at his feet. The piece was one of six that had been commissioned by a gallery owner in Mackinaw City. The other five had been lost in the fire. Ellie had planned to use the money from the sale for the children's Christmas presents.

She couldn't keep taking charity, but the alternative was even less acceptable. If necessary, she would apply for government assistance, but only as a last resort. Her family had never been on welfare, and she didn't want to be the first.

Ellie glanced at her watch. The kids wouldn't be home from school for almost two hours. She pulled on her donated coat, found a pair of gloves and her keys and headed for the one spot where she'd always found some measure of peace.

ELLIE PARKED THE CAR at the intersection of the well-traveled county road that ran between North Star and Sault Ste. Marie and an abandoned logging road a mile outside of town, and headed for the beach. She took her time. The day was a little warmer than the day of the fire, the snow had melted and the rusty-brown leaves that carpeted the rutted track were wet and slick. Soon, the low, steady drumbeat of waves along the shore overrode the sighing of the wind in the treetops, and the chatter of squirrels racing along the bare branches of the white birch and poplars. Quickening her step, Ellie turned off the logging road to follow the curve of a stream until it emptied onto a narrow, rock-strewn beach, and the full splendor of Lake Superior lay spread out before her.

Ellie inhaled deeply. The wind off the lake was cold and sharp. An old log, wide and smooth, spanned the little stream. Ellie crossed it carefully, arms outstretched. At seven months, she was far enough along in her pregnancy that the baby sometimes got in the way, and she didn't want to lose her footing and end up in the shallow but ice-cold water.

A hundred yards beyond the stream, a pile of house-size boulders stood sentinel at the water's edge, a section of the low bluff broken away in some long-forgotten upheaval thousands of years before. Since Ellie's childhood this had been her special spot, her place. In summer, she had reluctantly shared it with tourists walking the beach searching for agates and trying to imagine where, beneath the sapphire waters of the lake, lay the remains of the doomed freighter *Edmund Fitzgerald,* and her crew.

Ellie climbed up among the boulders and settled on a sheltered ledge a few feet above the waves. When she was younger, she had preferred climbing right to the top, no matter the wind or the weather. It had been her throne, her aerie, the place where she could see forever. Her older siblings had used the boulders to play pirate games, and pretend they were *voyageurs* or brave Indian scouts. She had preferred to sit and watch the waves and the seabirds overhead. There she would weave stories of the important, interesting things she would do with her life.

Instead, she met Lonny Lawrence who was back in town after four years in the army, when she was seventeen years old and married him just ten days after graduation from high school. She had never left North Star, and now, a dozen years later, she didn't want to.

The baby kicked strongly inside her and Ellie dropped her hand to her stomach, soothing the tiny one through the fabric of her coat. Soothing herself with the sight and sounds and smells of the vast inland ocean moving restlessly all around her. She took in the deep blue of the autumn sky, the muted green of pine and spruce, the squat white tower of the Chippewa Point lighthouse, picture-postcard pretty, perched on its rocky ledge half a mile down the beach.

Her thoughts snagged and lingered on the building and the man who lived there. Ben MacAllister was as solitary and as isolated as the lighthouse in which he lived. He hadn't shown his face in North Star since the fire. She hadn't been able to thank him properly for saving Spock's life that awful afternoon. She'd thought about searching him out to let him know how deeply grateful she was. But somehow she hadn't got round to doing it yet.

Movement at the corner of her eye caused Ellie to drop her gaze from the sunlight glinting off the tower windows. A man and a dog were coming steadily down the beach toward her. The man wore faded jeans and a hooded, dark blue, military-style parka that obscured his features. Ellie didn't have to see his face. She knew at once who it was. Ben MacAllister. The setter romping at his side identified him beyond a doubt.

Ellie leaned back into the shelter of her stone perch, her good intentions dissolving before the awkwardness of actually putting her feelings into words. Actually talking to the man. Besides, she remembered the way he had looked at her, at her stomach, at her obvious pregnancy, and she felt the awkwardness even more strongly. If she stayed very quiet, he would probably pass landward of where she sat and move on down the beach. Then, once he'd rounded the curve of Agate Point, he would be out of sight again, and she could make her way back to the woods before he returned.

But she hadn't reckoned on Riley's formidable, but erratic, nose. Moments later, the setter bounded up to Ellie's perch and executed a perfect point, feathered tail erect, nose quivering, gorgeous brown eyes fixed unblinkingly on Ellie's sneaker.

"Shoo!" Ellie hissed. "Go away! There are no grouse here. I'm a person. Not a bird. Can't you tell? Shoo!" She stamped her foot. It was no use. Apparently, to Riley's poor brain, her sneaker looked like a grouse. And one that wasn't going to fly away before his master could get to it. He intended to stay no matter how much she protested.

"Riley!" The sharp command rang out over the water. Riley's eyes gleamed but he didn't move a muscle. "Heel, you damn mutt!"

"Uh—oh. He sounds mad," Ellie whispered. She stood, then leaned around the edge of one of the big boulders that screened her from Ben MacAllister's sight. "Hi," she said, hoping the breaking of a wave, large enough to send foam swirling almost to the base of the cairn, would hide the quiver in her voice. "Your dog seems to have mistaken my sneaker for a bird."

He stopped walking, watching her from the shadow of his parka's hood. The November afternoon, though cool, wasn't cold enough to warrant such a heavy coat. Had he chosen to wear it because the hood hid the scars on his face? Or because like her, he owned only one?

"Shoo!" she repeated, waving her hands at Riley. The animal stayed glued on point.

"Dog!" This time Riley obeyed the summons, reluctantly. She could tell that from the way he ambled toward his master, looking over his shoulder now and then to check if his quarry had flown away. Ellie stayed put. This was the perfect opportunity to thank the man, but she couldn't think of a word to say.

"You can come down from there," Ben assured her. "He won't bite."

Ellie laughed. "I know that. He's a cupcake."

"Then why are you still standing up there?"

Ellie blinked. He'd leaned a little forward so that he could see her better without getting his feet wet, presenting the unscarred side of his face to view. In all the excitement the other night she hadn't realized what a very good-looking man he was. He was probably about her ex-husband's age, in his early thirties, three or four years older than she was. He was six feet tall, give or take an inch. His jaw was lean and hard, beard-shadowed at this time of day. He had high cheekbones and straight, dark eyebrows, and dark brown hair, a little long for Ellie's taste, with more than a hint of a wave in the heavy lock that fell across his forehead. And, of course, the MacAllister nose, a truly impressive beak, giving his profile the look of an old Roman statue, some long-forgotten warrior god, or maybe a Highland chief setting out on a border raid.

She wondered what he would look like in a kilt.

"Hey? Did you hear what I said?" He'd moved closer while she studied him.

"I'm fine," she said, bullying her wayward thoughts into order. "It's just that it's quite a scramble to get down. I might as well stay here if you're just passing through." *Now why had she said that? It was as though she was challenging him to remain and talk with her.* Or challenging herself not to let him get to her.

"I am just passing through," he responded, and Ellie felt herself flush. His words must have sounded harsh even to him, for he qualified them by saying, "I'm glad you're feeling well enough to walk the beach."

"I don't get much chance to do that any more, but today I just couldn't stay away." That much was true, at least.

"It's hard not to want to be out here on a day like today."

"There won't be many more like this," Ellie agreed. The sun had wheeled into the west. Already, the shadows were starting to lengthen, and the air had grown uncomfortably chilly, reminding her that winter lurked just around the corner.

"No aftereffects of the fire?" he asked. "The...the baby's okay?"

"The baby is fine."

"I'm glad to hear that." He didn't come any closer, but neither did he walk away. He'd shoved his left hand into the pocket of his parka. The right, the unscarred hand, remained in view. "And Spock. She didn't swallow too much smoke?"

"We had to clip some singed fur." Ellie wrinkled her nose at the memory of the smell of burnt dog hair. "But she's fine. Mayor Carmichael offered to keep her and Muffin at his place until we get out of the motel. Captain Larson doesn't allow pets at the Safe Harbor."

"I imagine Tim isn't happy about that."

She smiled a little sadly. "No, and neither is Carly, but they're doing okay. We're all doing okay," she said, taking a deep breath, aware that she might not get another chance to talk to this solitary, enigmatic man. If she waited too long, he was liable to turn on his heel and disappear down the beach the way he'd disappeared into the woods the night of the fire. "I...I want—"

Ben jumped back. "Sh—" He looked at her, a rueful twist to his lips. "Sorry," he mumbled. A wave had washed over his shoes. The wind had definitely strengthened since she'd arrived on the beach. Water was beginning to bridge the sand wall at the base of her rock aerie. She was going to have to leave her perch soon, whether or not she wanted to—or wade out, not an attractive prospect at this time of year.

Especially when she had only one pair of shoes to her name.

At the thought, despair threatened to overtake her again. Ellie bit her lip and lifted her chin. When she looked down, she saw Ben MacAllister looking up, studying her. Unexpectedly, he lifted his arms, hands outspread. "Let me help you down."

Ellie hesitated. Although she was perfectly capable of getting down herself, it would be an awkward scramble, as she'd told him, and she didn't want to make a fool of herself. "Thank you," she said.

He stepped forward into the swirl of water and shifting sand at the foot of the boulders. She leaned into his arms, her hands braced on his shoulders. His hands went around her waist—or where her waist should have been. She saw his gray eyes widen slightly in surprise. He stepped back with a slight grunt, but swung her easily to the ground.

"Are you all right?" he asked, his hands still on her waist.

"Yes, thank you. I'm fine." She stepped away, unsettled by his touch, the strength of his grip and the warmth of his hands. "Are you all right? You didn't strain...anything, or pull a muscle, did you?" she asked in turn, the heat in her cheeks increasing. "I...I should have warned you. I...I've gained fifteen pounds with the baby and..."

He shook his head, shoving his hands back into his pockets now that he was certain she could stand on her own. "I...it's not that. I didn't hurt *you,* I didn't...squeeze you too tight, or...anything?" he finished in a rush.

"Oh." The baby was moving strongly within her, arms and legs, elbows and knees all in motion, it seemed. Ellie put her hand on her stomach and laughed a little breathlessly, coaxing a hesitant smile to curve the corners of his firm, straight mouth. Ellie felt her breath catch in her throat. Even with the scar that marred the left side of his face, his smile was magical. "Did you feel the baby move?" she blurted out, amazed and alarmed by her visceral, and very feminine, response to that smile.

He nodded.

"Don't worry," she assured him, striving for a nonchalance she didn't feel. "You didn't do anything wrong. He's just waking up from his nap. Stretching. Doing somersaults. You know."

"Do you know it's a boy?"

"That's what the doctor thinks. Me? I'm not so sure. Carly was just as wild and rambunctious as this one." She tilted her head, watching him. "You don't have children of your own?"

"No." The word was clipped. "I've never been married." The smile disappeared, as though he realized he'd been on the verge of a conversation with her.

"Oh." Ellie's smile died away, as well. Was there a love affair gone bad in his past? She could sympathize with that. She didn't know much about Ben MacAllister, only that he was Eldor's cousin and that he'd been living in the lighthouse since early that summer. And that he kept to himself. He didn't have a job, at least not one that anyone knew about. That gave him and Ellie something in common. She looked up and caught him watching her again.

He was frowning.

"I...I'm interrupting your walk," she said. "I really should be getting back to town. The kids will be coming home from school soon and Mrs. Carmichael has invited us for dinner. It'll be nice to have a home-cooked meal."

He didn't turn and march down the beach as she'd expected him to do. "Getting tired of eating at the Jack Pine?" he asked, one dark eyebrow lifting slightly.

"No...of course not. The food at the Jack Pine is quite good. But—" she shrugged a little helplessly "—I miss having my own kitchen."

"I'm a lousy cook. I'd loan you mine if we could get it in the back of my truck," he said.

"Thanks," she said, risking a grin. "But our motel room's as crowded as it can get."

"How did you get out here?" he asked. "I didn't see any cars parked at the trailhead." Although the government had sold Eldor MacAllister the lighthouse and the property around it, the county still maintained the approach road in return for Eldor's allowing access to the bluff path for summer tourists and winter snowmobilers. Most of them parked at the trailhead, where the county road ended, just past the lighthouse. "Where's your car? I'll walk you to it."

"It's on the old Shurmansky logging road. The path comes out on the other side of Agate Creek."

His eyebrows pulled together again. "That's close to a mile from here."

"I'm pregnant not incapacitated," she retorted.

Again that reluctant and incredibly sexy smile curved the corners of his mouth. "I'll try to remember that. I'll walk with you to the creek."

"All right." Surely she could manage to spend that much more time in this man's company without making a fool of herself. She turned around and started walking, unusually aware of his nearness, of the sound of his breathing and her own. The going was harder once they were off the hard-packed sand, onto the shingle. She made herself pay attention to where she put her feet, trying not to think about the man at her side.

The silence lengthened between them. Riley ranged ahead, nose down, quartering the beach, following the scent trail of a deer or raccoon, perhaps even a black bear, although Ellie hadn't noticed any tracks earlier.

Ben must have noticed the length of the silence, too. "I take it you haven't found a place to live," he remarked as they skirted a fallen tree trunk.

"No. I...I might have to move to Newberry—" the county seat "—or even the Soo," she said reluctantly. "The Soo" was how everyone in the area referred to the small city of Sault Ste. Marie, Michigan—and its sister city, Sault Ste. Marie, Ontario.

Apparently, he noticed her reluctance, too. "I take it you're not cut out for city life?"

Ellie smiled. "Nope. I've always lived in North Star. Guess I'm a country girl at heart."

"There's nothing available in North Star?"

Ellie shook her head. "So far, nothing's come up. At least that I can afford." They were almost to the log crossing. Ellie wished he hadn't brought up the subject.

"What about your husband—"

"Ex-husband," she corrected.

He swung his head in her direction for just a moment. "Ex-husband. Can't he help get you back on your feet?"

She laughed, because if she didn't laugh she'd cry. "Lonny never has two extra nickels to rub together. He's in Louisiana working on an oil rig in the Gulf. At least that's where his last support check was sent from." It had arrived in August, but she didn't tell Ben MacAllister that.

They were at the creek bank. Ellie looked down at the brown-stained water tumbling over stones and boulders on its way to the beach. This man had risked his life to save her and her children and there was no way she could repay him. Words would never be enough but she had to try.

She held out her hand. After a moment's hesitation, Ben folded his big, strong fingers around hers.

The contact was brief but the effect on her nerve endings made her curl her fingers into her palm. "Thank you," she said, swallowing a clot of tears that threatened to block her throat and choke off the words. "Thank you for everything you did for us."

Then she stepped onto the log and made her way carefully to the other side, all too aware how awkward and ungainly she must look. Once more safely on dry land, she walked into the woods and taking a page from his book, she didn't look back.

BEN SAT at the bar in the Jack Pine nursing a beer and listening to Eldor and his wife argue in the kitchen. Riley was asleep at Ben's feet. Ben had crossed Agate Creek on the log bridge a few minutes after Ellie Lawrence had walked into the woods. He'd headed up the beach into town, and had been here for an hour or so.

The Jack Pine Bar and Grill sat right on the water. A big window behind the bar looked out onto the small, sheltered harbor that made North Star an attractive summer anchorage. Cottages—mostly uninhabited at this time of year—dotted the shoreline for a mile in either direction. Behind him, across Main Street, were half a dozen stores and businesses. To his right was Lars Larson's motel/general store/bait-and-tackle and video-rental place. On his left was the post office and town hall, where Baldy Carmichael presided as both postmaster and mayor, but the Jack Pine was the center of North Star's social life.

Just then, His Honor entered the bar from the side door that opened onto the parking lot, and stood blinking, adjusting his eyes to the dim light. The clanging of pots and pans in the kitchen intensified. Baldy ambled across the uneven wooden floor and took the stool beside Ben's. He looked around. "Who's tending bar?" he asked.

"Eldor." Ben took a swallow of his beer. He was as comfortable with these people as he was with anyone these days, but still, when the bar was full, evenings and weekends, he usually stayed away.

"Who's cooking?" Baldy folded his hands together and cocked his ear toward the altercation in the kitchen.

"Mrs. Eldor."

"Damn, Farley's not back from Brimley, eh?" he muttered, sliding off the stool to circle the bar and snag a beer mug off the mirrored shelf. He filled it with the expertise of a connoisseur, dropped a dollar bill beside the register and resumed his seat. "I was looking forward to a good meal. Martha Mac-Allister's a fine woman, but a lousy cook. Is Farley still off playin' the slots?"

"Farley's on his way to Florida," Ben revealed. "Eldor just told me."

"Florida?" Baldy repeated in the same tone he might have said "the moon."

"Lars, did you hear that?" The cadaverously thin, former freighter captain had followed his longtime pal into the bar. Ben nodded a greeting and the older man returned it with a half salute, three fingers touching the bill of his baseball cap. "Listen to this," Baldy said. "Old Farley Tall Trees has taken off for Florida."

"What?" Lars sat down at the bar. "Who's in charge here?" he asked. Every day at four o'clock, Lars Larson came into the Jack Pine for a double bourbon and cola. He was a methodical man, punctual and precise and he didn't like his routine disrupted. "Innkeeper! I need service."

"Oh, draw your own, Larson," Baldy fumed. "Go on, Ben, tell me what the hell's going on with Farley."

Ben gave the elderly man a sideways look. "Haven't you heard?"

"Heard what? I'm only the mayor of this burg. No one tells me anything."

"Farley won the progressive jackpot on the dollar slots at Brimley," Ben informed him.

"Like hell!" Baldy slapped the counter, a delighted grin on his red face. "Lars, did you hear that?" he bellowed.

"It would be hard not to. Tell us the rest, Ben," Lars said, leaning forward on his stool to look past Baldy.

"I was here when he came in. He already had his suitcase packed. Told Eldor he'd be back in the spring. Or when the money runs out."

"Well, I'll be damned."

"We'll all be damned if my wife takes over the cooking in this place," Eldor said gloomily, coming through the swinging doors leading to the kitchen. He went immediately to the bar and poured a double shot of bourbon into a glass, added cola and set it in front of Lars. "She's a fine woman. But one lousy cook."

"Amen to that," Baldy mumbled in his beer. "What are you going to do about it? Us bachelors got to eat somewhere and my cholesterol's too high for bacon cheeseburgers every damn night this winter. I'll have a stroke before the ice is off the lake."

"I'll be divorced or dead long before that," Eldor declared, more gloomily still.

"Hire someone else," Ben suggested.

"Who? Farley took most of his pay in room and board. On top of everything else, now I got an empty cabin out back, all winterized and snug as can be."

"What about Ellie Lawrence?" Ben heard himself say.

"Ellie Lawrence?" Eldor glanced first at Ben, then his lifelong friends. "Ellie Lawrence," he repeated.

"She sure needs a place to live," Baldy agreed, frowning into his beer.

"And a job," Lars contributed. "Since her Santas all got burned up in the fire, she has no income to speak of."

There were those Santas again. At least now Ben knew what Lars was talking about, because Eldor had told him that Ellie carved Santa figures for a living. She had contacts with a Midwest distributor that supplied Christmas ornaments and decorations to stores all over the country.

"I don't know, eh?" Eldor hedged. "I'd have to consult Mrs. Eldor on this one . . . Does anyone know if she can cook?"

"If she can boil an egg without setting fire to it, she can cook better than Martha," Baldy said.

"I heard that, Lucifer Carmichael," Mrs. Eldor hollered from the kitchen. "I can cook if I want to. I just don't want to. Hire the girl, Eldor. We can stow Farley's stuff in the garage and she can move into the cabin tomorrow." She appeared in the doorway, cheeks flushed, a tomato sauce–stained apron tied around her ample middle.

"B-but Ellie's going to have a baby," Eldor stammered.

"Not until after Christmas," Lars clarified.

"She needs the work and she's too proud to take charity," Mrs. Eldor went on as if he hadn't spoken. "She comes from proud stock. Jane and Hank Gibson are good people. Ellie's the only one of their kids to stay around North Star. Thought for a while she'd be the making of Lonny Lawrence." She shrugged and made a disgusted face. "I hate to say this. Patty Lawrence was a good friend of mine, may she rest in peace, and that boy of hers was the apple of her eye. But you can't make a silk purse out of a sow's ear. And in my opinion Lonny Lawrence is a sow's ear."

Lars nodded his head in agreement. "Between us I think you're right, Mrs. E. Ellie's got a tough row to hoe, but she's better off without that ne'er-do-well."

"She likes to cook," Ben surprised himself by saying. He didn't want to hear about Ellie's ex—good or bad. "She told me she misses her kitchen."

"When did you talk to her?" Mrs. Eldor demanded, her piercing dark eyes turned in Ben's direction.

"This afternoon. On the beach." People were starting to drift into the bar. Ben could feel their eyes on his back. He didn't like being around people, not yet. Maybe someday. Someday, when he could forget about the scars on his face and hand, and the guilt in his heart. Sweat broke out between his shoulder blades. He grabbed his coat off the stool beside him and shrugged into it.

He didn't know what had possessed him to tell them he'd talked to Ellie Lawrence. He wasn't responsible for her livelihood or her future just because he'd happened along and pulled her kid's dog out of a burning building. Helping her and her children should be her ex-husband's job. Or the father of her baby. He didn't know if the two men were one and the same. And he wasn't going to ask. He was responsible for no one anymore. No one but himself.

"Look, I have to go," he said to the older men. "I walked into town. I want to get back to the lighthouse before dark."

The others were used to his abrupt appearances and departures. Eldor and Baldy just waved goodbye, Lars raised his half-empty glass, but Mrs. Eldor stared at him with narrowed eyes. "Goodbye, Ben. And by the way, thanks for suggesting Ellie to take Farley's place," she said mildly. "I'll go talk to her right away." She had turned back toward the kitchen, but her words were clearly audible, at least to Ben. "Having her around here could be a good thing for all of us, eh?"

CHAPTER THREE

ELLIE LOOKED UP from the stainless-steel table where she was quartering carrots for venison stew, Wednesday's lunch special at the Jack Pine. Movement outside the back door of the restaurant had caught her attention and she wondered who could be out there at this time of night. Not that it was terribly late, a few minutes before nine o'clock, but the restaurant closed at seven in the off-season. Although the restaurant was closed, the bar stayed open for business. Almost no one used this entrance except herself and the MacAllisters, both of whom were tending bar out front. Her gaze remained fixed on the door, a carrot in one hand, her paring knife in the other.

"Who's there?" she called, feeling a little foolish but wary all the same because she hadn't locked the door.

Ben MacAllister, wearing his blue parka, opened the door and stepped inside on a swirl of cold, damp air. He stopped short at the sight of her. "Hi," he said. "I didn't think there would be anyone in here at this time of night."

"Hi," she responded a little faintly. Her heart had kicked into overdrive, and although she wanted to blame it on being startled by an unexpected visitor, she knew it wasn't the truth. Her heart had acted the same way when they'd met on the beach three weeks earlier.

"What are you doing here?" Ben asked, not moving any farther into the low-ceilinged room, redolent of cooking odors.

Ellie fought to regain her equilibrium. *She had just ended her marriage. She was seven months pregnant with her third child. She was not attracted to this man. She couldn't be.* "I w-work here now," she stammered, exactly like the teenage girl she most assuredly was not. "Didn't you know? I thought everyone in North Star would have heard the news by now."

Ben didn't smile, but at least he wasn't frowning. "You're right. Everyone's heard the news. What I meant was, what are you doing here this late? With the door unlocked? The restaurant's been closed for two hours."

"Pumpkin pies," she said, indicating the pastries cooling on the huge, black cookstove.

"I'm missing something," he said, the frown making its appearance between his eyebrows.

Ellie laughed. "Thanksgiving. I've been baking pies for the Veterans of Foreign Wars' community dinner and I didn't get the vegetables for tomorrow's special cleaned earlier." He was still frowning. "Thursday is Thanksgiving," she prompted. "Don't tell me you've forgotten the holiday?"

"No, I haven't forgotten the holiday. I just don't pay much attention to it." And then, perhaps realizing how isolated that statement made him appear, he went on, "My family wasn't much for big family dinners. Turkey and all the trimmings, that kind of thing. Actually, I'm going back to Ohio for the weekend. I have business there." Low and whiskey-rough, his voice, like the rest of him, both intrigued and dismayed her. Intrigued her by its consummate maleness, dismayed her for exactly the same reason.

"I'm sure you'll have friends to visit there," Ellie said, rushing her words.

"There are people I have to see."

Something in his voice caught her attention. "Don't you have a family?"

He didn't respond for a moment, as though deciding how much to tell her about himself. "Eldor and Martha are all the family I have left. I'm an only child. My mother died when I was two, my dad died five years ago. My stepmother remarried and moved to Alaska. I haven't seen her in two years."

"I'm sorry."

"Don't be."

"But you're coming to the community dinner at the VFW, aren't you? Eldor and Martha invited me and the kids to join them. I've never attended before. We—we always had Thanksgiving with—with my husband's family."

"You don't have family, either?" She couldn't very well ignore his question about family when he had answered hers, however reluctantly.

"Not in North Star. My parents live in Florida. My older brother and sister are in Detroit and Minneapolis. My mother-in-law died suddenly last March..." She let the words trail off, unable to trust herself not to start crying. Ellie hadn't been able to stay married to Patty Lawrence's son, but she had loved her mother-in-law dearly, and mourned her loss.

"I'm sorry. I can tell you miss her."

"A great deal."

He changed the subject abruptly. "I came to get some ground venison from the freezer. The refrigerator at my place is as old as Methuselah." He made a square with his hands about the size of a brick.

"Help yourself. It's unlocked." She cut a carrot in two, slipped it into a bowl full of cold water beside her and picked up another, but her thoughts weren't on her work. *Alone at Thanksgiving. And most likely at Christmas.* The thought made her sad. How empty a holiday season it must be for someone like Ben MacAllister who spent every holiday alone.

"Do you like working here?" he asked unexpectedly.

She lifted her eyes to his. Ben stayed where he was. He wasn't wearing gloves but the hood of his parka shadowed his face. "It's different," she admitted. "It's hectic sometimes, but I'm getting the hang of it." She tilted her head, considering. "Yes, I do like it. I've never cooked such large quantities of food before, of course. But everyone's been patient and Eldor's waitresses know how all the regulars like their food. That's a great help."

She was talking too fast and too loud. The job and the cozy furnished cottage behind the restaurant were a godsend, but she didn't trust her voice enough to say the words aloud. She was too emotional these days. Too unsettled by the baby, and heaven help her, by this man.

She picked up another carrot, then laid it down. *Her hands were shaking.* She didn't want him to see that. She narrowed her gaze, straining to read his expression, decipher the emotion in his eyes. "Was it your idea to have Eldor and Martha hire me?" she asked. Just like that, like the clichéd light bulb going on over her head, she was suddenly certain that he'd had something to do with the job offer.

Ben ignored her question and crossed to the chest freezer under the window. He opened the lid, rummaging through the institutional-size packages of vegetables and fruits, the stacks of steaks and chops and vacuum-packed chicken breasts. After a moment, he found the two small packages of ground venison he'd been searching for.

"Ben, answer me."

"I might have mentioned you told me you like to cook," he said at last.

Ellie covered the carrots with plastic film and set the bowl in the big refrigerator next to the containers of potatoes and onions and celery stalks she'd already cleaned.

So she owed this man her job and the roof over her head as well as her life. She didn't want to be beholden to anyone, not ever again. She had to be strong, invincible, for her children's sake, as well as her own. Right now she didn't have any strength left over to deal with men. Any man. This man in particular. Her hands were shaking harder than ever. She wiped them dry in the folds of her apron, pulled down the sleeves of her bright red pullover and smoothed her hair. Anything to hide the tremors. She leaned against the refrigerator door. "It seems I'm in your debt once more."

His gaze flickered to her belly, then back to her face and away. "Forget it," he said roughly. "It was serendipity. I walked the beach on into town the day I saw you out there. Farley Tall Trees had just headed south, leaving Eldor and Martha high and dry. I mentioned that you'd said you like to cook. And you sure as hell needed a place to live. Martha picked up the ball and ran with it, that's all."

Ellie wasn't about to be cowed by his grudging tone or his frown. "I'll think of some way to repay you."

He was across the room in five long strides. Ben moved so fast the hood of his parka fell back onto his shoulders. For a moment, Ellie was free to study his face, the hard line of his jaw, the high sharp cheekbones, the dark fringe of lashes above charcoal-gray eyes. The ridged scars on his cheek and temple stood out in angry relief against the bronze of his skin. The one on his temple ended at the very edge of his eyelid. She guessed that the injury that had caused those scars had come very near to taking his sight.

And then he was so close there was nothing she could focus on but the lightning flashes of anger in his eyes. Ben reached for her so quickly she couldn't step away. He curled his long strong fingers around her arms. His touch wasn't rough, there was no pain, but she doubted if she could free herself without a struggle. "You don't owe me anything," he said between clenched teeth. "Nothing."

"I do," she insisted. "You saved Spock's life. That dog is just about all Tim has left of his old life. Do you know what it would have been like for him to hear...to watch his dog die?" The color drained out of her face. "I'm sorry. That was a stupid thing to say. Of course you realized that. And you knew I'd feel the same way. That I . . . I would have tried to go back after her."

"No, you wouldn't. You have too much sense for that." His voice was harsh, a sandpaper rasp that filled the quiet room, raised the short hairs at the nape of her neck. He gave her a little shake to emphasize his words.

"I'm not so sure," she said. "Mothers sometimes do crazy things when their children are in pain."

"Don't make me out to be a hero, Ellie Lawrence. I'm nothing of the sort."

She wasn't frightened by his near violence because violence was not what she saw in his eyes. She saw what she knew he didn't want her to see—sadness and regret. She knew because she had seen a measure of that same pain reflected in her mirror more than once during the last two years. "You are a hero, whether you want to admit it or not. You're Tim's hero. And Carly's. Captain Larson thinks you should be nominated for North Star's Man of the Year award."

"No more," he growled.

"Don't," she whispered. She meant, "Don't do this to yourself," but he must have thought he had hurt her. Ben froze. He released his grip, smoothed his palms down her arms, then up to cup her face in his hands.

"I'm sorry, Ellie," he said. The pads of his thumbs traced the line of her mouth, and his voice softened. "I didn't mean to frighten you."

She shook her head defiantly. "I'm not afraid of you, Ben MacAllister. Why should I be?" But she lied. In her heart she knew this man could be very dangerous—not to her body, but to her bruised and battered soul.

"Because I'm not the man you think I am." He held her face captive between his rough palms. *Lord, was he going to kiss her?* He leaned closer, as though he couldn't help himself. His mouth was only inches from hers. She could feel his breath, his heat, the scent of soap and cold, clean air on his skin, and her body responded in kind. Ellie stiffened in his arms. *She couldn't let this happen. She couldn't.*

"Mom!"

"Mama!"

Tim and Carly erupted into the kitchen through the swinging doors that led to the bar, followed more sedately by their Sunday-school teacher, Danelda Larson, Lars's wife. The children stopped short at the sight of Ben. Tim muttered a tentative hello but Carly only smiled and hurried to Ellie's side.

Ben's eyes narrowed and he pulled the parka hood back into place. Ellie noticed the gesture and a protest pushed its way into her throat, but Danelda spoke first, "Here they are, Ellie. Safe and sound. Oh, hello, Ben." She nodded a welcome, her faded blue eyes widening slightly in surprise at finding him in the Jack Pine kitchen.

"Hello, Mrs. Larson," Ben responded. Somehow, in the blink of an eye, he'd moved halfway across the room.

"Sorry we're so late." Danelda was in her mid-sixties, almost as tall as her husband, with short, salt-and-pepper hair and a smile that lit up her plain, wrinkled face. "The rehearsal ran overtime. As usual, I might add. Every year I swear I will not direct another Christmas pageant and every year Reverend Young sweet-talks me into it."

"I'm going to be King Balthazar," Tim announced. "One of the Wise Men, you know."

Ellie smiled. "I know. And that's wonderful, Your Majesty."

"And I'm going to be a shepherd girl," Carly said. Her round little face puckered for a moment and her brown eyes filled with tears. "I wanted to be an angel but Erika Shurmansky started crying like a little baby, so I said I'd trade with her."

"That was nice of you, sweetie." Ellie gathered her close. Carly laid her head against her stomach, one hand patting the rounded firmness. "Mrs. Larson said I can be an angel next year when I'm bigger and the wings will fit me better. Right, Mrs. Larson?"

"I promise, Carly. I won't forget. Now, I simply have to run." With another wave, she was gone.

"Thanks, Danelda," Ellie called as the door swung shut behind her.

"Mommy, do you suppose Daddy will come home to see us in the play?"

Ellie's heart ached for her children. Even though it had been over a year since he left town, they still kept hoping that Lonny would come back into their lives.

"Happy Thanksgiving, Ellie." Ben's voice broke into her thoughts. He already had his hand on the door.

"Ben, wait." She didn't want him to think that Carly had been frightened of his scars.

"It's late," he said. "Riley's out in the truck. He's probably chewed through the dashboard by now."

"You've got your dog with you?" Tim asked, not quite meeting Ben's eye as he planted both hands on the stainless-steel work table where Ellie had been cutting vegetables.

Ben nodded. "Yeah, he's with me. Eldor and Martha are going to keep him while I'm out of town." The elder MacAllisters lived in a comfortable flat above the bar. "I'm going to put him in the kennel right now."

"Cool. Can I pet him while he's here?"

"Sure. Just don't let him off his chain. He likes to wander off and I don't think Eldor will want to be spending a lot of time chasing him down."

"I won't," Tim promised, venturing a smile. "It'll be great to have him to play with." A stricken look came over his face. He gave Ben a quick glance. "Not that Spock isn't a great dog. She is. And I'm real, real glad you went back into the house to save her. But—"

"But she doesn't like to chase sticks and catch Frisbees as well as she used to, right?" Ben prompted.

"Yeah, right."

"Spock sleeps on Tim's bed," Carly chimed in. "She doesn't like it out in the kennel with the other dogs."

Tim ignored the little girl's comment with an older brother's practiced disdain. "I wish I had a hunting dog. Spock can't hunt. She only pushes us around with her nose. She thinks we're sheep." He sounded so disgusted he surprised a laugh out of Ben.

"That's what Border collies are bred to do."

"She bites me on the butt when I don't go where she wants me to," Carly informed him from the sanctuary of Ellie's embrace.

"Oh, Carly, she does not," Ellie admonished. "And don't say 'butt.' Say 'bottom.' It's more polite."

"I don't care what you call it." She shot Ben a glance and a tiny smile. "She bit me, didn't she, Tim."

"You stepped on her foot."

"Mom. The baby kicked me. Right on the hand," Carly yelped.

Ellie laughed, and put her hand over her daughter's. "I felt it."

"I have to go," Ben said, an edge of panic in his voice. "Good night."

"I'll help Eldor watch out for your dog for you," Tim said.

"Thanks, sport." Then he disappeared into the frosty darkness of the November night.

"He called me sport, Mom." Tim threw out his narrow chest with pride.

"Why didn't he stay and visit?" Carly looked crestfallen. "I like him. He saved Spock's life."

"He's a busy man. And it's late," Ellie said, wondering why she felt compelled to make excuses for Ben's leaving so abruptly. "Hey. Look at the time.

There's school tomorrow, so why don't you two help me clear up the mess here and we'll go home.''

"Okay," Carly said, amenable as always.

"What happened to his face?" Tim asked, standing on tiptoe to look out the window above the sink.

"I don't know," Ellie said truthfully.

"It must have hurt a lot," Carly said, retreating to the haven of Ellie's arms once more. Ellie stroked the little girl's hair and squeezed her hand. Carly needed so much more reassurance these days. Ellie was her only anchor in a scary new world that now included a soon-to-arrive competitor for her mother's affection. "How did it happen?"

"I truly don't know." For such a garrulous couple, Eldor and Martha had been pretty closemouthed about Ben MacAllister. Probably at his urging. Ellie supposed she knew as much about him as anyone else in North Star. Rumor had it that he'd been a policeman somewhere farther south in Ohio.

There had been an accident of some kind, in the line of duty. Ben refused to discuss it. He'd come to North Star to recuperate, and even though he was fully recovered, the scars on his face and hand—and on his soul—remained. And he'd stayed on, alone and solitary in his lighthouse above the ice-blue waters of the lake.

"I like him," Carly repeated.

"So do I," Tim agreed with a nod.

Ben had saved Spock's life, it was true, but beyond that he had hardly spoken to Tim and Carly, shown them no special attention. Yet they both professed to like him, to want him for a friend. There was no understanding how a child's mind worked. Unfortunately, there was no understanding how a thirty-year-old woman's mind worked, either. The fact remained, her children liked him. *So do I,* Ellie said in her heart. *God help me, so do I.*

BEN'S HEART was pounding from his encounter with Ellie Lawrence and her children. He could hear it as he unloaded Riley's water dish and favorite blanket and shut him in the kennel in Eldor's garage with his father and mother and the new litter of puppies she had just produced. Riley ran back and forth in his cage, but Ben's mind was not on the dog. He was still picturing Ellie's little girl, frightened and clinging to her mother's waist. He couldn't blame the child. Even adults were repulsed by his scars. But he should have talked to Carly, asked her something simple like what grade she was in? Or did she like pumpkin pie? Instead, he'd turned tail and run.

Riley's father came up and exchanged greetings, then snapped at the younger dog through the chain-link fencing when Riley got too familiar. His mother stayed in her nest with the pups and bared her teeth. Riley trotted back to Ben and sat on his haunches, looking crestfallen and pathetic.

"Looks like what the writer said is true," Ben observed. "You can't go home again. I don't know why the hell I'm even trying." He should never have told Linda Novak, his partner's widow, that he would come back to Columbus to speak at the dedication of a new athletic facility at the church the dead man had attended all his life. He didn't want to go back there, talk to his old friends, his fellow state troopers. He didn't want to pretend, as they would, that the scars on his face and his psyche were not there. He didn't want to lie and say that he would be back on duty soon, when they all knew that wasn't going to happen.

He couldn't take the chance that some other routine traffic stop might go terribly wrong, as it had that spring night. Two deaths on his conscience were more than any man should have to bear.

No, he wasn't anxious to go home.

But at the moment, he wasn't anxious to stay in North Star, either. Not when he risked running into Ellie Lawrence every time he came into the Jack Pine. He spent entirely too much time thinking about Ellie Lawrence, dreaming about Ellie Lawrence. He'd deliberately stayed away from her since the fire, but it hadn't done much good. He could barely keep his hands off her tonight.

He could tell she didn't like him. She was jumpy and nervous around him. She'd looked frightened as a rabbit when he'd touched her tonight. Hell, why wouldn't she, alone in a bar kitchen with some guy that probably reminded her of the Phantom of the Opera.

No, he had to be honest about that, at least. She didn't seem afraid of him, or his scars, or his bad temper. But she was definitely leery of being alone with him. Hell, for all he knew, she was still in love with her ex-husband. She might as well be wearing a sign that said Hands Off in big red letters.

He was becoming obsessed with her, but he wasn't so far gone that he didn't realize nothing but heartache would come from falling in love with a woman who was seven months pregnant with another man's child.

CHAPTER FOUR

HE HADN'T THOUGHT it would be this hard. Or take this long. It seemed like State Trooper Ben Mac-Allister had fallen off the edge of the earth.

Until today.

Matt looked down at the newspaper that someone had left lying on the table at Mickey D's. He ignored his hamburger as he read. Bingo! It was right there, in the Reynoldsburg paper, all laid out in black and white, with pictures and everything. The pig had been in town all weekend and Matt hadn't known anything about it until right now. He read on. There was a lot of stuff about dedicating a church recreational facility, about loyalty and duty and friendship that lasted beyond the grave. Matt nearly puked, but he kept on reading.

He had never seen the other cop whose photograph was alongside MacAllister's, but he remembered the picture. It was the same one he'd studied from his hospital bed in the infirmary at the juvenile detention center all those weeks. It was the picture of the man who'd been behind the whole nightmare chain of events. At least as far as Matt was concerned. But he was dead and buried, just like Eric, and beyond retribution.

Sergeant Brian Novak, that had been his name. Older than MacAllister, fatter, staring out of the picture like John Wayne in his Statie uniform and the flag in the background. Sergeant Novak. He was the cop driving the patrol car the night Matt had talked Eric into joyriding in Eric's mom's car. He was the one who'd chased them off the highway onto that narrow county road south of the city.

Novak. He was the one who'd been riding their tailpipe when the tire blew and sent the patrol car into a spin that caused both cars to leave the pavement. Novak had been burned to a cinder, just like Eric, in the resulting crash and explosion. Ben MacAllister, who'd been in the second cop car, had pulled Matt out, too, smashed leg and all. Supposedly, he'd tried to get Eric free of the tangled mess of metal and broken glass, but the smoldering hulks had blown up in his face and it was too late. Too late.

Matt held his breath, not wanting to remember the smell of seared paint and burning rubber, and *God help him,* the smell of burning flesh. *Whose had it been? MacAllister's? Eric's? His own?* Those last-ditch heroics didn't make a difference. They didn't make Ben MacAllister any less guilty for Eric's death. MacAllister could have stopped the old guy. He could have radioed him to slow down, stop chasing them. They *would* have stopped. He, Matt, would have reasoned with Eric, calmed him down, talked him into pulling over when he saw the Staties backing off. *He knew he would have.*

If the old guy would have given them a chance.

If Ben MacAllister had made him.

Matt jumped up from the table and stormed out into the chill November night. He stuck his hand in the pocket of his varsity jacket. The one with the big C embroidered on the front, the letter he'd earned playing football at Central High the fall before the accident. A whole lifetime ago, when he thought he'd be able to make something of himself. When Eric had been there to listen and talk him through the bad times. Now, the only thing that kept him going was his need for revenge.

"Man, if I'd only known he was in town for that damned church dedication I could have done him then." Matt limped as he walked, the brace on his left leg feeling more like a lead weight than the state-of-the-art polymer that it really was.

He slowed down because his leg hurt like hell, but his brain kept on racing. He shoved his hand deeper in his pocket and found the handle of the eight-inch switchblade he'd bought off a drunk, homeless guy he knew from the old neighborhood. He'd got it in Nam, he'd said, kept it all these years, real sentimental value, but he'd sold it to Matt for the price of two bottles of cheap booze.

North Star, Michigan. That's where Trooper MacAllister was recuperating from his injuries, the paper said. Some little burg no one had ever heard of. It had taken Matt half an hour to find it in the atlas at the library. It was way the hell up in the Upper Peninsula, right on Lake Superior. As far as Matt could tell, about a hundred miles from nowhere. He didn't have a car and the bus was too damned slow. That meant he was going to have to hitchhike as far as he could. Good thing it was the weekend. There were a lot of cars heading up the interstate.

He'd wanted to buy a gun. But it hadn't been as easy as he thought, no matter how they kept yakking on TV about how any little first-grade kid could get one if they wanted one. Well, Matt hadn't had that kind of luck. At least not for the amount of money he was willing to pay. He needed to keep as much money as he could to get to North Star and then to Detroit or Chicago. Someplace he could lose himself for good.

Forever.

The knife would have to do.

ELLIE WAS UNLOADING laundry from the back seat of the car on the Monday evening after Thanksgiving, when Ben MacAllister drove into the parking lot behind the Jack Pine. He was wearing jeans, hunting boots, and his dark blue parka open over a flannel shirt, whose color was impossible to determine in the blue-white glow of the security light. It was snowing, big, fat flakes that stuck to everything including the dark waves of his hair.

"Hi," she said as he got out of his truck.

"Hi." The greeting was unenthusiastic. She had the distinct impression he would have driven right past her and out the other side of the looping driveway if he could have got away with it.

"Let me help you with that," Ben said. "You shouldn't be carrying that kind of load in your condition."

"It's the maid's day off," Ellie countered, determined not to let him see how startled she was by his sudden appearance. She'd thought of him off and on over the long weekend, wondering where, exactly, he was spending the holiday and with whom.

Ben laughed at her shopworn joke, a short, sharp bark of a laugh, but a laugh, nonetheless. The first she'd ever heard from him. The laughter creased the corners of his full, well-shaped mouth and caused a sudden tightening low in her stomach. Her pulse rate sped up, and the baby gave a jump of reflexive surprise. Ellie jumped, too. She just couldn't seem to keep herself from reacting physically to this man. That was a bad sign, a very bad sign. It had been the same with Lonny all those years ago.

"Where are the kids?" Ben asked picking up the three plastic baskets full of clean, folded clothes, holding them all easily, it seemed, as he waited for her to go ahead of him into the cottage.

"At pageant practice," she answered as she scooped up the detergent and bleach bottles, tucked the dryer sheets under her arm and kept her eyes averted from the top basket, resting just under his chin, the one with her underwear piled on top.

"It's the chef's day off, too, I see."

The restaurant was closed on Mondays, although the bar was open for business, as usual. "Microwaved sandwiches and pizza are the specials on Mondays," she explained, needing something to say, although he was as familiar as she was with the schedule at the Jack Pine. "Mrs. Eldor doesn't mind that kind of cooking, and Jackson Tall Trees, Farley's brother, has agreed to help out behind the bar. Here, let me get the door." Feeling as big as an elephant, she lumbered past him. She hesitated for just a heartbeat with her hand on the worn iron doorknob.

A man in her house.

She'd begun to allow herself to think of the little cottage as home, because on Saturday a letter from Farley Tall Trees had arrived, informing Eldor that the cook had met—and married—a well-to-do Florida widow, and that he had no intention of returning to North Star. At least not until it was warm and sunny and black-fly season was over.

Ben MacAllister in her house.

Ben seemed to fill the small living room as he stepped inside, depleting the oxygen supply. Ellie flipped the light switch, wondering if he had heard the news about Farley, but she couldn't seem to get enough control over her breathing to ask the question. She dumped the laundry supplies on the counter that separated the living space from the minuscule, utilitarian kitchen, then hurried to move the Santas she'd been carving so that he could set the clothes baskets on the table. Ellie bit her lip, hoping the table's bad leg didn't give out under the added weight.

She couldn't take off her coat. She felt as if she'd gained a ton over the holiday weekend. And she couldn't just continue to stand there like an idiot saying nothing. "How was your Thanksgiving?" she managed to ask.

"Fine," was the one-word reply.

"Did you spend it with friends?"

"Yes." Again, a terse reply. Ben set the clothes baskets down and the table wobbled alarmingly just as she'd feared.

"Darn, I'm going to have to get that fixed." Ellie made a grab for the last of the six, tall, pencil-slim Santas she'd carved the day before as it rolled toward the edge of the table.

"I can work on it for you," Ben offered, taking the top two baskets and setting them safely on the floor.

"No!" Her response was too harsh. She was determined to make it on her own, but she didn't have to sound quite so inflexible. "I can fix that myself," she said. "But not the washing machine. The repairman's coming tomorrow. It'll be a relief not to have to go to the Laundromat anymore." She was babbling and she hated it. "Would you like a cup of coffee?" She had never entertained a man in her home before. Especially one who kept her as off balance as Ben Mac-Allister. One who made her heart speed up, and her breathing difficult. Who made her think of things entirely inappropriate for a woman seven months pregnant with her third child. It was a very strange feeling. She didn't know quite how to act around him.

"No, thanks. I just came to pick up Riley."

Small talk helped. Kept the conversation general, casual. "Did you just get back in town?"

"About an hour ago."

"He's missed you," Ellie said. "But Tim kept him company. I think Riley liked having him around."

"Tell Tim thanks for me, will you?"

"Yes," Ellie said, smiling, knowing how pleased Tim would be that Ben had mentioned him. Her son had so little contact with men he could admire. It worried Ellie sometimes, but she did the best she could to be both mother and father to her children.

Ben reached out his hand for the Santa. Ellie hadn't realized she was still holding it. She gave it to him, taking care that their hands didn't touch. He turned the carving over and studied the face, the pointed hat, the suggestion of a smile on the lips. "This is good," he said.

"Thank you."

He balanced the Santa on his big palm. "Balsa?" he asked.

She shook her head. "No, I use basswood. It's a little heavier, a little tighter-grained. But it's still quick and easy to carve and there are a couple of gift shops in the Soo with year-round Christmas displays that pay me eight dollars for each Santa. With any luck, I can have two dozen apiece for them by next Monday."

He looked at her sharply. "Even if they're quick and easy to make, they must take at least a couple of hours."

"Yes, that's about right." Actually, when she wasn't as tired as she had been lately, it took far less time, but she didn't tell Ben MacAllister that.

"Even at eight dollars a pop, that's less than minimum wage."

"Beggars can't be choosers," Ellie said, holding out her hand for the Santa.

"What about this one?" He moved to the cheap pressed-wood bookcases that flanked the Franklin stove, the cottage's main source of heat. The bookcases were empty except for a few photographs, du-

plicates of favorite family snapshots her mother had
sent from Florida to replace those destroyed in the
fire, and a sleepy Muffin curled up on a lower shelf.
The small ginger cat opened one eye, glared balefully
and rolled over, pointedly disapproving of the human
interruption of her nap.

Ben tickled the cat's ears, then picked up a Santa,
the one she'd saved from the fire. He turned the figure over and over in his hands. The Santa was carrying a sack of pinecones and holly with a sleeping fawn
at his feet. He hefted its weight. "Oak?"

Ellie moved around the table. She still wasn't at ease
in his presence but she'd managed to gain control of
herself. "Yes. I found it in my toolbox. I...I was
working on it...when the fire started."

"Don't tell me this one took two hours to carve."

She held out her hand, taking the Santa from him.
"No," she said quietly, running her fingers over the
smooth-grained wood. "It took much longer. But then
again, I would have gotten a lot more money for it."

"May I ask how much it's worth?"

"They sell for about four hundred dollars," Ellie
said.

"That's more like it."

She smiled. "That's not all profit, either."

"I know. But at least it's not sweatshop labor."

"No," she said. "But it's the only one left. And I
have no more suitable wood." Ellie sighed, the smile
fading as she thought of the five lost oak Santas, and
the dozens of pine and basswood figures that had been
destroyed along with them.

"Who taught you to carve, Ellie?" He wasn't used to making small talk, that much was evident, but he was trying.

"My grandfather." She smiled. "He lived with us when I was a little girl. He was always whittlin' away—that's what he called it—at some piece of wood. When I was old enough, he gave me a penknife of my own. When he died, I quit carving for a long time. But after Carly was born, I couldn't find a job that paid enough to justify hiring a baby-sitter so I started again. It was Christmastime and Santas seemed just the thing to carve. It's grown from there. Thank goodness it's not a business that requires a lot of overhead."

"What other wood do you work in?" Ben asked, sticking his hands back in the pockets of his parka after she took the Santa from him.

"Pine," she said. "I love to work in white pine, it makes the whole house smell like a forest, but the white pine was logged out of here years and years ago, and it's expensive to buy from the lumberyard." She looked down at the Santa. "But there are other woods almost as good. And I'd rather find my own."

"What do you mean by that?"

"I usually spend time in the woods each spring, looking for just the right fallen tree. It has to have the bark on, no woodpecker holes, no knots. A friend of my dad's has a small sawmill. He hauls in the wood, and planes it down, slices it and cuts it in pieces anywhere from six to sixteen inches long and up to about seven inches wide." She used her hand to sketch the sizes in the air. Then she looked up and found him watching her with an unfathomable expression. She stumbled over the words but kept on talking. "But wood takes at least a year to cure and season properly. And what he's storing for me now won't be ready until April or May, depending on the weather." She shrugged, embarrassed, feeling she had said too much. "I'll manage somehow. I always do."

He reached up and touched a curling tendril of hair that had escaped from beneath her knit cap. "You shouldn't have to manage all by yourself, Ellie. What about your ex-husband? Or the father of your baby? Why haven't one or the other of them been around to help you?"

Ellie stiffened. Somehow, it hurt that he believed she not only had an ex-husband and a lover, and that they were both men she couldn't count on. Losers—did that make her a loser, too? Instinctively, she put her hand on her stomach, sheltering the new life there. "My ex-husband is this baby's father," she said coldly, lifting her chin. "I'm not in the habit of jumping from one man's bed to another."

The hand he'd lifted to her hair dropped to his side. "I'm sorry," he said. "I didn't mean to imply anything." He didn't move an inch, but Ellie felt as if he had. She couldn't step away. The rickety table was at her back and there was no room in the small dining area to create any distance between them.

"I'm not ashamed of this baby, Ben MacAllister. I . . . I made a mistake, but it's not his fault."

"I'm not judging you, Ellie. God knows I've made enough mistakes in my life." His face was deeper in shadow than it had been before, his expression hard to read. His voice was low and quiet but the words carried an arctic chill, a bitterness that she realized with a start was directed inward, not at her.

"Maybe not." She couldn't back down, couldn't let go of her anger or she'd burst into tears in front of him. "But you're asking yourself why, aren't you? Wondering how I got myself in this situation?"

"It's none of my business." He started to turn away, but she reached out, grabbed the sleeve of his coat and made him stay.

She laughed, short and hard. "You're not from a small town, are you? In North Star, it's everybody's business," she blurted out, appalled to feel the sting of tears behind her eyelids. She blinked furiously to keep them at bay. "I'll save you the trouble of asking around. Like I told you, my mother-in-law died suddenly last spring of a massive stroke. I loved her dearly. So did Lonny. We were both devastated. He didn't want to be alone..." She lifted her eyes to Ben's, dark pools of obsidian that watched her closely, weighed her words and probed her emotions, threatening the protective barriers she'd erected. "I didn't want to be alone."

"You don't have to tell me this, Ellie."

She shook her head. "It's not a secret. Anyone in North Star who can count backward can tell you when this baby was conceived."

"But maybe not why?" he asked, his voice taut, the words clipped and unwilling.

"Loneliness is a terrible thing," she whispered. "I knew it was a mistake as soon as it happened, but I tried to talk myself into giving Lonny one more chance." She looked up, meeting his shadowed gaze, defying him to disapprove. "He's not a bad man. I want you to know that. But he's..." She managed a smile. "He's Lonny, that's all. We reconciled for less than a week. Then he began to get restless. He wanted to move us all to Louisiana so that he could go back to work on an oil rig. I knew... I knew it wouldn't work. I signed the divorce papers the same day I learned I was pregnant."

"You are one hell of a woman, Ellie Lawrence." Her hand was still on his sleeve. He looked down at it, then lowered his head until his lips were mere inches from hers.

She closed her eyes, shook her head, but it was too late. It seemed as if once he had moved toward her, they were both powerless to stop what happened next. He kissed her. And for the space of less than a dozen heartbeats, she resisted the warmth and strength of his mouth on hers.

Then something changed, some chemical reaction began to sparkle in her veins, run in fine tremors along her nerve endings. *Desire. Passion. Need.* Emotions she had long denied and certainly wasn't prepared to feel in her present situation—or condition—coalesced in a pulsing fireball that seared her body and her brain.

Ben moaned low and deep in his throat. And Ellie knew he felt it, too, that incredible surge of lightning that communicated itself through bone and muscle. She could also tell he was no more happy about it than she was. But his arms came around her, moving to her shoulders, pulling her closer. He tightened his hold, adjusting himself with effortless grace to the rounded intrusion of her stomach.

The pressure of his mouth on hers increased. He touched the tip of his tongue to the corner of her mouth. He tasted of peppermint and coffee. He smelled of spice and snow and warm, clean skin. Ellie's thought processes shut down, her feelings took over.

She parted her lips with a sigh. He took immediate advantage of that small surrender. His tongue slipped inside, explored the soft moistness. But when she raised her hands to his face to hold him close, bring him even closer, Ben tore his mouth from hers. His hand closed over hers, holding it away from his face, refusing to allow her to touch the scars that marred the strong, clean lines of his cheek and jaw. She'd been about to cross a line, an invisible barrier past which he wouldn't let her go.

"I think we'd better slow down," he said, his voice low and husky. "This could get out of hand."

"I...I think you're right." Ellie's mind reeled with the implications. She was glad the inadequate overhead light hid her expression from him nearly as well as it obscured his face from her. "I...I don't know what came over me." Ellie's eyes followed his, looking out into the snowy darkness beyond the window. Now she was blushing, she could feel the heat of it coloring her throat and cheeks. What would she have done if the kids had walked in on her in Ben's arms. "I think it would be better if you go now."

"Don't worry, Ellie. It won't happen again." He stepped away, moved around the couch toward the door.

She nodded a little shakily. "I know that."

Ben stopped with his hand on the doorknob. I just remembered something Eldor said when he was showing me around the lighthouse after I moved in. He said there were some timbers in one of the outbuildings. They were probably left over from when the light keeper's house was built. And it's built of Michigan white pine. Do you suppose they'd be of any use in your carving?"

"I don't know." It would be a small miracle if they were.

"Why don't you stop out sometime and take a look?"

Her pulse rate accelerated once more. The baby gave a lusty kick and rolled over, nearly taking away what was left of her breath. "I'd like to see what you've got out there, but it's hard for me to get away from the Jack Pine most days." Ellie hesitated, then made up her mind. The kids were at pageant practice and Danelda Larson wouldn't be bringing them home for over an hour. He wasn't a seventeen-year-old teenager in thrall to his hormones and neither was she. They'd shared a kiss—albeit an earthshaking, volcanic eruption of a kiss—but that was all. "Maybe...would it be too much trouble if I came out to look at the wood tonight? There's a Coleman lantern around here some—"

He was silent for so long Ellie thought he would turn her down. "If you want," he said at last. "And don't bother with the lantern. I've got a couple of good flashlights in the truck.''

"I'll follow you in my car. And Ben, just so there's no misunderstanding. If the wood is suitable, I'll pay you what it's worth.''

CHAPTER FIVE

BEN GLANCED at the headlights of Ellie's car in his rearview mirror for at least the tenth time since he'd pulled out of the Jack Pine parking lot five minutes earlier. Snowflakes whirled and danced around him, buffeted by a cold wind off the lake. The road was snow-covered but not icy, and his truck had four-wheel drive, but he doubted if Ellie's beat-up old car did.

"What the hell am I doing, Riley?" he asked the attentive setter beside him on the bench seat. It was below freezing outside, snowing like the dickens and the steering wheel was like ice, but the palms of his hands were sweaty. "What the hell's come over me, dragging a pregnant woman out on a night like this? Why didn't I just tell her I'd load up the beams and bring them into town, let her look them over? If they weren't any good for her carving, she could have had them cut up for firewood for the stove."

Riley whimpered in sympathetic response.

Ben clamped his teeth shut before he answered himself aloud once more, but that didn't stop his brain from answering. *I dragged her out into the night because I couldn't get enough of her, that's why. I wanted to be with Ellie Lawrence. I wanted to talk to her, listen to her. I wanted to hear her laugh, make her life a little easier, hold her, kiss her*— He silenced his traitorous inner voice with ruthless self-discipline, wiped his sweaty palms on his thighs, one at a time, deliberately flexing his stiff, left hand, feeling the pull of scarred skin and the weakness of destroyed muscle and tendon, constant reminders of his failures and his guilt.

He pulled off the county road and drove up the curving, tree-shadowed lane that led to the outbuildings of the lighthouse. He lowered the snowplow that he'd attached to the front end of his truck earlier in the day, and cleared the narrow road as he drove, just as he'd done an hour before on his way out.

He glanced in the rearview mirror one more time. Ellie was following him at a prudent distance, driving slowly but with assurance. She pulled into the shelter of the barnlike brick building that had originally housed the gasoline generator that supplied electricity to the powerful lamp in the tower. Chippewa Point light station had warned ships away from the treacherous shoals offshore for seven decades until the light was taken out of commission twelve years before.

According to Eldor, the Fresnel lens, a huge, faceted, compound lens that had surrounded the lamp itself, was still in use in a lighthouse on the coast of Chile. The generator was probably there, too, for all Ben knew. All that remained here were this building—a small, brick privy that would outlast time—a cold and drafty light keeper's house and the empty light tower itself. The last was a solid stone structure, seventy feet high with a steep, spiral iron staircase leading to a narrow catwalk. The spectacular view of

Lake Superior and the three-hundred-foot dunes rising to the west made the arduous climb more than worthwhile.

Ben turned off the truck engine. Silence—now that the lake was frozen—flowed in to meet him as he opened the door. Before getting out, he reached under the seat and grabbed a long-handled, heavy-duty flashlight, switched it on and directed the beam downward. The narrow pathway of yellow light that arrowed through the snowy darkness would help keep Ellie from taking a dangerous misstep on the half-buried stones that lined the sidewalks. Riley bounded off the seat, and jumped to the ground. The dog circled the truck, growling low in his throat and then stood barking at the dark bulk of the light keeper's house.

"Heel, Riley," Ben ordered. "And watch your step," he cautioned Ellie with the same breath. "The Coast Guard had a thing for marking every sidewalk or pathway around here with big fat stones."

"I'll be careful." Ellie stopped in her tracks. "What do you think he's barking at?" she asked, peering into the gray-tinged darkness.

Ben shrugged. "Probably a coon in the garbage can. Or maybe a coyote. I heard one howling last night."

"Do you think it could be a wolf?"

"I don't think so."

"I suppose not." Ellie sounded more disappointed than frightened. "I've never seen one." Gray wolves, once numerous in this part of Michigan, had disappeared from the area years ago. The Department of

Natural Resources had reintroduced them in the western Upper Peninsula, but so far none had been spotted as far east as North Star. "Maybe, someday," she added a little wistfully.

"Maybe," Ben agreed. "The wood's in here." He grabbed a defiant, still barking Riley by the collar and dragged him over to the building. "Riley, heel!" he commanded. "You're not going tearing off after a raccoon and end up tipping over the garbage can."

"Or a skunk," Ellie said, a warm thread of amusement lacing her voice. "A skunk would be worse."

He handed her the flashlight and swung open the door. The rusty, unoiled hinges protested violently. Ellie played the flashlight over the half-dozen, ten-foot-long beams while he held on to Riley.

She bent awkwardly and ran her hands over the gray, weathered wood. "This one is split," she said. "That's too bad. I might be able to get some smaller pieces from it, though. But the others seem to be in good shape. Of course, I can't tell for sure right now, but I think it is white pine. And once the old wood's cut away..." She looked up at him. "For me, this wood is worth its weight in gold. Thank you, Ben," she said simply. Tears sparkled on her lashes like snowflakes glittering in the moonlight.

Her tears were almost his undoing. He forced himself not to kneel at her side, reach out and take her in his arms. "Glad I could be of help," he said gruffly. "If you'll give me directions to the sawmill, I'll drop off the wood tomorrow." He knew that this small gift was all she would accept from him.

God, what kind of man was her husband to leave her to fend for herself and her kids this way? The thought made the blood pound in his head, his hands knot into fists.

"Ben?" He heard his name beyond the rush of anger through his veins. He blinked, shook off the darkness and looked down to see her holding out her hand. "I'm sorry. I need some help," she said, in a choked little voice. "I can't get up by myself."

Automatically, Ben held out his hand to help her rise. As he did, he realized he had offered his scarred hand. He looked down at the red ridges, the dead white skin and cursed himself for his carelessness. But before he could snatch it back, Ellie curled her fingers around his.

Thanks," she said, sounding a little breathless as he lifted her to her feet. "I keep forgetting how hard it is to move this stomach around." She kept the flashlight angled down, but even in the near darkness he could see the blush that stained her cheeks and throat. "I must look like a beached whale," she said faintly.

"Are you fishing for compliments?" he asked before he could stop himself.

She laughed, and her laughter was like sunlight, touching the cold, dead places in his heart. Inwardly he flinched from its warmth. He didn't want to start feeling again. He was getting comfortable with the emptiness inside him. It was better than the guilt and the pain.

"I'm definitely not fishing for compliments," she said, handing over the flashlight. "Compliments imply looking good and that requires entirely too much time in front of a mirror."

Ben couldn't help himself, he reached out and touched the tip of his finger to her cheek. "You don't need to waste your time in front of a mirror to look good."

He felt the heat rise beneath her skin even though he couldn't see it. "Ben—" A frown had drawn the delicate arch of her eyebrows together. "I...I think I'd better be going."

"I'll walk you back to the car," he said.

"I can manage."

"There's no security light," he said woodenly. "I don't want you to slip and fall." Ellie's reply was inaudible as Riley's head whipped around, his lips curled back, and he began growling at the open doorway.

She put her hands over her ears to block out the noise, and looked at Ben. "The raccoon must be right outside."

The short hairs at the back of Ben's neck stood on end. Instincts he hadn't used in months stirred to life. His skin tingled, the muscles in his jaw tightened and electricity danced along his nerve endings. "Stay put," he said, shifting his grip on the flashlight. It wasn't much of a weapon, but it was better than nothing. He turned it off, plunging them into intense darkness. Ben closed his eyes for a moment, adjusting to the lack of light.

"Ben! Wait!" Ellie's voice was barely more than a whisper, but it held an edge of fear. She had her hand clamped on his coat sleeve, trying to hold him back. "What's wrong?"

He shrugged her off. "Nothing," he said, willing the tension out of his voice. "I don't want you walking into an ambush by an angry skunk, that's all."

"It's not a skunk you're expecting out there," she said.

"Just being careful." He let go of Riley's collar. The setter was gone like a shot, running straight for the front door of the light keeper's house. "Oh, hell," Ben said. "Stay put." He stepped through the doorway and immediately sidestepped to his left, into the darker shadows beneath the overhang of the steeply pitched roof, but he didn't move quickly enough.

Out of the corner of his eye he saw a figure barreling out of the tree line at a clumsy, uneven run. Ben spun around, preparing to meet the attack, but the other man cannoned into him, knocking them both off balance. Ben hit the frozen ground and rolled, coming up on top of his assailant, but he lost his grip on the flashlight and it skidded out of reach.

Riley reappeared out of the falling snow, standing a few feet away, feet braced, barking at the top of his voice. Ben's opponent was slight but strong, and he fought with desperate ferocity. With a grunted oath, he wrenched loose from Ben's grasp, and lunged to his feet, aiming a kick at Ben's head. His movements were slow and stiff, and he missed by a mile.

Ben grabbed his leg and jerked. The other man went down like a ton of bricks. Ben grabbed him by the collar of his coat, swung him around and hauled him to his feet, wrenching his arm behind his back and immobilizing his head in the crook of his elbow. "One more move and I'll snap your neck," Ben growled.

"You and who else." His captive's tone was defiant, but his voice cracked and rose on the last word.

The mugger was a kid.

His hunch was verified when Ellie hurried out of the building, retrieved the flashlight from a snowbank and turned it on. "He's just a boy," she said in disbelief.

Ben hadn't been expecting Ellie to move so fast. Bright spots of color danced before his eyes, temporarily blinding him. "Don't shine that light in my eyes," he snapped. It might have been seven months since he wore the uniform, but at the moment he was all cop. "Riley, shut up."

The barking stopped. Riley sat whimpering in the snow.

"I'm sorry," she said. The flashlight beam lowered to the level of his chest. "What is he doing here? Why did he attack you? Do you suppose he escaped from the prison in Marquette?" Ellie was holding the big, heavy flashlight with both hands and it was shaking, but her voice was steady, her tone indignant. "Where's your phone? I'll call the sheriff."

"I'm no con." The kid started struggling again, and Ben jerked the boy's arm higher between his shoulder blades. He let out a ragged yelp of pain and went still.

"Let's get him inside," Ben said, shoving the kid toward the house. "March!" He half pushed, half dragged his captive toward the pale circle of light above the front entrance to the light keeper's house.

"Who is he?" Ellie wanted to know. "I've never seen him before. I don't think he's from around here." She was walking backward. "Do you know him?"

"Ellie, turn around and watch where you're going," Ben said in exasperation, still half-blinded by the flashlight.

"What? Oh!"

The next ten seconds were a blur of motion and confusion. Ellie stumbled over the snow-covered stones lining the sidewalk. Ben took half a step in her direction, loosening his hold on the boy. The kid bucked like a wild horse, breaking free with a lunge that sent him careening into Ellie. She went down in a flurry of arms and legs. The flashlight fell from her hand, the light shining golden on the snow. Riley ran into the fray, barking and jumping. Ben took one step toward her, then stopped dead in his tracks, his blood running cold.

Ellie was on her knees, the boy beside her, his hand locked around her neck as Ben's had been locked around his just moments before. In his other hand, Ben caught the gleam of steel. A long, thin knife blade hovered inches from the pale skin of Ellie's throat. "Don't try anything," the kid yelled. He was shaking so hard Ben was afraid the knife would slip and he would hurt Ellie even if he didn't mean to.

He held out his hands. "No one's going to try anything. Let her go."

The boy shook his head. His cap tumbled off his head, a baseball cap, no protection at all from the cold. A small, detached portion of Ben's brain, his cop's brain, cataloged the details. The boy wasn't wearing gloves and his jacket didn't look heavy enough to block out the arctic wind. His cheap running shoes weren't made for wrestling in the snow and he was having trouble keeping his balance as he struggled to haul Ellie to her feet.

"Shut that damn dog up," the boy demanded.

"Riley, heel," Ben said, and miraculously the dog did just that. "Let her go," he repeated. "Whatever you want with me has nothing to do with Mrs. Lawrence."

"Shut up," the kid said, looking wild, his head swinging back and forth like a trapped bull. "Shut up. I don't want to hurt her, but I can't let her go or she'll call the cops."

"I won't," Ellie whispered. "I won't. Just let us go. Take my car if you want to. Just go away."

"No." The boy's voice rose, in hysteria or desperation, or both. "No. I came to kill you, Ben MacAllister, and that's what I'm going to do."

"Why?" Ellie's eyes flew to Ben's. Ben kept his gaze focused unblinkingly on the kid . . . and the knife.

"Because I promised Eric. On his grave," he whispered. "This pig killed my friend. The best friend I ever had. He's gotta pay, man."

He took a step forward. Now he realized why the boy had seemed familiar. He was taller, a little broader in the chest and shoulders than he'd been seven months before, but the shape of his face and the long, lean look of him were the same. "You're Matt Westrick."

"Yeah. Eric Baden was my best friend. And because of you and your gung-ho Dirty Harry cop buddy, he's dead. It's your fault."

Ben shook his head. "You stole a car and tried to get away."

"Damn it, it was Eric's mom's car. We were just taking it for a *ride*. She would have never called the police if she knew he had it. *You* got him killed over a joyride."

"You know as well as I do there'd been a juvenile car-theft ring operating in the area. You guys were just in the wrong place at the wrong time." *God, what a feeble excuse.* He knew it. The kid knew it. And, from the horrified look in her eyes, so did Ellie.

"He burned to death, man." The words were half scream, half sob. The kid was nearly at the breaking point. There was no telling what he'd do next.

"Oh. Help me, please." Ellie dropped her hands from Matt's forearm to her stomach. She groaned. "Help," she repeated in a weak, fade-away voice.

Matt stiffened, his eyes were big dark holes in his white face. "What's wrong, lady?"

"Pain," Ellie said in a strangled voice.

"What's wrong with her?" Matt shouted at Ben.

"The baby," Ellie moaned. Her voice was convincingly weak and frightened, but her eyes, fixed on Ben's face, were steady and clear.

"Baby! Jeez, what are you talking about? What baby?"

"She's pregnant," Ben said, his voice as cold as the north wind. "Can't you tell?"

"I . . . I thought she was just fat."

"Let her go. You may have hurt the baby."

Ellie moaned again.

"No! I didn't mean to hurt no baby." Matt staggered back, setting Ellie free so suddenly she stumbled and fell to her knees. Ben launched himself at

Matt the instant the teenager loosened his grip. Ben drew back his fist, prepared to knock the boy sense-less and disarm him before he could recover his balance. But Matt wasn't moving. He lay huddled on the ground where he had fallen, the knife gleaming dully in the snow a few inches from his hand.

Ben kicked the lethal switchblade farther into the yard, and hauled Matt to his knees by the collar of his coat. "Stand up, damn it," Ben commanded, but the boy seemed incapable of following the order. He stayed where he was, head bowed, hands clenched between his knees.

"Ben, he's half-frozen," Ellie said, reaching out.

"Don't touch him," Ben growled. Her hand dropped to her lap. "Are you okay?"

"I'm fine," she said, managing a smile.

"Are you sure? The baby?"

She laughed, a little shaky and high-pitched, but a real laugh, all the same. "You haven't been around pregnant women much, have you? I'm fine, just a lit-tle scared."

"This was more than a little scare," Ben said roughly. His heart was pounding like a sledgehammer. The kid could have killed her, or harmed the baby.

The smile left her face. "I know, but I'm fine, re-ally."

"I didn't mean to hurt the baby," Matt mumbled. "You just got in the way." His voice was slurred, the words thick and slow. "I only wanted to pay Mac-Allister back...for Eric...I couldn't do it." His head dropped forward.

Ellie's glance sharpened. "Is he hurt?" she asked. "Did he cut himself with the knife?"

Ben hauled Matt upright. He was a dead weight hanging on the end of his arm. "I don't think so. There's no blood. He's probably high on something."

Ellie shook her head. "I didn't smell any liquor or pot on his breath."

"How do you know what pot smells like?"

She gave him a long, level look. "My ex-husband smoked it regularly. Of course, he could be on something else. Something more dangerous." She frowned, touching Matt's hand again, shaking his arm. There was no response. "I don't like this." She frowned harder. "He sounded perfectly normal a few minutes ago."

"Ellie, he had a knife at your throat," Ben said in exasperation. "How can you call that normal?"

"Don't be ridiculous. You know what I mean. I think he's sick. Or—" she reached out and gently touched Matt's clenched fist, despite Ben's instinctive snarl of protest "—or he's half-frozen to death. Ben, we'd better get him inside. He's got all the symptoms of hypothermia."

CHAPTER SIX

"DAMN IT, you're probably right. Open the door for me, will you? I'll carry him inside. But first, get the knife." Ben pulled the boy upright and lifted him over his shoulder with a grunt.

Ellie picked up the flashlight and swung the beam across the snow, willing her shaking hands to function. Yellow light gleamed off the sinister weapon. She reached down, picked it up and fumbled to find the catch that released the thin, deadly blade. She shut it with a snap and dropped it into her coat pocket, then hurried up the steep, narrow stairs to open the heavy door.

She'd never been inside the old lighthouse. The front door opened directly into a narrow hallway that appeared to run the length of the living quarters. It was cold, unheated and bare of furniture, but there was a faint light above the kitchen sink straight ahead. She hesitated for a moment, letting her eyes adjust to the new play of light and shadows then headed toward the kitchen. There was a closed door on either side. One of them would be to Ben's bedroom. Her heart gave a funny little jump at the thought.

"There's a couch in the kitchen," Ben said, kicking the door shut behind him. "I'll put him there." His words echoed in the shadowy darkness.

Ellie found the light switch, one of those old-fashioned, button-type ones, and pushed it. The kitchen was fairly large, with two double-hung windows at the far end that faced out onto the lake. The view would be beautiful during the day, but tonight there was nothing to be seen but a swirl of snowflakes against the glass. A round table piled high with books and magazines, a worn leather armchair, reading lamp and a small woodstove exuding blessed warmth gave evidence that this room must be where Ben spent a lot of his time.

While Ellie was looking around, Ben lowered the boy to the sagging leather couch, twin to the armchair—the pair of them relics of the fifties. Matt sat there, shivering violently, his eyes seeing nothing.

"We have to get him warmed up," Ellie said worriedly. "Do you have a hot-water bottle?"

Ben looked at her as if she'd spoken a foreign language. "A hot-water bottle?"

"No, I suppose you don't. How about those big plastic bags that zip shut? They work just as well."

"I don't do much cooking here."

Ellie bit her lip. "Blankets then?"

"That I can manage. I'll get them." He held out his hand. "Give me the knife."

Ellie frowned, but stuck her hand in her pocket and pulled out the weapon. "He's in no condition to harm anyone now."

"Maybe," Ben said. "But I'm not taking any chances."

She handed over the knife and his flashlight. "Hurry," she urged, looking around, spotting the bulky, old-fashioned bottle-gas range along the far wall. "We have to get him warmed up. From the inside out, too. He looks like he's been outside in this weather for hours." There was a teakettle sitting on the burner. Ellie picked it up. It was full. There were matches on a shelf above the stove. She lit the burner and set the teakettle over the flame, then went back to the silent boy on the couch.

"Matt," she said, reaching out to touch his shoulder. He flinched. Ellie jerked her hand back, not because he had rejected her touch, but because his flimsy satin jacket was soaking wet and icy cold. She glanced down at his legs. His jeans were old and worn thin, soaking wet, as well. He wore a lightweight, nylon and velcro brace on his left leg. It too, was soaking wet. His shoes were caked with snow. "Matt," she said more loudly. "How long were you waiting out there?"

He didn't respond immediately. "A long time," he said at last.

"You have to get out of these wet clothes. You'll catch pneumonia."

He looked at her for the first time. His brown eyes were pools of misery. "I don't give a rat's ass," he said, his voice breaking, rough with swallowed tears. His teeth were chattering so violently she could barely understand what he said. He pushed his fists into his eyes and dropped his head to his knees, shutting out the world. Dry sobs racked his body.

Ellie's heart contracted. He had the look of a man, the height, the breadth of shoulders, the beginning of fuzzy stubble on his chin. But he was still a boy. She put her hand on his shoulder, at a loss how to deal with such abject misery. Despite what he'd just done, something inside told her Matt Westrick wasn't evil. He was desperate and hurting and very, very scared. "Yes, you do care what happens to you, Matt."

He shrugged her off. "Let me go."

"Ellie. Get away from him." Ben's voice was a whiplash. Ellie jumped backward, startled by the sudden interruption.

She put her hand on her heart. "Don't do that again. I'm liable to go into labor right here in your kitchen." The scars on his cheek and temple stood out in bold relief. He caught her staring, and his mouth hardened into a tight line. He dropped an armload of blankets on the couch beside Matt and handed her a terry-cloth-covered oblong article.

"It's one of those microwave gel things you can heat up. For muscle sprains and stiff necks," he explained. "I forgot I had it. Will that do in place of a hot-water bottle?"

"It'll do fine. Where's the microwave? How long shall I set it for?"

"Over there, by the fridge." He shrugged out of his coat and tossed it over a chair. "Never mind. I'll do it. It'll save time."

"Okay." Ellie turned awkwardly toward the stove, dismayed at not being able to control the direction of her eyes. She was angry with herself for causing him distress, but angrier still because it wasn't his scars that had drawn her gaze, it was her need to see him, to really see him without the protective shadows behind which he always hid. And God help her, she liked what she saw.

The kettle was beginning to whistle, a welcome distraction. "Do you have tea?" she asked.

"No." The door on the microwave slammed shut, the motor started to whir.

"Oh." *Silly,* how many men did she know who actually preferred drinking tea? She opened a cupboard door. It was almost empty. There was salt and pepper, chili powder and small bags of sugar and flour, nothing else. She opened the next one. Plates, saucers, three thick white coffee mugs, half a dozen jelly glasses, all of them of the same vintage as the cracked black-and-white linoleum and round-shouldered refrigerator.

She opened the cupboard above the stove. Instant coffee, dry creamer and, best of all, half a dozen foil envelopes of hot-chocolate mix. "Excellent," she said, just to break the uncomfortable silence. The microwave beeped. She grabbed a chipped china mug and the hot chocolate.

She worked quickly, turning around, holding the mug of chocolate carefully in both hands as Ben finished wrapping Matt in the blankets. He looked up, his eyes dark as the winter sky before a snowstorm. "Give me that." Ellie handed him the drink. "Matt." Again that whiplash tone of command. "Drink this."

The boy shook his head. Ellie wondered how old he was. Fifteen? Sixteen at the most, she guessed. "Get the hell away from me," he said, pulling the blanket tight around his shoulders. "Give me back my clothes." His hands were still shaking, but his voice was a little stronger, his words less slurred.

"I said, drink this," Ben told him. "I'm not going to let you die of hypothermia just so you don't have to go to the trouble of getting out of bed every day."

"Ben." Ellie sucked in her breath. She had seen the despair in Matt's eyes. What if something Ben said pushed the teenager over the edge?

"I know what I'm doing." He held up a restraining hand, never taking his eyes off Matt's pale, blotchy face. "If you don't drink this now, I'll call 911 and they'll send an ambulance out here to haul you off to the hospital. The way they'll warm you up is a damned sight more embarrassing and uncomfortable than this."

The threat got through to him. Matt took the cocoa and drank. "There." He stuck the mug in Ben's face, but Ben didn't take the cup. "Now. Give me back my clothes. Let me get out of here."

Ben stood up, towering over the seated boy and Ellie's own smaller frame. She realized what a formidable figure he would have made in his state trooper's uniform. "You just tried to use a knife on me, buster. You threatened Mrs. Lawrence with assault. What the hell makes you think I'm going to let you get up and walk out of here?"

"Go ahead, call the cops," Matt said, trying to sound belligerent, but only sounding scared. "I don't give a rat's ass what happens to me anymore."

"I know," Ben said. "That's why I'm not going to do it."

"What?" A flicker of dismay crossed Matt's face.

"Does anyone know where you are?"

"I don't have to answer that. I don't have to tell you anything."

"No," Ben acknowledged. "You don't have to say a thing. But I'll find out anyway."

Matt looked down at the empty cocoa mug. Ellie stepped forward and tugged it gently from his hands. "Would you like a refill?" she asked.

Matt raised his head. Once more, the misery hiding beneath the tough mask he wore seared her soul. The thought struck her that Ben and this kid were a lot alike. "Yeah. Please," Matt added hastily.

"I'm waiting," Ben said, with steel in his voice.

"No one knows where I am. I left Ohio two—no, three—days ago."

"Were you in foster care?"

"A group home. I doubt they even noticed I'm gone," he said bitterly. Then after a moment's silence, he repeated. "I don't have to tell you anything."

"You don't have to say a word," Ben agreed. "I can find out for myself."

"You're not calling the cops?" Matt didn't seem to see the refilled mug of cocoa Ellie offered. He sat staring up at Ben, his eyes focused just about at the level of his chin, not quite bold enough to meet his gaze head-on.

"Not tonight."

Matt's eyes narrowed. "You can't keep me here."

"I can do damned well almost anything I please," Ben informed him, his face grim. He took the cocoa from Ellie and shoved it into Matt's hand. "I've got your clothes. I've got your knife and your wallet and I've got a real vicious dog I can sic on you."

Matt's mouth flopped open. "Vicious dog? Where?"

"Right there," Ben said, leaning down to scratch Riley behind the ears. The setter's mouth flopped open just like Matt's, his tongue lolled out, his eyes closed in pleasure.

"That's a vicious dog?"

"Yep," Ben drawled.

"You've got to be kidding."

"Want to take the chance?" Ben inquired mildly.

Matt clenched his fists, panic in his eyes as he obviously realized Ben meant every word he said. "I'm not staying here," he said from between clenched teeth.

"You don't have a choice—" Ben's tone was as implacable as his words "—unless you want to go to jail."

Ellie thought she knew where Ben was headed. He meant to keep Matt here with him, to keep him from doing anything more desperate than he'd already attempted. She didn't think that was a wise decision.

"Drink your cocoa," Ben told Matt. "I'll be back as soon as I see Mrs. Lawrence to her car. She needs to get home to her children." Ellie glanced at her watch. Ben was right. Carly and Tim would be home in less than thirty minutes, and it was a fifteen-minute drive from the lighthouse back to the Jack Pine.

Ben scooped up Matt's wet clothes and shoes and the leg brace. "Not my clothes—"

"I want you here when I get back. Stay, Riley." The setter woofed in reply, tongue still lolling as he gazed soulfully at Matt. Riley bumped the teenager's arm, thrust his muzzle onto Matt's lap. Reluctantly, the boy reached out and patted Riley's head. The dog whined and wiggled closer in ecstasy, his tail slapping against the leather couch. "Yeah, some vicious watchdog you are."

Ben motioned Ellie to follow him out of the kitchen.

For another long moment, she studied Matt's bent head, his slumped shoulders. Her heart ached for his loss and the pain that had driven him to such desperate acts, but still she was uneasy. Ben was waiting, tall, composed, silent. She looked at him, and he didn't flinch from her scrutiny. He knew what he was doing. She turned and led the way down the hallway, into the shadows.

Ben reached around her to open the door. "You don't have to walk me to the car," she said, laying her hand on his arm. She kept it there, even though the shock of touching him arced along her nerve endings like a live current.

"I don't want you slipping on the ice."

"I won't slip on the ice," she assured him, dropping her hand. "You can stand here and watch me from the doorway, if you insist, but I don't think you should leave Matt alone."

"I don't intend to leave him alone. I'll sleep in the chair by the window. He can bunk down on the couch."

Cold air swirled around them, snowflakes floated in the yellow light above the door. "Is that safe?"

"Do you mean, is he going to try and pull a knife on me while I'm asleep?"

"I..." Did she? It seemed as if the rage had drained out of the boy, but she couldn't be sure. She wasn't trained to make those kinds of judgments. "I don't think that will happen," she said at last, trusting her heart.

Ben didn't smile, but neither did he look quite so grave, so remote as he had moments before. "I don't think so, either."

"But what if he's a danger to himself?"

"I'll keep an eye on him."

"Shouldn't he be with someone who knows about these things, someone who's trained to deal with troubled teenagers?"

"Trust me on this one, Ellie. I've got a hunch, a gut feeling that dumping this kid back into the system will be the last straw for him. He'll shut down, he'll walk the walk and talk the talk till he can get out on his own. And then—"

Her breath hissed out between her teeth as images she didn't want to contemplate lanced her mind. She shivered. "What, Ben?" she made herself ask.

"He'll disappear. Somewhere big and mean and dangerous. And sooner or later, there will be a gang fight, or an overdose, or something else and we'll lose him forever."

"And you'd blame yourself for that, too, wouldn't you?" Ellie wondered if she'd gone too far. "What happened that night, Ben?" She lifted her hand toward the scars on his face.

His hand shot out, circled her wrist and held her captive. "Don't," he said. She dropped her hand to his chest, waiting. She could feel his heart beating beneath her palm. His jaw tightened.

"How did you get these scars?" she whispered, moving a little closer, determined to learn what terrible memories this man shared with the angry, sorrowing boy in the other room. "I want to know, Ben. I think you owe me that after what happened tonight."

The slow, steady drumbeat of his heart beneath her fingertips increased. He ignored her demand, changed the subject. "Did he hurt you? Were you telling the truth? The baby?" He searched her face, looked down at the roundness of her belly, let his gaze linger for a moment, no more.

A slow warmth spread through her, pooled in her womb. The baby rolled and stretched inside her as though he, too, felt the fleeting caress of Ben's eyes. "No. I'm fine. Really. Both of us are fine." She mustn't let herself be distracted from her quest, by thoughts of what might have been if she'd met Ben long ago instead of only last month. "Ben—"

"You aren't going to let go of this, are you?"

"No. Not until you tell me what happened that made that boy want to kill you."

The fragile bond created by his concern for her unborn child was broken with the harshness of his next words. "I'm exactly what Matt accused me of being. I'm responsible for his friend's death. And my friend's death, into the bargain."

"I don't believe that," Ellie said so fiercely she surprised herself.

The grip on her wrist tightened. "Believe it."

"That's not an answer. It doesn't explain anything."

He released her wrist, bracketing her face with his hands. For once, he made no attempt to hide his scars. "They used to call this kind of interrogation the third degree. It's illegal."

"I want to know why you feel you deserve to be punished. Why you're willing to shield a teenager who just threatened your life."

"Are you always this stubborn?" he asked, desperation tingeing his words.

"Always," she whispered.

"You'd make a hell of a cop."

"What happened?" she urged softly. "What happened to you and to Matt?"

"Not tonight, Ellie."

"Yes, tonight. If you expect me to cooperate with this mad scheme, I have to know why you're doing what you're doing."

His breath hissed out between his teeth in a gusty sigh. He looked past her down the long hall, avoiding her eyes. "One night last spring, Matt and his friend, Eric Baden, went joyriding in Eric's mother's car. Matt's been in trouble most of his life, but Eric was one of those squeaky-clean kids who help old ladies cross the street, or rescue kittens from trees. Good student. Good citizen."

The kind of kid Ben himself might have been?

"And he was Matt's best friend?"

"Opposites attract." He shrugged. "Maybe Matt's recklessness appealed to Eric. Maybe Matt was drawn to Eric's stability. Anyway, Eric and Matt were supposed to be camping out with some other kids that night. Eric's parents had planned to be away, too, but his dad wasn't feeling well and they came back home to find the family car gone. Thinking that Eric, who was only fifteen and didn't have a driver's license, was camping out at a state park fifty miles away, they reported the vehicle stolen."

"Oh, God," Ellie said, anticipating what would come next.

"There had been a rash of car thefts in the area, a teenage gang out of Columbus, moving into the suburbs, snatching cars right out of the owners' driveways. Eric's parents had read about the thefts and figured that was what had happened to their car. So did the local cops. They notified the highway patrol to be on the lookout for the Baden vehicle."

Ellie could feel the strain in his body, hear it in the flatness of his low, rough tone as he fought to keep his voice level. "Someone made a terrible mistake that night, didn't they?" she said.

Ben nodded. "Brian Novak, my best friend, was patrolling that night and spotted the Badens' car. He thought if he could apprehend whoever was in the car, we might get a break identifying the leaders of the ring. He radioed for backup. I was closest. The Baden car turned off the state highway where Brian had spotted it, heading into the hills south of Columbus. Brian gave chase. It was a muggy spring night. There had been storms during the day. It was foggy in patches. The roads down there are narrow and twisting—"

"You didn't think it was a good idea, did you?"

"No," he said fiercely, and she knew the guilt he carried with him was as heavy and tormenting as if the events he was relating had occurred only hours before, instead of over half a year ago. "I radioed Brian to stay back, wait for me to catch up, but he didn't. I came into visual range just in time to see the accident."

"What happened next?"

"It was hard to tell, even afterward. From what I remember, Brian's cruiser was right on their taillights. Then something happened, a tire blew? One of them hit something lying in the road? Who knows? Both cars left the pavement, crashed into the trees along the berm and caught fire. Matt was thrown half out of the passenger side. I pulled him out. His leg was a mess but he was still breathing. I tried to get the Baden boy out, but he was pinned behind the wheel. There was no pulse, but I don't think Matt ever believed that."

"And Brian? Your friend?"

Involuntarily, his fingers lifted halfway to his face, as though to touch the scars that marred the strong, clean lines of his profile. "Brian never had a chance. The cruiser blew up—" he gave a short, harsh bark of sound, laughter with no humor, only misery "—literally in my face. The burning debris ignited the gasoline in the Baden car. It was an inferno."

"And that's what Matt remembers about that night, isn't it? His friend, still in the burning car, and you watching, not doing anything."

"Yes."

"Even though you were seriously injured your-self?"

"He'd lost a lot of blood. He was in shock and I was the only one left standing. A cop, just like the one that had chased Eric to his death."

"I don't know if you can help him deal with those memories, Ben. Should you even try?" She knew the answer he would give before the question left her mouth.

"I have to try, Ellie," he said quietly. "Now, go on home, back to your kids. I'll watch over Matt, and I promise no harm will come to him tonight."

CHAPTER SEVEN

"I'M GOING to make a Christmas tree with purple icing and red and green sprinkles and those little silver balls on it," Carly announced. She was perched on a high stool in the Jack Pine kitchen, watching Mrs. Eldor roll out cookie dough.

Ellie's employer was making sugar cookies for the Sons of Gitche Gumee Auxiliary's annual bazaar to benefit the North Star library fund. The event was the traditional kickoff to the holiday season in the area. Mrs. Eldor's sugar cookies were also tradition, hard as rocks and heavy enough to be used as doorstops. But no one was ever rash enough to point out those flaws, so every year she made six dozen, and every year they sold out, giving the birds and squirrels in North Star backyards an unexpected Christmas treat.

"Carly, you can't make Christmas trees purple," Tim objected. "Mom, tell her she can't make purple trees."

"I can if I want to." Carly's voice had that little catch in it that meant she was going to start sniffling and then burst into tears. Carly could cry buckets at the drop of a hat.

"Tim, you make your trees green," Mrs. Eldor ordered before Ellie could say anything. The older woman had been a sergeant in the Woman's Army Corps during the Korean War, and she'd never lost the knack of command. "And let Carly make hers purple. You can say they're California Christmas trees or some such thing. Everyone knows they do strange things out there, even for Christmas."

"More like Martian Christmas trees," Tim muttered under his breath. "That's where she belongs, anyway. Goofy little sister from Mars."

"I heard that," Ellie said, wiping flour from her hands as she finished cutting out biscuits for next morning's breakfast crowd. "Let your sister be creative. Let her do what makes her happy. That's the Christmas spirit, after all," she reminded him gently as she covered the baking sheets with plastic film and slid them onto the shelves of the big double-door refrigerator.

"Your mother's right," Mrs. Eldor chimed in, "And don't forget, Santa's elves are watching and keeping track of how you treat your sister."

"Hmmph." Tim folded his arms across his narrow chest. He looked a great deal like his father when he did that, intelligent, quick-witted and completely, utterly, arrogantly male. Ellie sighed. She just hoped she had better luck instilling a sense of responsibility and self-discipline to go along with that quick wit and intelligence than her mother-in-law had had with Lonny.

"Tim," she reminded him, "Christmas is getting closer every day."

"I suppose purple Christmas trees aren't so bad."

"That's better."

Ellie wasn't altogether sure Tim still believed in Santa Claus, but he hadn't come right out and said he didn't. She suspected he was still clinging to his faith in the legend because of the upheavals in his life over the past couple of years. She didn't blame him. She could use a little of that kind of magic herself.

"There," she said. "All finished." She'd pop the biscuits into the oven first thing in the morning.

She looked out the kitchen window for a moment. It had been snowing all day. The first real, pile-up-in-drifts-and-stick-around-for-a-while snowfall. The snowmobilers were out in force. They'd been pulling into town all day. The motel was full, so were some of the winterized cabins along the lakeshore. Tomorrow there would probably be a big demand for hearty breakfasts, like sausage gravy and biscuits and blueberry pancakes, before the eager adventurers set off into the woods on their sleds, so she'd made a double batch.

She was getting the hang of this restaurant thing. She'd learned not to panic when the dinner special sold out before six-thirty, or the delivery truck with the French fries and frozen appetizers was a day late, or the price of lettuce went up seventy-five cents a head from one week to the next. She improvised, made do, made over or did without, just the way her grandmother had done during the Great Depression.

And from Mrs. Eldor, Ellie had learned never, ever, to let anyone know things hadn't turned out exactly as she'd planned. If the gravy on the venison stew wouldn't thicken up to her satisfaction, she changed the menu to read, Venison Vegetable Soup, and stirred up a batch of corn bread to go with it, and accepted compliments from the patrons as if she'd planned it that way from the beginning. Cooking at the Jack Pine restaurant was hard work, but a lot more fun and challenging than Ellie had ever imagined it would be.

She had enough money to pay her health and car insurance premiums and her most important bills. She had finished the pencil-slim Santas for the stores in Sault Ste. Marie, so she could let the kids look through the Penney's Christmas catalog without saying no to everything they wanted to put on their Christmas lists. And even though she would miss her parents this holiday season, she had the kids and she was among friends, not alone and desperate like Matt Westrick.

Thinking of the teenager also made her think of Ben. She hadn't seen him for three days, but that didn't mean he wasn't in her thoughts. He was. Far too often. Day and night. That wasn't a good sign.

"Okay, kids," Mrs. Eldor announced, flourishing a baking sheet of stars and bells and Christmas tree–shaped dough, interrupting Ellie's musings. "It's into the oven with these beauties. Now run off and wash your hands, put on those aprons over there, and in ten minutes we'll be ready to frost the cookies that are cooling on the other counter."

"All right," Carly squealed, happy again. Her mood brightened as quickly as it had fallen. Carly was like sunshine and shadow chasing each other across the lake on a cloudy day, Ellie thought as a smile played at the corners of her mouth. Carly's emotions were close to the surface and she acted on her feelings, instead of bottling them up, as her brother tended to do.

"No apron," Tim insisted.

"If Mrs. Eldor says you wear an apron, you wear an apron," Ellie seconded the command. "Or you can head back over to the cabin and clean up your room and make your bed, instead of frosting cookies."

"It's seven o'clock at night," Tim groused, clearly sensing defeat. "Who makes their bed at seven o'clock at night? Girls," he said with a hiss, giving Carly a surreptitious poke.

"Mom," Carly screamed, clutching her arm as though it were going to fall off. It was a bravura performance. Ellie swallowed a smile.

"Hey," she said, "cut that out. Or you will be cleaning your room, whether you want to or not."

"Sorry, Mom." Tim gave her a big, toothy smile, lopsided and boyish now but with the same potential as his father to charm any girl in the country in ten years' time.

If he grew up like his father. Which she intended not to let happen.

Like small tornadoes, both kids took off for the swinging double doors leading into the dining room.

"Use the 'out' door," Ellie called, causing them to swerve to the right, just in time to avoid a collision with Eldor as he came through the "in" door.

"Whoa!" he called, spinning like a roly-poly top, holding an empty cardboard box aloft as the children launched themselves through the proper door, barely breaking stride. "What was that? Did a herd of moose just go running through this kitchen?"

He pitched his voice to carry through the swinging door.

"Sorry about that," she apologized.

"They just about had me that time. A man my age could fall, break a hip," he said, only half joking. He was wearing a fur-lined, hooded parka that was at least as old as Ellie, and a red-and-black-checked cap with earflaps that made him look like a caricature of an old-time lumberjack.

"A man your *weight* could fall and break a hip," his wife amended.

"I weigh exactly the same as I did ten—"

Mrs. Eldor cut him off. "How was Ben? Is he okay? What about that boy? Is he still out there with him?"

"He's still there," Eldor reported with a concerned frown. "All the boy does, it seems, is eat and sleep." He upended the cardboard box that Ellie and Mrs. Eldor had packed full of food not an hour earlier, to show it was empty.

"Well, if he's eating and sleeping, at least he's not trying to murder Ben. Did he seem . . . normal?" his wife demanded.

"As normal as can be expected with that long hair and earrings . . . two of them. In the same ear." Eldor shook his head. "But he was quiet and polite enough. Thanked me for the food," he admitted conscientiously.

"I'm still worried about Ben," Mrs. Eldor repeated, waving the frosting spoon above the bowl. "I don't like the idea of him out there alone with that young thug. That boy might get violent again."

"Ben doesn't think so."

"He attacked Ben and Ellie with a knife. He might have harmed the baby." His wife brandished her spoon. "He should be behind bars."

Ellie spoke for the first time. "I don't think he's still dangerous," she said, wishing she was more sure of her opinion. "He was desperate and hurting and half-frozen to death that night."

"That's no excuse," Mrs. Eldor retorted with a definite snort. "I think you and Ben should have called the sheriff."

Ellie ran her hands over her swollen belly, smoothing the wrinkles from her enveloping white apron, taking comfort from the baby's movements. "I don't want to press charges against him."

"I think you're making a mistake. Both of you," Mrs. Eldor said portentously. "Mark my words. That boy will bring Ben nothing but grief."

MATT WATCHED Ben MacAllister from the corner of his eye as he drove along the snowy county highway heading west from Sault Ste. Marie. There wasn't much traffic even though it was Saturday afternoon, a half-dozen cars, a van or two, a couple of pickups pulling trailers with snowmobiles loaded on behind. Ben pulled out to pass one of them, and Matt drank in the sight of the sleek snow machines from narrowed eyes.

Now, *there* was something that he could probably get into if he really lived here. Snow racers. He'd seen them compete once or twice on the sports channel. Streamlined and fast as the wind. Yeah, real rad. If he lived here, he'd have to have one of those.

If he lived here.

Bile rose in Matt's throat. He did live here, now. He slid Ben another hooded glance. *Jeez, this guy was his temporary guardian.* How the hell had it happened? What kind of clout did he have back in Ohio to cut through all that red tape in one morning? And on a Saturday, to boot. Abracadabra! Poof! Here are the papers. Sign this. Notarize that. The guy was some kind of damn magician.

Okay. Maybe it hadn't been quite that easy, but Ben had definitely pulled some strings. He'd had to. Matt had only been here five days. The system just didn't work that quickly. He'd spent his share of time with social workers and bureaucrats. Most of them didn't work on Saturday if they could help it. None of them, to his way of thinking, ever did anything without checking with someone else, sometimes a lot of someone elses. But here he was, signed, sealed and delivered to Ben MacAllister—and all before noon on a frigid December Saturday.

He rested his head against the window. On his right, past the yellow sand beach, Lake Superior was frozen solid along its shoreline, snow-covered and deserted as they headed back to North Star. But far out on the lake, where there was still open water, a long low-riding ship steamed slowly southward. In grade school, he'd read about the sailors who worked on lake freighters, and about the wreck of the ore carrier *Edmund Fitzgerald.* He was good at math, good with his hands. His sixth-grade teacher had said he'd make a good merchant seaman, or maybe he should even consider applying to the Coast Guard academy.

But that had been a long time ago, when he'd still been pretty good about showing up at school every day. A lot had changed since then. He hadn't spent any more time in school than he'd had to since his second stepdad left—the one who cared about his good grades and his playing football—and his mom started bringing home a new guy every few months. School was just a drag then, a place to go when the weather was bad. The truancy police had threatened to send his mom to jail if she didn't make sure he showed up at school every day, and she'd washed her hands of him. That's when he'd really started learning about the way things worked when you were a kid with a lot of trouble behind you, and even more ahead of you. He'd ended up in foster care, and then the group home, and they'd marched him up to the school doors every morning. But it hadn't done much good.

Until he'd met Eric. And some of that stuff had been fun again. His grades got better. He made the junior varsity football team his freshman year.

Then he'd talked Eric into going for a joyride in Eric's mom's new car. Eric had died and Matt didn't know if he'd ever walk without a limp, so why dream about working on a lake freighter someday? Now he was trapped here in the back of beyond with the cop who'd killed his best friend.

Trapped with the enemy.

And he still hated Ben MacAllister with every breath he took. But he couldn't up and *off* the guy in cold blood. He'd tried that once and he hadn't been able to go through with it. He just wasn't a murderer. He wasn't enough of a man to do it for Eric. For his friend. He was nothing.

Matt shuddered and huddled down into his coat. His brand-new coat that Ben had just bought for him. Jeans and shirts, underwear, socks and shoes and boots and gloves. Matt had lost track of how much it all cost. Now he even owed the guy the clothes on his back. He was trapped like a scrawny rat in a cage, until he could figure out a plan to get the hell out of here and head for Detroit or Chicago.

He didn't know much about small towns, but he knew it was going to be a hell of a lot harder to get out of North Star than it had been to get into it. He wasn't going to be lucky enough to find some garrulous old coot to give him a ride out of town in broad daylight the way he had at Thanksgiving. An old geezer who'd been so glad for the company, he hadn't stopped talking long enough to ask Matt a single question about who he was or what he was doing heading for North Star.

In a matter of hours, everyone in the burg would know who he was, and where he should be. He'd bet on it.

No. He was stuck in North Star. Stuck with Ben MacAllister in charge of his life.

At least until Christmas.

He needed that much time to plan, and to find a way to earn some money. He could probably steal it from Ben MacAllister, and he would if he had to, but he couldn't chance waiting till the last minute and finding Ben didn't carry more than a few bucks in his wallet.

They were getting close to town. There were only a half-dozen streets in North Star. Streets with names like Main and Schoolcraft, and Pine and Cedar and Elm and Maple. Most of the businesses were on Main Street, facing the small half moon–shaped bay. The fire department, a couple of small churches and the school were up on the hill, on Schoolcraft.

He watched the buildings go by from beneath the bill of his cap. Matt had never been in such a small town in his life. Not that Columbus, Ohio, was the center of the universe, but it sure seemed like it compared to North Star, Michigan.

"You warm enough?"

"Huh?" Ben's question cut into his thoughts like a knife.

"I said, are you warm enough? I can turn up the heat." Matt darted a quick look at him out of the corner of his eye, afraid what he'd been thinking showed on his face, but Ben wasn't looking at him. His eyes were on the road.

"I'm fine." He was still a little cold from spending the morning in his too-thin jacket, and the low temperatures made his bad leg ache, but he wasn't about to admit it. He wondered if the cold made the scars on Ben's hands and face ache, too. They probably did. And it served him right, Matt reminded himself. He wasn't about to start feeling sorry for Ben Mac-Allister. Not when he remembered how he got those scars.

The old man Matt had hitched with had said Ben's scars were bad enough to scare little children and pregnant women—like Ellie Lawrence.

Matt had asked Ben about them last night, trying to pick a fight, trying to get Ben to kick him out of the lighthouse, but it hadn't worked. He'd sneeringly accused the highway patrol of getting Ben some cut-rate plastic surgeon who'd botched the job on Ben's face.

Ben hadn't turned a hair. He'd just looked right through Matt and said that he'd had a very good doctor, but that he'd developed an infection, one of those kind that sweep through hospitals now and then. The skin grafts they'd planned for his face and hand hadn't worked. The scars had remained. Maybe, someday, he'd try plastic surgery again. And maybe it would work better. And maybe not.

Matt hated the stares he got because of the brace on his leg, but at least it wasn't permanent. Ben's scars might very well be. Ben would have to look people in the face every day for the rest of his life, catch them watching him and frowning, see them turn away in embarrassment and disgust. And pity.

Matt knew about pity and he didn't like it.

But that didn't change anything. Ben MacAllister had killed Matt's best friend. He could never forget that.

Riley whined softly when he heard Matt speak, likely hoping to get his ears scratched. The dog was sitting between them on the bench seat, his head in Matt's lap, his tail thumping lazily against Ben's thigh. Riley grunted again, and Matt buried his fingers in the dog's silky fur.

"How cold does it get here, anyway?" He didn't want to start a conversation with Ben, but the silence was driving him crazy. Ben hadn't turned on the radio and Matt wasn't about to ask him to.

"Thirty, forty below in January and February," Ben informed him.

"Jeez." Ben's answer surprised a response out of him before he could bite it back. "That's the windchill, huh."

"No," Ben said, his eyes still on the road. "That's the temperature."

"God," Matt grumbled. "I'll freeze my gonads off."

"Not if you keep them covered," Ben said dryly. "I've got some insulated coveralls back at the lighthouse. If you dress in layers, you'll be fine."

"Yeah. Sure." He didn't intend to be here in January or February, but he didn't dare tip his hand. He had to stay on his guard, had to remember Ben MacAllister was a cop. And you didn't play head games with a cop.

CHAPTER EIGHT

BEN SLOWED the truck as they headed down Main Street. There was a lot of traffic in North Star for a Saturday afternoon, cars and pickups parked haphazardly along the sandy shoulders on both sides of the street for almost a block on either side of the VFW hall.

"What are we stopping here for?" Matt asked suspiciously.

"I need to get a few dollars out of the bank machine. It won't take long."

"If you're hinting that the clothes you bought me tapped you out, I'm planning on paying for them."

"I didn't say that. I'm a little low on cash, that's all." Ben didn't let his surprise show, although Matt's offer to reimburse him for the clothes was the last thing he expected. It would be a miracle if Matt possessed that much of a sense of responsibility the way he'd been raised. While Ben had been pulling strings in Columbus over the past five days, he'd learned a hell of a lot about Matt Westrick's life. The kid had had it pretty tough the last half-dozen years. He'd been in trouble, sure, plenty of it, but nothing violent, nothing really hard-core.

"I don't expect you to pay me back."

Matt slid onto his tailbone, his arms folded across his chest. "Yeah, sure. You're doing all this out of the goodness of your heart."

"Okay. I'll save the receipts. You can pay me back when you get a job."

Matt snorted. "What the hell kind of job am I going to find in this sorry burg?"

"Ask around," Ben said.

He opened the truck door and stepped out into the clear cold afternoon. He'd bought Matt three pairs of jeans, two sweatshirts, a pair of slacks, two shirts and a V-neck pullover, running shoes—an off-brand but still expensive, underwear, socks, a coat, boots, gloves and knit pullover cap—and toiletries. And he'd damned near maxed out his credit card. He wondered how in blazes people managed to feed, outfit and educate more than one kid. It seemed like a sure trip to the poorhouse.

What if Matt had been a girl? Ben suspected he would have had to spend even more to outfit one of those.

God, how did Ellie manage with only sporadic support payments from her ex?

Ellie. She was always on his mind. He caught himself listening for the sound of her voice, the echo of her laughter on the wind. He wanted to be with her. He wanted to touch her, kiss her—

"I'll be right back." He slammed the truck door on his thoughts and Matt's scowl, but not before he heard the teenager mutter something about not being beholden to anyone.

The kid wasn't much of a conversationalist.

But then neither was he. Not anymore.

Neither one of them had talked much in the last five days, if you came right down to it. Matt, in fact, hadn't done much of anything but eat and sleep.

The first night, Ben hadn't slept much, either. He'd sat in the chair by the window, watching the snow diminish to flurries. Watched the clouds break up, hurrying in tattered wisps before the cold, Canadian wind. He'd watched the moon come out and drop away beyond the horizon as dawn lightened the eastern sky.

When it was light enough, he'd switched his gaze to the sleeping teenager and wondered if he'd made the right decision, or the biggest mistake of his life by not calling the authorities right away. He knew it was risky following his gut instinct instead of his brain, and he knew just as well his decision could backfire at any moment and get him seriously hurt or killed.

But he didn't think Matt Westrick had it in him to be a killer. He was just a kid, a hurting, mixed-up kid. Ben knew what it was like to be hurting and alone. He knew how hard it could be even to get up in the morning to face the guilt, and he was a hell of a lot older—and supposedly wiser—than Matt.

"Hey, Ben. Just the man I wanted to see," Eldor called out as Ben turned away from the bank machine. He hadn't noticed his cousin drive up and park in front of the bank. "Help me unload this stuff and carry it over to the bazaar, will ya?" the older man asked.

"Bazaar? So that's what all the cars and the comings and goings are about?"

"Sure. The Sons of Gitche Gumee Auxiliary's Christmas bazaar. You know. To make money for the library fund. Martha's the president this year. She's pretty much in charge. And I'm her number-one go-fer. I know I told you about it last time you were in the Jack Pine."

"I don't remember," Ben said, feeling his gut tighten. The last thing he wanted was to go inside the ugly, gold-colored, metal building and have the good citizens of North Star trying not to stare at him.

"I need some help unloading these cases of soft drinks," Eldor told him. "They're running low in the kitchen. Got a real good lunch crowd this year."

"I—" If it just meant carrying the soft-drink cases in through the kitchen door, he could handle that. He could handle a beer or two at the Jack Pine in the middle of a weekday afternoon, this wasn't much different. "Okay."

"I need to restock the pop machine in the vestibule, too. We'll just take it all in through the front door."

Ben's heart started pounding like a trip-hammer. He wasn't ready to face a crowd again. Not so soon. It had taken everything he had to attend the dedication of Brian's memorial in Columbus. It had been the hardest thing he'd ever done. He'd made himself stand there before Brian's family and friends as a kind of penance. He hadn't been able to save Brian Novak's life. But he could honor his memory. And he had. But not this. Not this ordinary, everyday gathering of North Star residents.

Eldor didn't seem to notice his reluctance. Or maybe he just plain didn't hear him; the earflaps were down on his red-and-black-checked lumberjack's hat. "Here you go. I'll buy you lunch for your help. Anything you want." He swung a case of soft-drink cans in Ben's direction. "Where's that boy? He can carry a couple, too. His leg ain't that bad, from what I seen of it. We can make it all in one trip that way. Hey, Ben. Are you listening to me?

"Matt's leg can take it." One of the calls he'd made over the past few days had been to the boy's surgeon. He'd told Ben that Matt's leg was almost healed and referred him to an orthopedist in Sault Ste. Marie who could monitor Matt's progress.

"Good." Eldor added two more cases to the one Ben already held. "Let's get him over here." Clearly pleased with his plan, Eldor looked over at Ben's pickup and signaled Matt to join them. "Yeah, that's a good idea, the three of us working together. We'll get this all over with at once."

ELLIE WAS IN CHARGE of the dollhouse raffle. She made change, tore off tickets, saw to it everyone put their name and phone number on the original and kept the duplicate, helped the little ones stuff their chances into the big wire barrel from which the winner would be drawn just before the bazaar was over.

It wasn't a difficult task. And at least she could sit down. People came and went in twos and threes, stopping to say hello, ask her how she was getting along, compliment her on the improvement in the food at the Jack Pine, even if they didn't want to buy a ticket.

Everyone was in a good mood. It was snowing and snow meant money coming in from snowmobilers, cross-country skiers and ice fishermen. One thing people in this part of the world dreaded was a cold, dry winter. North Star's winter mantra was, "Let it snow. Let it snow. Let it snow."

And Christmas was coming. Lights were starting to show up on trees and rooflines. The village workers were stringing red-and-green-colored lights across Main Street. The community tree, decorated with oversize handmade ornaments, would be turned on in front of the firehouse up on the hill next weekend. It was Ellie's favorite time of year.

"Mom." Carly was standing in front of her, a dollar bill clutched in her hand. She had been carrying the money around for almost an hour, looking for just the right treat to spend it on. "Mom. Ben's here. And there's a boy with him. A boy who can't walk very good. He's got this thing on his leg like Erika Shurmansky's brother wore after he hurt his knee playing football. Who is he?"

Ellie looked in the direction of the vestibule. Her line of sight was partially blocked by shoppers browsing through the baked goods, Christmas-tree decorations, carved wooden toys and crocheted pot holders. But she managed to catch a glimpse of Ben's flannel-clad back and broad shoulders. Directly behind him, facing her, looking a whole lot cleaner, but still wary and apprehensive, was Matt Westrick.

"Who's that boy?" Carly demanded a second time.

"He...he's a friend of Mr. MacAllister's," Ellie said. That explanation would suffice for Carly and Tim, and anyone else who might ask about the teenager. She had the feeling, though, that just as many people—probably more—would like to ask questions about Chippewa Point's reclusive resident suddenly showing up in their midst.

Ben turned to face her and Ellie stared, transfixed, unable to look away. He'd had a haircut, and the short style suited him. The muted browns and golds of his plaid flannel shirt complemented the warm earth tones of his skin. Just then, he glanced her way, his gaze drawn by Carly's frantic welcoming wave. He smiled back at Carly, a quick curving of his lips, nothing more, then lifted his eyes to Ellie's, and suddenly she couldn't breathe. She waited for him to frown or look away.

Ben did neither but for a moment she thought she saw that same hunted look, the same wariness that glittered in Matt's gaze. But only for a second, and then it was gone and there was nothing, no expression, no emotion. Ben began to make his way through the crowd, Matt trailing a step or two behind.

How hard had it been for him to shrug off the protective shell of his heavy coat and leave it hanging with all the others on the rack in the vestibule? The parka was so much more than mere protection from the cold. It was his armor against the curious, staring eyes of the world.

She thought she knew, at least a little, how difficult it was for him. She'd felt something of the same need to hide herself when her pregnancy first began to show. It wasn't easy being single and pregnant—and old enough to know better—in a close-knit, conservative community like North Star.

Suddenly, Ben and Matt were standing in front of her. Ellie made herself smile, as though seeing him there was the most ordinary sight in the world. "Hello, Ben," she said, hoping her voice didn't sound as nervous to him as it did to her. She didn't add anything else. It was a miracle she'd got the mundane greeting past her lips without stumbling over the simple words. His eyes were the color of a rainy summer day. His gaze flickered over her face and, once again, she could hardly breathe.

"Hello, Ellie. Hi, Carly." He didn't exactly smile, but he no longer looked quite so remote.

"Hi," Carly said, leaning against Ellie's shoulder. "Where's your dog?"

"He's in the truck. I don't think Mrs. Eldor and the Auxiliary ladies would appreciate having him as a customer."

The little girl leaned a little forward and gave Ellie a conspiratorial grin. "He could eat Mrs. Eldor's cookies."

Ellie denied herself the smile that tickled her lips. "That's not nice, Carly" she said quietly. "You'll hurt Mrs. Eldor's feelings if she hears you say that."

"I won't say it to anyone else." Carly said contritely. "It's just our secret." Her gaze flickered past Ben to fix on Matt's frowning face. "Who's he?" Carly demanded. "Mom says he's your friend. What's his name?"

Ben nodded. "I'm sorry. I should have introduced you right away." Ellie could see the tension in the muscles of his neck and shoulders, thought she heard its echo in his voice. But he acted as if he didn't see the second glances people cast his way, the quick sympathetic frowns.

"Okay," Carly said with a gracious nod.

"Carly Lawrence, meet Matt Westrick."

The little girl narrowed her gaze and looked Matt over from head to toe. "Is your real name Matthew?"

Matt shuffled his feet, looking as if he might bolt. "No," he said. "It's just plain Matt. Nothing fancy."

"I'm Caroline, really, but I hate that name." She shot Ellie an accusing glance then looked back at Matt. "So don't call me that, okay?"

"Okay," Matt promised, eyeing the pigtailed little girl who barely reached his waist as if she might go off like a bomb.

"I have money to spend," Carly continued, undaunted by the teenager's monosyllabic answers. "My brother spent his already, so he went home to watch TV. But I saved mine."

"Rad," Matt said, shoving his hands into the pockets his obviously brand-new jeans. "How much?"

"A whole dollar." Carly waved the bill in front of his face. "That's four quarters. I'm going to buy books at the library table. They're a quarter each, so I can get four of them. Come with me."

"Huh?"

"Carly, Matt . . . might not want to go to the book table with you."

Matt's head swung in her direction. His face was expressionless, but he couldn't quite keep the pain from his eyes. He was steeling himself for her rejection. Ellie knew without being told that he had experienced many such rejections and that he had perfected survival techniques a long time ago. "The book table is only twenty feet away. You don't have to worry," he said defiantly. "I'm not going to take off with your kid and hold her for ransom or anything."

"I didn't think you would," Ellie said, accepting his unspoken challenge, holding his gaze for an extra second. She knew Ben was watching her as closely as Matt, waiting for her decision. He had taken the boy into his home, made himself accountable for him. Could she do less than give Matt the benefit of the doubt? As he'd said, they would only be twenty feet away.

"You may *ask* Matt if he would like to go to the book table with you. You don't tell him he has to go. That's not polite."

Carly made a face, then turned to Matt, her face transforming itself into a brilliant gap-toothed smile. "Please, would you like to go to the book table with me?"

"Sure," he said. He looked at Ellie again, not avoiding her eyes this time. His expression was still wary, guarded, but his gaze was clear and steady, a marked contrast to the flat, haunted stare of that first night. "I'll watch out for her," he said stiffly.

Ellie smiled. "Thank you, Matt."

"Is it okay with you?" he asked Ben grudgingly.

"Okay. But we'll be leaving soon."

Matt stared at Ben's scars. "Yeah. I figured you wouldn't want to stay here too long."

Ellie knew Matt's cruel remark must have hurt Ben. But he said nothing.

"You got your ear pierced," Carly said admiringly as she held out her hand to guide Matt to the next aisle of tables. "Did it hurt?"

"Nah."

"I want to get my ears pierced. When I'm eight."

Ben watched the unlikely duo walk away. "Thanks, Ellie," he said.

"You've made yourself responsible for the boy, haven't you?"

He didn't answer immediately. He pretended to study the four-room, log-cabin dollhouse that the residents of North Star's seniors housing development had built and furnished for the fund-raiser. Ellie waited. Finally, Ben looked at her, and a flicker of vulnerability flashed through the depths of his gray eyes like lightning through storm clouds. He had never let her see what he was thinking quite so clearly before, and Ellie felt the jolt of that small intimacy pass along her nerve endings as though the lightning's charge had passed from his body to hers. "Yes. I have."

"How did you manage that?"

"I have friends in the right places. I made some phone calls. Signed some papers, that's all."

"It's a big responsibility."

"I'm aware of that."

"Did you also pay for his new clothes and shoes?"

One of those rare, fleeting smiles she'd begun to crave like a drug curved the corners of his mouth. "Yes. God, raising a kid could bankrupt a person."

She smiled, too. "Tell me about it," she said dryly.

"I couldn't send him back to Ohio, Ellie." He leaned a little closer, both hands braced on the table. "It would be..."

"As though you had failed to save him, too, like the other boy in the accident, and your friend?" she asked quietly.

He straightened, the barriers dropping into place in the flutter of a heartbeat. "Yes," he said softly. "It would be like signing his death warrant one way or another."

"I understand." She thought of the residual anger and animosity in Matt's gaze. "How long will he be with you?"

"I've got temporary custody until the first of the year. They'll reevaluate the case then. They want Matt back in school, although they agreed he didn't have to enroll until after Christmas vacation. They want him in some kind of therapy."

"Do you think he'll agree to that?"

"Not now, not today, that's for sure." He raked a hand through his hair, stirring the short brown waves. Ellie watched, fascinated, as they settled into place again. Again, he leaned both hands on the table. "I'm flying blind here, Ellie, but I've got to give it a try."

"I know you do." Under the table she smoothed her hand over her stomach. The baby was active again, small fists pummeled her, an elbow or knee poked against her side. The little one always seemed to know when Ben was around. Perhaps he already recognized his voice, or perhaps he was only reacting to her excitement, the increase in her pulse rate and her breathing whenever the man was nearby.

"I'm no psychologist or social worker. I'm just a cop. I've never been married. Never had a kid of my own."

"You're doing fine, Ben. I can see a change in him already." She touched his hand, a brush of her fingertips, light and quick, over his knuckles, nothing more. "I just hope it isn't too late."

THE TINY KITCHEN in Ellie's cottage was fragrant with the smell of yeast and cheese and tomato sauce. Ben sat at the counter and watched her making pizza crust, and tried to determine exactly how he had ended up where he was. Shortly after Matt and Carly had returned from the book table bearing her treasures, Ellie had asked Danelda Larson to take over her duties at the raffle table, and invited Ben and Matt here for pizza, so quickly and so smoothly neither of them had time to object.

He glanced at Matt sitting in front of the TV watching a Disney video, the ginger kitten curled on his lap, Carly on one side with the JCPenney's Christmas catalog open on her knees, while Tim hung over the back of the couch. Spock was napping in her usual spot in front of the woodstove. Riley had been banished to the pen in the garage in deference to the older dog.

"Do you like pepperoni?" Ellie asked, pulling two round pizza pans out of a cupboard.

"Sure."

The oak Santa was sitting on the counter. Ellie had obviously been working on it. The wood had taken on a rich patina from hours of polishing. He picked up the carving. The wood was warm to the touch, almost as if it glowed from an inner life. He studied the Santa's lined, careworn face. The expression was benevolent, the attitude one of caring and compassion as he bent slightly toward the fawn at his feet. It was a beautiful piece. Ben had thought it was on its way to a gallery in Mackinaw City.

Ellie looked up and saw him holding the carving. "Looks like that particular Santa will be spending the holidays with us, after all," she said. Her voice was light, but it held a false note of cheer.

"What do you mean?"

"The gallery owner decided he wanted to wait for a full complement of the old boys."

"How long will it take you to carve the rest?"

"I don't know. My schedule's pretty full." She smiled again, a smile that didn't quite reach her eyes. Before he could say anything else, she changed the subject. "Matt?" She raised her voice slightly, smiling at the boy. "Do you like pepperoni?"

"Yeah. I mean, yes, sure. That's fine."

"Good." She straightened from rummaging in the refrigerator, her hand on the small of her back, a slight frown between her eyebrows. "I'll make one pepperoni and one with the works."

Ben didn't like that frown, it spoke of fatigue and stress, maybe even pain. He walked around the counter into the narrow little kitchen. "Are you okay?"

She looked at him, puzzled. "I'm fine," she said. "Why do you ask?"

"You—" He didn't know anything about pregnant women. He'd never been around one, not intimately. Not one he cared enough to worry about. "You were rubbing your back. You...you looked as if you might be in pain."

Ellie grinned. "You'd look pained too if you were carrying a five-and-a-half-pound whirling dervish around inside you," she said.

Ben felt his neck get hot. "Yeah," he said, grabbing the jar of olives she was trying to open. "I guess you're right. Here, let me do that." He dealt with the olive jar with one fierce twist, then handed it back.

She touched his hand, quick and light, just as she'd done at the bazaar, and again the fleeting touch burned against his skin. "Thank you for asking. Go, sit down," she said, sounding a little breathless herself. "This kitchen is too small for both of us."

She cooked five nights a week at the Jack Pine. He shouldn't be sitting here while she cooked for him on her night off. "I don't like you waiting on me," he said, knowing as soon as the words left his mouth they didn't sound the way he'd meant them to. He'd never felt this way about a woman before. Protective. Possessive. Aroused. All at the same time.

She ignored his tone. "I'm not waiting on you. I swore off waiting on men when my ex-husband moved out." A faint hint of color rose in her cheeks, and she looked down at the lump of dough she was kneading with floury hands. "Let's do it this way... You're in charge of sauce and toppings. I'll do dough and cheese." She gave him a level look that failed to hide her vulnerability completely. Her color was still high and her body language, the tension in her arms and shoulders, told him not to ask questions about the marriage and the ex.

God, was she still in love with the bastard?

She was pregnant with his kid, so she probably was. He may not know her well, but he'd bet his life Ellie Lawrence wasn't the kind for a one-night stand. She was the kind of woman for a lifetime, the kind of woman a man could build a future around. "Sounds like a fair deal to me."

"Good." She picked up the dough and began twirling it between her hands. "The cheese grater's in the cupboard above the fridge. You can start with that."

"I thought you were going to do the cheese?" He kept his voice light, friendly, but nothing more. He didn't want her to know she had made him start thinking of all the things he couldn't have.

"House rules," she said, laughing. "I said I'd put it on the pizza. I didn't say I'd grate it." Her laugh was as intriguing as the rest of her, with a throaty quality, full and rich. He walked past her, inhaling the flowery scent of her hair, almost brushing her bottom in the narrow confines of the cottage kitchen. He sucked in his breath. A sharp ache tightened inside him. He grabbed the metal grater from the cupboard and a chunk of mozzarella from the counter beside her.

He wondered what it would be like to hold her close, molded against him, his hands on her belly, both of them marveling at the movement of the child within, and teasing each other with memories of how they had made that child, and how they would make love again when he no longer came between them.

"Hey! You've got enough cheese there for six pizzas."

Ben looked down at the counter. He'd shredded nearly a pound of cheese. "Sorry," he said, trying to make a joke of it. "Guess I don't know my own strength."

"That's all right. It'll freeze." She indicated a box of freezer bags. "You can put what's left in there for now."

"Okay." Ben still felt dazed by the power of his fantasies. His thoughts had been sexual, that he could handle. Ellie was a very sexy woman, even pregnant. It had been the other thoughts that really threw him, the thoughts of home and hearth and family.

A family of his own.

A family like this one.

This family. These kids. This woman.

A phone rang in the living room. "Get that, will you, Tim?" Ellie sang out. "I wonder who it could be. Eldor and Jackson Tall Trees should have everything under control at the restaurant. It's steak night. They get a big kick out of grilling over the fireplace."

Ben remained silent. He still didn't trust his voice.

"I really hope nothing's wrong at the Jack Pine," she said, that tiny adorable frown he was beginning to recognize furrowing her forehead. "I . . . I was hoping we could spend a nice quiet evening."

"It's probably nothing." He hadn't meant to let himself get lost in her eyes this way again but he couldn't help himself. They were green and blue and brown all mixed together, with specks of gold floating deep inside, like sunlight filtering through leafy branches onto the surface of a swift-moving stream.

Her eyes, and her smile. That's what had got him through the crowd at the VFW hall this afternoon.

She was so close he could feel the warmth of her skin through his shirtsleeve, smell the flowery scent of her shampoo. "You've got flour on your nose," he said, the ringing of the telephone drowned out by the rush of blood in his ears. He reached out to brush the smudge away with the tip of his finger.

He hadn't meant to let his touch linger, to turn it into a caress. His fingers grazed her cheek, the curve of her lips, molded themselves to the silky column of her throat.

Ellie made a little sound of protest, but swayed toward him, her belly brushing up against him. Her lips parted, her breathing was quick and light, as though she was waiting for his kiss. Ben dipped his head. Ellie's eyes drifted shut. The phone kept ringing.

Carly's shrill scream broke the connection between them. "Let me have it. It's six o'clock. That's when they were going to draw the ticket for the dollhouse. Maybe I won! Let me have it."

Ben dropped his hand, jerked himself upright. Ellie blinked as though coming out of a trance, then leaned over the counter and issued a command. "Stop fighting and answer the phone," she called, sounding as breathless as he felt.

Ben moved away, blindly backing around the breakfast counter so that he wouldn't be tempted to touch her again.

"Here, baby," Tim muttered, handing Carly the receiver. Matt sat stiffly between the warring siblings, looking comically desperate as the battle waged around him.

"Lawrence residence," Carly said primly, sticking out her tongue at her vanquished brother. Suddenly dancing up and down like a jumping jack, she called, "Mom! Daddy's on the phone!"

CHAPTER NINE

ELLIE COULDN'T BELIEVE this was happening. Lonny was back. Dumping his dirty laundry into her hamper, sticking his feet under her kitchen table. Trying to charm his way back into her bedroom.

"Hey, Ella Marie, where are my clean socks?"

"They're in the washer," Ellie said, keeping her irritation masked for the children's sake.

"Didn't you put them in the dryer before you went over to the Jack Pine?" Lonny asked, coming out of the bedroom he was sharing with Tim. He was wearing jeans that fit his long legs like a second skin and a western shirt with mother-of-pearl buttons and a stitched yoke that probably looked right at home in Texas or Louisiana, but was out of place in North Star.

His hair was longer than she remembered, too, but it was still as black and thick and lustrous as it had always been. Twelve years ago she'd thought he was the handsomest boy she'd ever seen. He was still a good-looking man, but now she saw him with a woman's eyes, and what she saw beneath the sweet talk and ingratiating smile was weakness and self-indulgence.

"I didn't have time. I was late for work and Carly didn't want to get ready for school. She didn't sleep well last night. You know she's got the sniffles." Carly's cold was slight, but it was the perfect excuse for moving her into Ellie's small bedroom.

"Well, damn, Ellie. What am I supposed to wear to the tree lighting? I'll freeze my feet off with no dry socks."

"Just put them in the dryer," she said. She felt as if she were talking to someone Tim's age, not a grown man of thirty-two. "They'll be dry in fifteen minutes." She didn't know how she'd got into this mess.

She hadn't had any choice, really. Lonny had simply announced over the telephone that the oil rig he was working on was being shut down for maintenance, and he would be home for Christmas. And since his mother was dead, and his brothers had moved away, he needed a place to stay. And if she made him stay in a motel, it would just make it more likely the check he'd given her for Carly and Tim would bounce.

"I'll put your socks in the dryer," Tim said, watching Ellie with a frown between his eyebrows. "I know how to do it." Tim was far more conflicted by his father's reappearance in their lives than his sister was. But then, he'd been disappointed by Lonny more often in the past. Carly loved everyone. She trusted everyone. She missed Lonny when he was gone, and she rejoiced when he came back home.

"Thanks, son." Lonny ruffled Tim's hair as he walked by. "I guess I'm just not one of them sensitive New Age kinds of guys that know how to run a washin' machine and all, eh?"

"Yeah, sure. It's kind of girly, but I help with the laundry so Mom can work on her Santas." Tim trotted off to the tiny lean-to utility room at the back of the cottage.

"Your mom and her Santas, eh?" He gave Ellie a megawatt smile. "Be respectful of a woman holding a knife, I always say."

Lonny had tolerated her carving because it brought in money. At best, he considered it a hobby. He didn't think of it as a livelihood, or as art. Carving was something for old men and little boys with pocketknives, and Ellie, if she had the laundry done and supper on the table.

"And fetch my boots when you come back, okay?" He grinned and pulled out a dollar bill and wiggled it in Tim's direction. "I'll make it worth your while."

"Me, too, Daddy!" Carly squealed when she saw the money. "Me! Me! I want a dollar, too."

"Sure, pumpkin. But you'll have to earn it. Come here and give your daddy a big old kiss." Living in Louisiana had had an effect on Lonny, Ellie noticed. His accent and inflection had definitely moved south.

Carly did as he asked, then bounced off his lap with a big smile and the dollar bill clutched firmly in her fist. "Mom, can we go shopping? I want to go shopping."

"Not tonight, honey. It will be too late by the time the tree-lighting ceremony is over," Ellie reminded her. "And tomorrow, I have so many things to do." Ellie glanced over at her Santas. She hadn't worked on them since Lonny arrived three days earlier. Even though it looked as though she could scrape by financially the rest of the winter by working at the Jack Pine, it limited her carving time. The baby's arrival in a month or so would limit it even more. If she intended to keep supplying her customers in Frankenmuth, a town in the Lower Peninsula that boasted one of the largest Christmas stores in the world, and those in Wisconsin on the beautiful, chic Door Peninsula, she had to keep up her production.

"I'll take you shopping, angel," Lonny drawled. "We'll go Sunday, right after Sunday school. How about you, Ellie, darlin', you want to go along?"

"I'm working," Ellie said, biting her tongue to tell him not to call her *darlin'*. "Martha's short of help this weekend, so I told her I'd fill in."

"Take the day off. Come with us. It'll be like old times." Lonny picked Carly up underneath her arms and swung her around in a circle. The little girl screamed with delight.

"Don't get her too excited, Lonny," Ellie cautioned. "She'll start coughing again." Both her ex-husband and her daughter looked at her with accusing brown eyes.

"I like Daddy to swing me," Carly said, and promptly started coughing.

Ellie didn't say I told you so, but she wanted to. She hated being the heavy all the time. It was hard enough when she knew that she had no choice, but when Lonny was around, it was even harder. He was a parent, too. He should act like one. Being a parent didn't mean being your child's best buddy or an unending fountain of gifts. It meant being an adult, a loving, caring, responsible *adult*.

And Lonny had never grown up. Never wanted to.

She couldn't help contrasting him with other men in her life. Strong men, loyal and hardworking and principled, like her father, like Eldor MacAllister and Mayor Carmichael. Men who got up and went to work each morning, came home every night. Men who didn't complain when things didn't go their way, men who sacrificed for their families, put others' welfare before their own. Men like—Ben.

"C'mon, darlin'," Lonny said, snapping his fingers in front of her nose. "What are you daydreaming about?"

"Nothing," she said, hastily pushing thoughts of Ben MacAllister to the back of her mind. She hadn't seen him since the night of the bazaar a week ago, but that didn't stop her from wondering where he was, what he was doing. How he was getting along with Matt.

"Then let's get this show on the road." Lonny pulled on cowboy boots over the socks Tim had just taken from the dryer, and grabbed his coat. Cowboy boots. With two-inch heels. In North Star. There was eleven inches of snow on the ground. He'd be lucky if he didn't slip and break his neck. "I swear my blood's thinned, working down there in the Gulf. It feels like the North Pole out here."

Ellie slipped her arms into her coat sleeves and sat down heavily on the couch to help Carly with her scarf and gloves. "It's not all that cold outside." Lonny had been complaining about the weather ever since he'd returned.

"Yes, it is. Ready, Tim?"

"Ready, Dad."

They were walking to the tree-lighting ceremony because the event always drew a crowd and cars would be parked along both sides of the street all the way up the hill. Even the Jack Pine parking lot would be full, mostly because a number of people would end the evening in front of the long oak bar.

Ellie took Carly's mittened hand as they picked their way across the snowy parking lot. Ellie walked carefully. The baby had shifted position sometime during the last week, dropped a little lower in her abdomen, and she felt even more clumsy and off balance than she had before. She didn't want to slip and fall so close to term. Lonny didn't offer his arm; Ellie would have been surprised if he had. It would have been out of character for him to worry about her.

But she didn't care. Lonny was no longer part of her family. Never again would she be dependent upon him—or disappointed by him. That was a promise she'd made to herself months ago.

And one she had every intention of keeping.

THERE WAS A KNOCK on the bedroom door. Matt ignored it, huddling deeper into the bedspread he'd wrapped around his shoulders. Damn, it was cold in here. He hadn't thought about not having any heat in the room when he'd shut himself inside three hours ago.

Ben knocked again. Harder this time. "Matt. It's time to leave for town."

"I'm not going to any lame tree-lighting ceremony." He wasn't going anywhere with Ben Mac-

Allister. He wasn't coming out of this room again until he hightailed it out of this hellhole. It would be just like that damned bazaar last week—people staring, whispering behind their hands.

"You will if I say so. Unlock the door or I'll break it down."

Matt hesitated. Would Ben really kick the door in? He didn't doubt for a moment that the man *could* kick the heavy door off its hinges, but would he?

"Matt. Open the door. Now." There was no anger in Ben's voice, just infinite, unrelenting patience. Ben walked like a cop. Talked like a cop. He expected to be obeyed like a cop. And all of a sudden, Matt wasn't ready to call his bluff.

"Just an effing minute." He threw the bedspread across the bed, slid back the flimsy old-fashioned bolt lock and swung open the door. "I said I'm not going to town with you."

"Oh, yes, you are."

"What for? Three hours ago you wouldn't let me set foot off the property." All he'd wanted to do was take the truck into North Star and rent a video. Ben's television only picked up one lousy station. And he'd already watched every video Ben owned. Not that there were that many. And most of them were old black-and-white movies.

"You're not driving my truck without a license."

"I'll be sixteen in April." He knew how to drive. Sure he didn't have a license. But North Star didn't have a cop. No one was going to know if he drove into town or not. It was no skin off Ben MacAllister's nose.

"Then we'll discuss it again in April."

"You son—"

"Don't push me, Matt. Get your coat. We're going to town."

"What's so damn important about this stupid tree lighting, anyway? We haven't spent fifteen minutes in that burg in the last week."

"It's time you started meeting some people."

Matt snorted. "Yeah. That'll be a good one. I can just hear them now—'Hey, who's that gimp over there?' 'Don't ya know, Earl? It's the crippled juvey Ben MacAllister took in.' 'Ben MacAllister? Who's that?' 'You know who he is, Earl. The hermit livin' out at Eldor's lighthouse. The one who looks like that Phantom of the Opera guy without his mask.'"

"That's enough, Matt."

"It's the truth, isn't it?" His voice cracked and he swallowed hard. "Admit it. You don't ever set foot in town in daylight if you don't have to."

Ben ignored Matt's gibes. "We're going because I say we are. And because Eldor called about an hour ago. He's got a job to offer you. But he needs to know tonight if you'll take it. It's up to you." He crossed his arms over his chest, waited for Matt's answer.

"What kind of job?"

Ben shrugged. "Helping out around the Jack Pine. Splitting wood, general cleanup, that kind of thing. Afternoons and weekends, mostly."

"How much does it pay?"

"I'm not your agent," Ben said. "You'll have to discuss that with my cousin."

"I'll call him on the phone."

"You don't do job interviews over the phone. This is a job interview. You'll do him the courtesy of meeting him face-to-face."

Matt ground his teeth. "How the hell am I supposed to get back and forth to this great job? We're not exactly living in the effing heart of North Star, ya know."

"I'm getting tired of your language," Ben said quietly, implacably. "I suggest you clean it up in future."

"Huh?"

"I said, clean up your language or I'm going to fine you a buck for every cussword that comes out of your mouth."

"I don't even have an ef—a buck."

"You will have if you take Eldor up on his offer."

"Man, I hate you."

Ben shrugged.

"How the hel—devil am I supposed to get back and forth to this great job you've lined up for me? Walk?"

"I've got a pair of snowshoes."

Matt slammed his fist into the door frame. "Oh, hell."

"Okay," Ben said, "that'll be a dollar. Now come with me. He jerked his thumb over his shoulder toward the front door. "I've got something for you."

Matt trailed after him, still seething, hating his cold, stiff leg, hating his helplessness, his lack of any means of getting out of this place. Hating Ben. Hating himself.

Ben opened the door and the cold air swirled inside. Ben pointed out into the yard. "There. Not too pretty. But she runs."

It was a snowmobile. Nothing like the state-of-the-art machines Matt saw on the road every day now, but not bad, either. Black with red pinstriping and a red leather seat, it was a little older, a little heavier, a little slower than the sleek beauties he coveted. But not bad. Not bad at all.

"Where'd that come from?"

"She's been in storage in one of the outbuildings. I'll show you how to run her tomorrow. It's too dangerous riding at night if you don't know the machine or the trails."

Riding at night, roaring across the moon-bright snow. Alone, in control of all that power and speed. A funny little pain darted through Matt's heart. "I can't afford that thing."

"I didn't say you had to buy it. Consider it a loaner."

"Why don't you want to ride it?"

"The scars on my face are too sensitive to the cold."

"Hel—" He remembered Ben's threat about the fines and swallowed the word. "Yeah. Okay." He wished he hadn't said anything. It was all a pipe dream, anyway. "I can't even afford to put gasoline in it."

"You will after you get your first paycheck. I'll stake you to the gas and motor oil till then."

"What's the catch?" There had to be a catch. There always was.

"No catch. Snow machines have the right of way on all the roads up here. And it's legal for kids your age to operate one. But I expect you to let me know where you are and who you're with when you're not working at the Jack Pine. No drinking and driving."

"I don't drink."

"Good. Keep it that way."

"What else?"

"Just that you take a safety course. There's one starting at the school next week. You can sign up tonight after the tree-lighting ceremony."

"I still didn't say I'd go to the da—darned thing," he said, catching himself again.

"You're not driving that thing until you agree to my terms. And that's the first one."

"Okay," Matt said. He wanted that snowmobile. He wanted it bad. "I'll go. But I don't have to like it."

BEN AND MATT WERE late getting to the tree-lighting ceremony because they couldn't find a place to park the truck and had ended up walking to the firehouse from the Jack Pine. But at least they were there. Matt was right about one thing. Ben was more comfortable among people if he didn't have to face them in the light of day. But he'd made himself do it more and more lately for Matt's sake.

And because of his own overriding desire to see Ellie Lawrence again.

Matt whistled between his teeth. "Jeez, how'd a nowhere burg like this come up with a radical tree like that? It must be forty feet tall."

"Trees are one of the things they do best around here."

"Yeah, I guess they do. I'm glad I don't have to pay the electric bill."

"Good point," Ben agreed. "I imagine there's a donation box somewhere around to help defray the cost."

"Yeah."

You couldn't exactly call it a rousing conversation, but at least Matt was speaking to him, which was more than he'd been doing an hour ago.

They passed under a streetlight as they made their way up the hill to the firehouse. Matt was wearing the heavy coat and boots that Ben had bought him, but his hands were bare and he still wore the grungy ball cap he'd had on that first night, backward, with the bill hanging down over his collar. It was just slightly above freezing, but the winds were calm and with his long hair the kid wasn't in any real danger of frostbite, but he was courting one hell of a cold.

Lord, he sounded like a parent.

The thought shook him. Ben decided against making a comment about the headgear. Every hour he spent with Matt was uncharted territory. The only guidelines he had were vague memories of the intensity of his own emotions at Matt's age and the conviction that a willingness to listen, firm boundaries, common sense and the patience of Job were the best tools for the job. Their relationship was still way too shaky to risk a confrontation every time he opened his mouth.

"Good thing we weren't here when they turned it on. It would've blinded me," Matt said. "I should have brought my shades. How many lights do you think there are on that thing?" Matt stopped in his tracks, craning his neck. The towering pine tree was indeed impressively festooned with lights and garlands of tinsel and snowflakes cut from heavy white plastic and covered with glitter.

As they approached, the high-school band began playing a medley of Christmas carols that carried over the frozen lake and echoed back from the surrounding woods. People stood in small groups. Children darted here and there, playing hide-and-seek in the shadows.

The public-address system squawked and a voice, barely recognizable as Baldy Carmichael's, announced that Santa was scheduled to arrive any minute in the town's brand-new fire engine. Children began to laugh and cheer, hurrying to be first in line.

But inside the fire station, the firemen were selling hot dogs, homemade vegetable soup and hot chocolate, and tables were being set up for the regular Friday-night bingo.

Ben knew he had to brave his own demons, walk into the lighted building and make his donation toward the lighting of the Christmas tree, whether he wanted to or not. He swallowed against the acrid taste of bile that rose in his throat. He'd made it through Brian's memorial service. He'd made it through the library-fund bazaar last week. He could make it through this.

"I'm going to check out the snowmobile they're raffling," Matt told him.

"Okay. I'll be over to take a look in a few minutes."

He watched Matt walk away, his limp barely noticeable.

"Are you handling all the excitement, okay?" Ellie asked playfully, suddenly appearing at his side.

He hadn't seen her approach in the noise and confusion, but subconsciously he knew he had been looking for her in every female face he saw. "I'm managing," he said, making himself smile. "Where are the kids?" He hadn't seen Ellie's children since Saturday. He was surprised to realize how much he'd missed them.

"They were..." She spun around. "Here they come." Carly came waltzing up, a candy cane clutched in her fist. Tim walked more slowly, careful not to spill the steaming cup of hot chocolate he held in his hands.

"Hi," Carly said, smiling and still dancing up and down beside her mother.

"Hi," Ben said, smiling back. Carly could coax a smile out of a stone.

"Here's your cocoa, Mom." Tim handed over the cup. "Hi, Ben."

"Hi, Tim."

"Where's Matt?" the youngster asked.

"Checking out the snowmobile the Lions Club is raffling off."

"It's awesome," Tim informed him. "Want to see it?"

"Okay," Ben said. "That is, if your mom wants to."

"Sure," Ellie said. Her nose was red. So were her cheeks. She didn't look a whole lot older than Carly, with her mittens, and her hair pushed up under a white knit cap. "But I'm not going to ride on it."

Carly giggled. "You might shake the baby out, right, Mom?"

"Right."

"We don't want that to happen 'cause he's not clear cooked yet, is he?" Carly giggled at her own joke.

"No," Ellie agreed, rolling her eyes in Ben's direction. "He's not clear cooked yet."

"There's Matt," Carly said. "I want to go say hi."

"All right. But don't make a nuisance of yourself."

"I'm going, too," Tim informed her. "I'll race you, baby." Tim took off running, Carly on his heels.

Matt was standing beside the snow machine at the side of the firehouse. Three other teenage boys were nearby, also inspecting the vehicle. Matt stood a little apart, not yet one of the group, but clearly being included in the discussion. Ben was relieved to see the interaction with kids who would probably be his classmates in the new year.

If Matt was still with him when school started.

Ellie must have sensed his uneasiness. "How's he doing?" she asked.

Ben shrugged. "Okay. We saw the orthopedist in Sault Ste. Marie a couple of days ago. She told him his leg was doing fine. He doesn't even need to go for physiotherapy unless the weather gets so bad he can't get out and walk."

"But?"

"He keeps to himself too much."

"Are you worried he still might run away?"

"It's a possibility. He's carrying a lot of emotional baggage. A lot of anger."

Ellie laid her mittened hand on his arm. "Ben, if—"

"Ellie. Hello. Ben. It's good to see you in town." Danelda Larson and her sister, Lenore, walked by, heading toward the firehouse. "Great night, isn't it?" Danelda observed. "Good crowd."

"Yes," Ellie said with a smile and a wave. "It's a great night. We're going to check out the snowmobile."

"Lars has already bought ten tickets. I don't know why. He's way too old for a snow racer like that one."

"Boys are never too old for their toys," Lenore said with a sniff as the twosome walked away.

"She's never been married," Ellie explained.

"I can see why."

She looked at him and laughed. "She does have a pretty sharp tongue."

Ellie began walking toward the crowd gathered around the snowmobile. Ben fell into step beside her. Carly had rushed over to Matt as though she'd known him all her life. Tim hung back, obviously awed by the older boys Matt was talking to. Ben found himself watching, waiting, to see what the teen would do when he spotted the kids. At his side, Ellie fell silent, as well.

Matt smiled at Carly, and appeared to admire the candy cane she held up to him. They were too far away to hear what he said to the little girl, but evidently Carly was pleased by the comment because she laughed and jumped up and down again. Tim sidled closer. Matt held out his hand, palm up. Tim hesitated a moment, then slapped his hand down on top of Matt's. He turned it over, and Matt returned the greeting. Tim's smile was so bright it shone through the murky darkness.

Matt said something to the group of boys he'd been with. They raised their hands in farewell. Matt did the same. He turned and headed to where Ben and Ellie were standing, Tim and Carly on his heels.

"Hello, Matt," Ellie said.

"Hi."

"It's a beautiful machine, isn't it," Ellie said with a slight inclination of her head. "I'd love to take it out for a spin, but my snowmobiling days are over for a while."

"Yeah, sure." A dark flush spread up Matt's neck as his gaze stole to Ellie's stomach. "'Cause of the baby, huh?"

"That's right. What do you think of the tree?"

"Rad," Matt said, swiveling his head to check it out once more. "The electric bill must be a bummer, though."

"You can make a donation inside," Ellie said, laughing.

Matt stuck his hands into his pockets and pulled them inside out. "Ben already hit me up. But I'm tapped out, man," he said.

Ellie laughed again. "Aren't we all?"

"Erika's brother Kevin said hi to me," Carly boasted. "He's the quarterback on the football team."

"I know that. Matt, what did you think of Kevin Shurmansky and his friends?" Ellie asked.

Matt looked down at his boots. "They're okay." After a long moment's silence, he said, "There's open gym at the school from six to eight every night. I might check it out. I doubt they have much equipment here, but it beats freezing my b...fingers off," he amended quickly, "walking along the beach to exercise my leg."

"Sounds like a good idea. Just don't overdo it, okay?" Ben's voice was soft.

"Okay," Matt said, nodding agreement. He lifted his eyes to Ben's. "Thanks."

"Carly!" A plump little girl in a red snowsuit and white mittens came running up. "Hi, Mrs. Lawrence."

"Hi, Erika."

The youngster gave Ben a distracted half smile but it was clear all she wanted to do was talk to Ellie's daughter. "Carly! Hurry! It's almost time for Santa to come. Are you ready?"

"Of course I'm ready. I've been waiting for you. Where have you been, Erika?"

Erika rolled her eyes. "Mom was talking to Mrs. Larson about the Sunday School pageant. She still *is* talking to her," Erika said in exasperation. "She said

Kevin has to take me to see Santa whether he likes it or not, but I can't find him.''

"He's over there. Looking at the snowmobile.'' Carly pointed to the trio of boys Matt had just left. "See. There he is.''

"Kevin,'' Erika hollered. "C'mon. It's time for Santa to come.''

Her brother waved her off.

"Mom said,'' Erika yelled even more loudly. Heads were beginning to turn. Ellie lifted her shoulders and smiled at the attention Carly's friend had drawn. "If you don't come right now I'll tell Mom you didn't just take the car to the grocery store last night. I'll tell her you—''

Kevin Shurmansky appeared at his sister's side as though by magic. "Okay, okay big mouth. I'm here.''

"Come on, Carly. You come, too.''

"Mom! We have to get in line.'' Carly started dancing up and down again. Her eyes, darker than Ellie's, more brown than hazel, were shining with excitement.

"Oh, honey. I'm so...'' Ben turned back to Ellie, hearing the fatigue in her voice. He ignored the jerk of pure sexual attraction that tightened his loins as he searched her face. There were dark circles under her eyes that hadn't been there the last time he saw her. And fine lines had etched themselves from nose to chin. She was clearly exhausted, and in her condition the last thing she needed was to stand in line, being jostled on all sides.

"I'll stay with them and wait for Santa Claus," Matt said unexpectedly. "You can go home and rest, Mrs. Lawrence."

"I..."

"I'll take good care of them. You can trust me," he said with just a shade of challenge. "And Shurmansky'll be with us. You know him."

Ellie didn't answer immediately. She tilted her head slightly, her clear, calm gaze holding Matt's. "Thank you, Matt. I am tired and it would be nice not to have to stand in line for another hour."

"Okay. I'll bring them straight back to your place as soon as they've talked to Santa Claus."

"All right. I'll make cocoa and pop some corn. How does that sound?"

"Radical," Tim said.

"I guess that means, okay?" she said, a smile turning up the corners of her mouth.

"Mom, don't be so bogus," Tim scoffed.

"Hey. Don't talk to your mom like that." Matt's voice was stern.

"Okay, Matt." It was obvious Tim had a new hero.

"Thanks for asking," Matt said, "but I won't have time for popcorn. I...I have an appointment with Eldor to talk about a job."

"Congratulations. And while we're at it, I think it's time you started calling me Ellie."

"Okay," he said. "Ellie."

"It's very nice of you to offer to stay with the kids... Their father was sup—"

"I'll walk you home," Ben said.

He had heard Lonny Lawrence was back in town, but he hadn't seen the man, hadn't met him. And didn't want to.

"You don't have to."

"I want to." Matt was watching them, but the two smaller children didn't seem to notice the tension that he suddenly felt swirling between them.

Ellie looked over her shoulder, then back into Ben's eyes. "All right. I'd like that."

"Listen! I hear a siren. Santa's coming!" Carly clapped her mittened hands. "Hurry. We have to get in line."

"We'll see you in an hour or so," Matt said, taking Carly by the hand.

"Bye, Mom."

"Bye."

"Be good," Ellie called to the departing group. "Mind Matt."

"We will," Carly promised. Tim lifted his hand in an assenting wave.

Then they were gone. So was the crowd that had been milling around them as people made their way toward the approaching fire engine and the visit from Santa. Ben was alone with Ellie.

He slipped his hand under her elbow as they started walking. It was a polite, innocuous gesture, a courtesy to a very pregnant woman walking on icy pavement, if anyone should chance to look their way. But for Ben it was much more. For him it was an excuse to keep Ellie close to his side, to breathe in the fresh flowery scent of her, precious memories of warmth and spring sunshine eddying around him in the cold air off the lake.

She tucked her arm more intimately within his as they walked down Birch Street. He wondered if she had missed his company this past week as much as he had missed hers. He had to be content to see her now, to tuck her close to his side and savor her proximity and the sound of her voice.

"Thanks for letting the kids stay with Matt. I know it must be hard for you to trust them to his care."

"It is, a little. But Kevin Shurmansky's a good kid. And I believe in my own good judgment. I don't think Matt's a bad boy. And he'll never learn to trust in himself if others don't show trust in him first." She looked up at him. "You believe that, too, don't you, Ben?"

"Yes," he said. At least he used to believe that goodness and caring could overcome all the bad things in life. He hoped that in Matt's case that was still true.

Ellie moved a little away from him again as they neared the business district. Cars and people were coming and going, picking up videos and last-minute grocery items. Jackson Tall Trees was holding down the fort at the Jack Pine, and the regular Friday-night crowd was beginning to pile in. Ben didn't try to hold her close to his side. That would imply that they were a couple, that they were more than just friends, and he didn't think Ellie would accept that sort of public intimacy. For his own sake, his own peace of mind, he'd do well to remember he had no claims on this woman, except in his heart and in his dreams.

CHAPTER TEN

"I HOPE THE KIDS don't give Matt too hard a time," Ellie said as they crossed the parking lot to the cottage. It was quiet here, without a hint of wind. Moonlight gleamed on the dark, open water far out on the lake, fractured into sparkling crystals on the ice close to shore. Twinkling, crystal Christmas lights outlined the door and windows of Ellie's cottage.

"He can hold his own," Ben said. He turned her to face him in the shadow of the cottage door. There were bits of starlight caught in the curling tendrils of hair that escaped her hat, and in her eyes. She smelled of cold, clear air and warm, soft woman. It was a dizzying combination. Ben sucked in his breath, willing his voice steady. "Thanks again for trusting him with your children."

"I do trust him," she said softly. "I told you that. If I didn't, I wouldn't have let them stay with him. But I'm worried about him."

Ben nodded. "So am I. Every morning I wonder if I'm going to wake up and find out he's taken off during the night. But every morning he's still there. I've been in touch with his caseworker in Ohio. She doesn't like giving long-distance advice, but she says to take it one day at a time."

"Does he still blame you for his friend's death?"

"Yes," he said. "I'm sure he does. But whatever he thinks about me, he blames himself more. A hell of a lot more. But I can't force him to deal with his pain. I'll lose him completely if I do that. In the end, it will be up to him."

"It's always up to each of us to deal with his own pain."

He knew she wasn't referring only to Matt's demons, but his own, as well. He didn't want to talk about death and guilt. Not tonight. Not when he had Ellie all to himself, even if it was only for a short time. He reached around her and opened the door. The cop in him spoke before he could censor the words. "You should keep this door locked."

"No one locks their doors in North Star, at least not during the day."

"It's night," he told her. They stood for a moment in the darkness, so close together he could feel the movement of the baby.

"It's evening. Very early in the evening." Her voice was soft and slightly breathless from the cold and the walk, but her words washed over him like silken petals.

"Thanks for walking me home, Ben." Over her shoulder he could see into the cottage's main room. The house was warm and smelled of cinnamon and spice. There were more tiny white lights strung along the bookcases and above the counter that separated the kitchen and living room.

"My pleasure." He leaned forward to brush a kiss across her lips. She took a step backward.

"I..." She hesitated. Ben's heartbeat turned erratic, painful. He straightened, rubbed his hand across his cheek, feeling the roughness of the scar tissue beneath his fingers. The unconscious action jerked him back to reality with an unpleasant jolt of sensation. She was reluctant to be alone with him. Her husband was back in town. Perhaps back in her life. The thought made him grind his teeth in anger and denial, but he didn't let the emotions show on his face.

"I'd better be going," he said. "I'll wait for Matt at the Jack Pine. Good night, Ellie."

"Ben..." She held out her hand, dropped it to her side. She took a deep breath. "Don't go. Come in. Have a cup of coffee."

He knew he shouldn't accept her invitation. She was a pregnant woman with an ex-husband in town. "Thanks. I'd like that," he heard himself say.

She stepped inside, leaving him to follow on his own. He shut the door behind them. A moment later, light blazed from a table lamp, dimming the Christmas lights, stealing a little of their magic.

Ellie hung her coat on a hook by the door. She held out her hand. He took his off, not letting himself hesitate for a moment. She took it and hung it beside her own. She moved into the kitchen with ponderous grace, her stomach round and full beneath the soft-woven turtleneck sweater she was wearing. It was a pale mint green that complemented the golden lights in her hair and eyes. He wondered what she would say, how she would react, if he told her he thought she was the sexiest woman he had ever seen.

She would color prettily, laugh and tell him he was crazy, but her eyes would darken, that little frown would appear between her eyebrows and her hands would move to soothe and be soothed by the precious life she carried within. As so often before, Ben speculated on what kind of man Ellie's ex-husband was. He knew he could ask Eldor or Baldy about Lonny Lawrence, but he didn't want to seem that interested, for Ellie's sake, as well as his own. His private, gut-instinct opinion was that the man must be an A-1 SOB to have turned his back on Ellie and his kids, and the baby she carried.

The baby Ben would have given everything he owned to claim as his.

The thought caught him unaware, stopped his breath in his chest with the same impact as a .45 slug.

He wanted another man's child to be his own?

Did that mean he was falling in love with Ellie Lawrence?

Did it mean he was already in love with her?

He was swimming in deep, shark-infested waters here. The last thing on earth Ellie needed was to know that a broken-down, burned-out cop was falling in love with her. Especially now that her ex-husband was back in town. Ben's hands balled into fists and he stuck them in the pockets of his jeans to keep Ellie from noticing his agitation. If she could read his mind, she would run as fast and as far as she could.

She was speaking to him and he forced his thoughts away from the emotional whirlpool they were circling. "Would you like a cup of coffee? It will be a little while before the kids get through the line. Especially if Carly bombards Santa with her entire wish list.''

"Wish list?"

She seemed to make a decision, motioned to a tablet of lined yellow paper on the counter with a slight movement of her head. "It's there. By the Christmas catalog. She spends hours looking through it, making lists. Gifts for Tim. For me and her father. For Spock and Muffin, Eldor and Martha. Even the baby.''

Ben picked up the tablet and sat down on one of the rickety bar stools on his side of the counter. Ellie was right. Carly had been making lists. There, in round, uneven letters, some of them backward, some of them twice the size of their fellows, were rows of names and gifts and the pages of the JCPenney's catalog where those gifts could be found.

His name was there.

So was Matt's.

Both of them followed by a whole squiggly line of what appeared to be question marks. Ellie looked down at the tablet from the other side of the counter and smiled, a half funny, half sad smile that seeped into his pores and pooled like warm honey in his loins.

"She doesn't know what to get you yet. You haven't been around this week, so she hasn't had a chance to pester you to look at the catalog. She'll try to waylay you before you leave. Consider this a warning.''

He answered lightly because there was a curious tightness in his throat. *Carly wanted to buy him something for Christmas.* "I have the sneaking suspicion telling her I could use a new pair of socks won't be what she wants to hear, right?''

"You catch on real quick."

She smiled again and the honey turned to liquid fire inside him. He shifted position on the hard stool, setting his jaw to keep his physical reaction from getting out of control. "I'll do my best to pick something more appropriate."

"Thank you. I hope Matt plays along. I haven't had the heart to tell her she can't really order any of those things." Ellie seemed to realize what she had said and her full mouth tightened into a thin line. She turned back to the stove and poured coffee for him and a mug of hot water for herself.

The oak Santa was still sitting on the counter, exactly where it had been the last time he was here. He picked it up, once more studying the ancient careworn features, the tiny, sleeping fawn at the base. He wondered if the gallery owner in Mackinaw City would wait for Ellie to complete more Santas. Was the commission secure, or was it only wishful thinking on her part?

There was something he could do to help her, but he was almost positive her reaction would be negative. Still, for the children's sake, he had to try. He looked up, caught her watching him holding the Santa figure. "Sell it to me, Ellie," he said. The words were out before he could call them back. They hung in the air between them, sharp and serrated, like icicles on the roofline.

Hot water splashed over the rim of the mug. She winced, then set it down on the counter. "No, Ben."

"Please, Ellie. Let me do this for you. I want you to be able to give the kids a real Christmas."

"No." She reached for the carving. Her hands were shaking. There was a tautness to her jaw, a tenseness to the set of her shoulders. "We'll manage."

He didn't release his hold on the Santa. Ellie's fingers brushed against his, warmth and softness against the ridges of scar tissue. She winced again and dropped her hands to the counter. He ignored the quick jab of anguish her reaction caused him. He'd gone too far to turn back now. He tried another tack. "If you let me buy the carving, Carly can buy her gifts, for everyone. Don't you want her to have that happiness?"

"Carly will have to learn she can't have everything." The little frown appeared between her sable eyebrows, the frown that he was beginning to know meant she was arguing with herself as well as with him.

He leaned toward her, moved his right hand to cover hers. Ellie's breath sifted out between her teeth in a little sigh. Her fingers curled into a fist beneath his, but she didn't pull away. Ben experienced the rush of heat he always felt when he touched her, but he kept his response under control, pressed his advantage. "You're going to tell her there's no Santa? That she can't give gifts to make others happy? That she can't have the things she wants for herself, too?"

Tears pooled in her eyes, drowning the desire, the sensual awareness that had flickered in the gold-green depths just seconds before. Ellie's chin came up. "I will if I have to."

"You don't have to, Ellie. Let me buy the Santa."

"No." She blinked rapidly, pulled her hand from beneath his, turned away. She picked up a tea bag and began blindly dipping it—in his coffee mug. Ben reached over and took the mug away from her. "Ellie—" Damn, he'd made a mess of things again. Why couldn't he keep his nose out of her business, let her take care of herself and her kids the way she wanted to do?

Because he loved her. There was no use lying to himself any longer. Somehow, some way, in the last month he'd fallen head over heels in love with every prickly, stubborn inch of Ellie Lawrence. And somewhere along the way, he'd fallen in love with her kids, too. All of them.

"The Santa isn't for sale," she said, not looking at him.

"All right. If you won't sell it, let me loan—"

"No." She spun around. "I will not borrow money from you!"

He'd never seen her so angry, so upset. "I only wanted to help, Ellie. I'll hold the Santa for collateral. I'll charge you interest. Same as the North Star bank, if that will make you feel any better."

"No," she said, her voice barely more than a whisper. "I won't take your money." She reached out and pushed the Santa a little closer to his hand. Once more, tears glistened on her dusky lashes. She dashed them away. "I want you to have it," she said. "It was going to be our gift to you." She nudged the carving an inch closer. "This isn't how I meant to give it to you. Merry Christmas, Ben. From all four of us. Please don't cheapen our gift by offering us money."

Ben didn't touch the Santa. "God, Ellie. I didn't mean to upset you. I didn't mean to insult you. I only wanted to help."

She lifted her head and met his anguished gaze head-on. "I'm sorry, too. I'm a stiff-necked fool sometimes. I know you meant well. But I have to do this on my own, Ben. I have to."

"No, you don't." He was up off the stool and around the counter before the sound of the words had died away. His throat was dry as a desert. His voice was a dusty croak. He knew as surely as he drew breath that these were the most important words he would ever speak. "Ellie—"

She held out a hand as though to ward him off. "No, Ben. Don't...don't say—"

Suddenly, the front door burst open in a swirl of cold air, snow and noise. "We have to go cut a Christmas tree tomorrow, Daddy. We have to. *Everyone* else has one up already."

Carly and Tim came rushing into the room followed by a man, taller, and about thirty pounds heavier than Matt. A man who looked a lot like Tim and treated Ellie's house as if it were his own. The father who had given Carly her sparkling dark eyes. Lonny Lawrence. There was no question that was who he was. But where was Matt? Then Ben spotted the teenager, his face a sullen mask, hanging back, just outside the door.

Lonny was laughing and talking as loudly as the kids, his accent a strange mixture of flat north woods vowels, and now and then a hint of Dixie drawl. Carly hung on his hand, Tim danced backward across the room, intent on the man's every word.

"Ellie, darlin', we're home. And I want to have a word with you. What the devil do you think you were doing letting our kids hang around—" He stopped dead in his tracks when he realized Ellie wasn't alone. The grin on his weather-beaten face disappeared. "Well, well. What have we here? A party?"

Ellie ignored the taunt. "Where's Matt?" she asked instead. From where she was standing, the teenager wasn't visible.

"Matt?" Lonny shot Ben a suspicious look. "Who's Matt?"

"The boy who was taking care of Carly and Tim. Where is he?"

Lonny indicated the doorway with a jerk of his head. "Outside."

Ellie brushed past him. Ben thought he saw her tense slightly as she focused on Matt's angry face, but she never missed a beat. "Matt, please. Come in."

"No," Matt said without preamble. "I just wanted to make sure the kids got home all right."

"Yes. They're fine. Thank you for taking such good care of them."

"Forget it."

"Please, Matt. Come inside." Ellie was smiling. Ben could hear it in her voice, but he could see tension in her neck and shoulders. Something was wrong and she knew it. Ellie's smiling invitation didn't help. Matt remained standing in the yard. "It's cold, Matt. I...I need to shut the door."

"No."

Ben took a step forward. "I'll meet you at the Jack Pine in five minutes," he told the boy.

Matt wouldn't meet his eyes. "Yeah."

"No," Carly wailed. "Matt's supposed to come in and pick out his present in the catalog. Daddy's going to take us shopping. Aren't you, Daddy?"

"Sure, sweetheart. I'll take you shopping."

"I don't want a present, Carly," Matt said. But his tone was softer, not so angry. "But...but thanks, anyway." He turned and walked away from the cottage. Ellie shut the door behind him, then spun on her heel.

"Lonny Lawrence, what the devil—"

"I won't have my kids watched over by no juvenile delinquent. I heard about that kid at the Steelhead." The Steelhead was an unsavory roadhouse about two miles out of town. He spread his feet and folded his arms across his chest. "Saw him walking with them down Main Street. He *said* he was bringing them home to you. But who's to know whether a kid like that is telling the truth or not. Have you lost your mind, Ella Marie, leaving our kids with scum like that?"

"That's enough," Ben said quietly. "Matt is my ward. I'll vouch for him."

"You will, will ya? Well, that plum sets my mind at ease."

"Lonny, that's enough," she said. "Ben, go after him. I...I want to apologize."

"I'll take care of it, Ellie," Ben said quietly.

She wasn't looking at him. Her eyes were blazing with anger, and Ben saw her hand trembling as she unconsciously smoothed her hand over her rounded belly. Carly and Tim watched the exchange between the adults in silence. "I won't have my guests insulted in *my* home, Lonny." The emphasis on the word was so slight, for a moment Ben thought he might have imagined it, but he saw Lonny stiffen slightly and knew that he had not.

"I'm sorry, babe. I was just worried about the kids, that's all."

Ellie's mouth tightened. She opened her lips as if to refute the man's claim. Then her eyes flickered to the silent, watchful children and he saw the fight go out of her. "Lonny Lawrence, this is Ben MacAllister," she said formally. "He's Matt's guardian. He's the man I told you about, the one who saved Spock's life the night of the fire."

Lonny had the grace to look sheepish. He smiled, but the smile never reached his eyes. They were dark and cold, stone hard and challenging. He didn't offer his hand. "Sorry," he said. "That boy having my kids sort of riled me up. Ellie told me about the fire. Thanks for what you did for *my* family."

To Ben, Lonny's message was clear. Lonny Lawrence had no intention of giving up his wife and children to any man. Certainly not to a scarred, battered ex-cop like Ben MacAllister.

He felt like punching Ellie's ex-husband right in the middle of his grin, but didn't let it show. For Ellie's sake. For the kids' sakes. "Glad to be of help," he said instead. "I have to be going. So long, kids."

Carly grabbed for his hand. "You can't go, Ben. You have to pick out your gift."

He hunkered down in front of her. "I tell you what, Carly," he said, reaching out to push a wisp of honey-gold hair behind her ear. "You pick something out for me and for Matt. I know it will be the best present I get."

"Okay," she said, smiling and nodding. "My daddy's here now. And tomorrow he's going to take me Christmas shopping. He says I can spend all the money I want and I can get something wonderful for everyone."

MATT WAS WAITING for him in the Jack Pine, sitting at a table along the wall, a can of Pepsi in front of him. Ben hadn't planned on the place being so crowded. His throat closed up, for a moment he couldn't catch his breath. Then he saw Matt was watching him standing in the doorway, and he knew he couldn't cut and run the way his gut was screaming for him to do. He made his way to Matt's table, looking neither right nor left.

"I didn't think you'd show up," Matt said, wrapping both hands around the soft-drink can. "Here, I mean. With all these people."

Ben didn't look around. He sat down at the table, his back to the noisy room. "I told you I'd be here," he said. "I usually mean what I say."

"Yeah. So I've noticed." Ben pushed back the hood of his parka, shrugged out of the sleeves. Jackson Tall Trees appeared at his shoulder.

"What'll you have?"

"A beer," Ben said. "Want anything to eat?" he asked Matt.

"No."

"Want another Pepsi?" Matt shook his head and Jackson ambled off to the next table. Matt went back to studying his soft-drink can.

Someone put a quarter in the jukebox. A country ballad wafted out of the speakers. The door opened and closed, letting in a half-dozen people who began shedding coats and gloves while looking for a table that would hold them all.

"What happened with Lawrence back there?" Ben asked when the group was settled and some of the commotion had died away.

Matt looked up. "Who said anything happened?"

"I did."

"I don't want to talk about it. The guy's an asshole." He looked at Ben defiantly. "You can go ahead and add that one to my tab. I'm not going to take it back."

"I think you're entitled to that one."

"I sure as hell am. He treated me like some ef—" He stopped talking abruptly, lifted his Pepsi can to his mouth and took a swallow. "He came up to me after me and the kids went through the Santa line. Got real huffy. Wanted to know what the hell—that's his word not mine—I was doing with his kids. That's when I decided I'd be better off not popping him one. It would have scared Carly. And it wouldn't be a good example for Tim."

"Good decision." Ben didn't gild the lily. Matt could have run. He could have opted to use violence. He'd done neither.

"Yeah. What is it they say? Discretion is the better part of valor," Matt said. "I never knew what that meant until tonight. Besides, he was with a couple of real badass-looking dudes. I told him I was a friend of Ellie's. That Mr. Eldor would vouch for me if he wanted him to. I told him I'd offered to stand in the Santa line with Carly and Tim so that Ellie could go home and rest. He quit hollering around then, but he still didn't act like he liked the idea of me being in charge of his kids. Said his friends had pointed me out. They said I just showed up in town one day and moved in with you. The lighthouse hermit. That's what he called you."

"I've been called worse," Ben said, taking a swallow of beer.

"Yeah, maybe," Matt muttered. "Anyway, he told the kids it was time to go home. He said he'd make sure they got back to Ellie's. Told me to be on my way."

"Then what did you do?"

"I hung around and followed him back to the cottage. You know the rest. Is he really the kids' dad?"

The question surprised Ben but he answered. "Yes, he is."

"Well, he looks like them, but I just wondered. My mom had about six different guys she wanted me to say were my dad. None of them were. Heck. They weren't even really my stepdads." He focused his gaze squarely on Ben. "Is he the baby's father, too?"

"Yes," Ben said again.

"Is she going to take him back? Because of the baby and all?"

"I don't know." Maybe she was. He was the kids' father. And he was a good-looking guy. Not a mark on him. Not a single hellish memory in his head to drench his dreams in blood and screams and keep him awake at night.

"I guess it's a good thing I didn't go ahead and pop him back there on Main Street."

"I think it probably is."

Jackson Tall Trees returned to ask if Ben wanted a refill. Ben shook his head. All he could think of was Ellie in Lonny Lawrence's arms, him holding her, loving her. His hand balled into a fist. He had to get out of here, away from the noise, away from the people. He shoved his arms into the sleeves of his parka, pulled the hood up over his head, then threw a couple of dollars down on the table.

Matt drained the last of his soda. "He's a jerk." He jammed his ball cap on his head. "But Ellie's a great mom. She'd do anything for her kids." Matt colored and looked past Ben. "I guess that sounds pretty hokey."

"No, it doesn't. As a matter of fact, I agree with you." The words came out in a kind of a low growl that he couldn't quite control. "Ellie will do anything for her kids." What if she did reconcile with Lawrence? If Ellie wanted her ex-husband back, she wasn't the woman he'd thought she was. He was better off with her out of his life.

"Yeah. She's pretty special that way. I know what happened tonight wasn't her fault. Hey, there's Eldor." Ben looked over his shoulder. His cousin had shed his fur-trimmed red coat and fake beard. He was wearing an old green-and-red-plaid shirt, suspenders and the red, fur-trimmed pants and black boots of his Santa suit. He was headed into the kitchen. "Will you wait a minute?" Matt asked. "I—" He crushed the aluminum can in his fist. "I'd like to ask him about that job, if you're not in a hurry."

"I'm not in a hurry. Go ahead. Take as long as you like."

"Thanks." Matt stood up, saw his reflection in the mirror behind the bar and stopped long enough to turn his ball cap around so that he was wearing it the way the manufacturer intended. "Wish me luck," he said, and headed for the kitchen.

Ben stared down at the residue of foam and beer in his mug. He'd turned a corner with Matt tonight. He didn't fool himself into thinking it was all going to be smooth sailing from now on. But at least they'd talked—Matt had talked—working through his anger and pain over the scene Lawrence had caused at the tree lighting, handling himself with restraint, following through on Ben's suggestion of asking Eldor for a job at the Jack Pine. It was a start, a good start.

It was also the end of a dream.

He'd almost fooled himself for a while there, thinking that if Ellie took Lonny Lawrence back, she wasn't the woman he'd thought she was. Illusion. Delusion. Wishful thinking, that wasn't going to hold up an hour past midnight. Ellie was exactly the woman he'd thought she was. Loyal. Caring. Devoted to her children. If Ellie took her ex back, it would be because she thought it was best for her kids.

Matt was right. There was nothing on earth that she wouldn't do for her children. And once she made up her mind, decided she was doing the right thing, there wasn't a force in heaven or on earth that could change it.

CHAPTER ELEVEN

IT WAS A COLD, crisp afternoon. School had been let out an hour early for a faculty meeting and Mrs. Eldor and Jackson Tall Trees were holding down the fort in the Jack Pine kitchen.

"C'mon, Mom. Let's go look for a tree," Carly begged for at least the tenth time in less than thirty minutes. "It's going to get dark if we don't hurry."

"We're waiting on Dad, snot face," Tim chided.

"Mama, he called me snot face," Carly wailed.

"No more names, Tim," Ellie said wearily. She was just about at her wits' end. It seemed as if the two of them couldn't say a dozen words to each other without coming to blows or tears. Maybe it was the bad weather they'd been experiencing for the past several days, dreary and wet, more sleet than snow. Maybe it was just the overload of Christmas excitement building toward the big day only a week away.

Or maybe it was the tension of having Lonny back in the house. She honestly didn't know. The children seemed to be glad to see their father. They certainly enjoyed his treats and the money he showered on them to play the video games at the Jack Pine, or to rent the latest Disney movie at the video store. But there were

also the disappointments caused by Lonny's carelessness and almost total self-absorption.

He still hadn't kept his promise to take Carly shopping for Christmas presents. He wouldn't even explain to her that she couldn't buy the expensive gifts
for everyone on her list. Ellie had been the one to ca-
jole her into becoming enthusiastic about making
splendid, one-of-a-kind Christmas cards for Eldor and
Martha and Jackson Tall Trees. Ellie had been the one
to bake and decorate gingerbread-men cookies for the
Larsons and Baldy Carmichael and Carly's teacher, to
get her to agree that a videotape copy of the Sunday-
school pageant would be a ''radically'' excellent gift
for Grandma and Grandpa Gibson in Florida. And
that while it was lots of fun to look through the catalog and make wish lists, that's all they were, just
wishes and not her real gift lists.

Tim had even pitched in to help. He carved a beaver
and a black-bear cub from Ellie's scraps of basswood, and offered them to his little sister with the
suggestion that she give them to Matt Westrick and
Ben MacAllister. The figures were amateurish but
recognizable, and Ellie had praised him lavishly. Then
she'd thrown her arms around Tim for a quick hug
and kiss, thanking him for giving the little figures to
his sister. He'd made a face as he pulled away from her
embrace, but his expression was pleased and proud.

''I would have made more of them, Mom,'' he'd
said earnestly. ''but you've been too busy to work with
me.''

It was just one more thing Ellie felt guilty about
lately. Tim had been watching her carve since he was

a toddler and was eager to learn the craft. But he was too young yet to be trusted with her knives and carving tools without some supervision, and these days, she was too bone-weary to spend more than a few minutes at a time helping him. Besides, she didn't want Lonny making fun of the boy's efforts, although, to give him credit, her ex had praised the bear cub and beaver figurines adequately, if a bit impatiently, when Tim had somewhat hesitantly produced his creations for Lonny's inspection.

"I know, honey," she said now. "Maybe we can find an hour this evening to carve together, okay?" She pressed both hands to the small of her back, arching her spine in a vain attempt to relieve the dull ache low in her abdomen. Ellie frowned as another twinge rippled across her belly. False labor already? She wasn't due for almost a month, but Dr. Makowski, her obstetrician had warned her that the false contractions might start early, and be more severe than she'd experienced with Carly or Tim. This was her third baby, after all. And she was almost thirty, she reminded herself with a wry smile. Her body would be showing the strain more than it had in the past.

"Not tonight," Carly insisted. "Tonight we're going to decorate the Christmas tree. You promised."

"Mom, it's getting late. When is Dad going to be here?" Tim was scowling at her from the sofa. "Everyone else in my class has their tree up but us."

"Daddy said he would take us to cut one down as soon as the sun came out. It's shining now. See?" Carly pointed out the window.

"We're not blind," Tim scoffed.

For days, Lonny had told them that he would take them out to cut a Christmas tree as soon as the sun peeked from behind the clouds. Instead, he'd gone off with an old high-school buddy he'd met out at the Steelhead one night, to run his traplines along the lakeshore, and still hadn't returned. As usual, it was up to her. "You're right, Carly," Ellie agreed, managing a smile. "It's a great day to cut a tree. Tim, get the hatchet." He bounded off the sofa. "And be careful with it."

"Aw, Mom. Don't worry. I know how to carry it the right way." He'd already pulled on his boots and was struggling into his coat. "We learned how in Scouts, remember?"

Ellie nodded, "Okay, but walk. Don't run."

"Mom—"

She shooed him out the door. "Carly, get your snowsuit and gloves. And your scarf. I don't want you getting the sniffles again so close to the holidays."

"Okay!" Brown eyes sparkling, she hurried to do as she was told.

"Okay, Spock," Ellie said, looking at the old dog stretched out in front of the Franklin stove. "Want to go along?" Spock opened one eye, seemed to consider the invitation, then closed it again and went back to sleep. Muffin, curled in her favorite spot on the bookshelves, didn't deign to twitch a whisker in response.

"I guess that's a no and a no," Ellie said, reaching for her own coat and boots.

"Should I help you put on your boots, Mom?" Carly asked, coming back into the room, looking like a colorful, roly-poly penguin in her shiny black snow-mobile suit and hat, with a red-and-white scarf wound around her neck.

"No, I'll manage," Ellie said, but she was more than a little breathless when the task was completed.

Twenty minutes later they were parked at the edge of the road half a mile from the lighthouse, at exactly the spot Ellie's father always used to come to find just the right tree. From where she stood, she could see the high, white tower with its red roof and windows spar-kling in the late-afternoon sun. And as always, the man who lived there hovered at the edge of her thoughts, even though she hadn't seen him since the evening of the tree-lighting ceremony.

She regretted both the argument over the oak Santa, and the scene with Lonny, even though she didn't see how she could have avoided either one. She couldn't accept money from Ben MacAllister, not even for her children's sakes. And Lonny *was* the father of her children. He would always be a part of her past, and because he was the father of her children he would play some part in her future, however marginal.

Yet, how did you speak of such things to a man who was everything that Lonny was not? A man who made her heart beat like a snare drum and her mouth go dry with desire and longing she'd never thought she'd feel again. It was a disorienting, confusing mixture of emotion and passion. She wasn't up to the challenge of dealing with it now.

Tim opened the trunk of the car with the keys he'd grabbed from the ignition the moment they stopped moving. He pulled out the small hatchet in its worn, leather case and the old-fashioned, wooden sled that Eldor had unearthed from the attic above the garage. It would come in handy for hauling the tree back to the car.

The throaty roar of a snowmobile broke the late-afternoon silence. Automatically, Ellie and the kids turned their heads in the direction of the sound as the snowmobile tore into view.

"Matt!" Carly squealed, waving her mittened hand wildly over her head. "Matt! We're over here."

It was Matt Westrick on a snowmobile, an old one, Ellie noted, a no-nonsense, dependable machine, a generation or two removed from the sleek snow racers favored by the winter-sports enthusiasts that flocked to North Star to ride the groomed trails crisscrossing the sparsely inhabited Upper Peninsula.

Matt skidded to a halt beside them, spraying snow over the car and the kids, who hollered in delight as the fine dusting of white settled on their heads and shoulders. He took off a beat-up helmet with goggles attached and placed it on the seat, between his legs.

"Where'd you get that old heap?" Tim hollered, giving the snowmobile a once-over with a connoisseur's critical eye.

Matt almost smiled. "Ben's letting me use it." He patted the nose of the snow machine, shouting over the roar of the engine. "I've been working on the engine. Hear that, purring like a kitten."

Ellie put both hands over her ears. "I can't hear a word you're saying over that noise," she shouted almost as loudly as Tim.

Matt shrugged, looking a little sheepish. He reached over and turned the key in the ignition. Silence descended with a rush. Ellie took her hands from over her ears, which were still ringing slightly. "That's better," she said, smiling, hoping to coax a real smile from the teen in return.

He was dressed in old canvas hunting pants and coat, and the hat and boots that Ben had bought him. His long hair, always clean and neatly pulled back in a ponytail these days, was pushed up under his knit hat. His cheeks and nose were red from the cold. He'd gained weight since he'd been living with Ben and Ellie noticed he wasn't wearing the high-tech brace anymore. If it wasn't for the hint of old anger and sorrow clouding his brown eyes, Ellie wouldn't have recognized him as the desperate, angry boy who had attacked her and Ben that night not so long ago.

"Hello, Mrs. Lawrence," he said politely.

"Hello, Matt."

"What are you guys doing way out here?" he asked, still astride the snow machine, forearms resting on the handlebars.

"We're going to cut down a Christmas tree. Mrs. Eldor said we could," Carly piped up.

"Rad. Cutting your own Christmas tree. Wow, real authentic Currier and Ives stuff, huh. I've seen it in the movies, but never for real," Matt responded. If there was any bitterness underlying the words, he kept it hidden from the children.

"I don't know about no Curry and Ivy. But you can come with us," Carly offered, giving him a brilliant grin.

"Yeah, you can help me cut it down." Tim brandished the hatchet, still in its leather holder. Ellie bit her lip to keep from voicing a warning in true worrying-mother fashion.

"I guess I could help you out for a while. I haven't got any other plans for the rest of the day. I don't have to be at work at the Jack Pine until seven."

"Rad," Tim said, imitating Matt's favorite expression.

"How is your new job coming along?" Ellie asked. She hadn't crossed paths with Matt at work. So far, Eldor had kept him busy chopping wood, rearranging the storeroom and cleaning the walk-in cooler. He seldom showed up in the Jack Pine kitchen.

"Not too bad. I get paid tomorrow." He hooked his helmet over the handlebars and brushed off the seat of his pants.

"I love payday," Ellie said.

"Yeah. I'm kinda looking forward to it myself."

"Unfortunately, I've always found they come too far apart to suit me."

"That's for sure. I already owe Ben for a tank of gas for this thing. I'm going to be broke again by Wednesday."

Ellie laughed. "Welcome to the real world."

Matt hesitated a moment as he swung his leg over the seat. His eyes flickered into contact with Ellie's and he turned just a little redder than the temperature warranted. "Yeah. I guess you're right."

"Matt." She wasn't about to pretend that the scene with Lonny had never happened. "I haven't had a chance to talk to you at the Jack Pine. I want to apologize for the way my ex-husband acted last week."

His jaw tightened for a moment, but all he said was, "It's okay."

"No, it's not," Ellie insisted. "He was out of line. I'm sorry that it happened."

Matt didn't avoid her gaze. He looked her straight in the eye. "I'd never do anything to hurt your kids."

"I know that."

"Then it's okay."

"I'm glad."

He gave a short little nod then changed the subject, directing his next remark to Tim. "Point the way to the world's most perfect Christmas tree and let's make like Paul Bunyan."

"Paul Bunyan?" Carly looked mystified once more. "Who are all these people, anyway?"

"Baby! You don't know anything. Paul Bunyan is a guy from the old days. A lumberjack who rode a giant blue ox and cut down trees all over everywhere," Tim lectured in his best big-brother voice.

"He's politically and environmentally incorrect these days," Ellie said, following Matt and Tim as they moved off into the trees. "Fallen from favor for clear-cutting trees and giving his ox a sexist name."

Matt gave a bark of genuine laughter. "Ain't that the truth."

Ellie laughed, too. For the first time, she felt Matt was comfortable in her company, coming out of his shell. They walked silently for about a hundred yards. The snow was clean and unbroken beneath the leafless trees, almost knee-deep, light and powdery despite the bad weather of the last few days. Not particularly hard going for anyone but Ellie, with her unwieldy belly and twenty extra pounds.

The big oaks and maples, second-growth trees because Paul Bunyan and his Lumber Baron cohorts had clear-cut their way across the Upper Peninsula almost a century before, began to thin out and give way to pine and spruce. The sun had wheeled into the west, and the tree shadows stretched out across the small clearing to meet them, blue-black against the dazzling white of the snow.

"That one," Tim called out, waving the hatchet at a short-needled pine that was at least ten feet tall. "That tree would be awesome in our living room."

"I don't think so," Ellie demurred. "We'd have to move into the garage to make room for that thing in the cottage."

"Aw, come on, Mom."

"Tim, we'd have to cut at least three feet off the top. Don't you think that would be a shame?"

Tim considered. "Well, I suppose..."

"Hey, man. What about this one?" Matt suggested, cutting Tim off in midwhine. He looked at Ellie, a slight twinkle in his eye. "It's pretty linear, in a conical kind of way, don't ya think?" The faint laughter in his eyes transformed his face. He was a very good-looking boy, Ellie realized.

"Huh?"

Matt walked around the tree, his boots making crunching noises in the snow as he inspected the fir. "What do you think, Mrs. Lawrence?"

"I thought we agreed you'd call me Ellie." She tilted her head to inspect the smaller tree Matt had pointed out.

"Okay," he said. "Ellie. I forgot." He ducked his head and turned his attention back to Tim. "Well, man?" he demanded. "What do you think?"

"It's okay," Tim admitted, looking wistfully at the bigger tree he'd spotted first. "But it's not very big."

"Our cottage isn't very big," Carly said.

"She's got a point," Matt concurred.

"It's a very nice tree," Ellie said. It was a nice shape and size, just right for the small table under the window in the main room of the cottage. "And I'm sure Matt would like you to show him the safe and proper way to cut it down."

"Sure. Show me how to do it, Paul Bunyan. I don't want to go chopping a hole in my foot."

"Okay." Tim allowed himself to be persuaded. "First, you check to make sure which way the wind's blowing—"

"Why?" Carly piped up.

"So the tree doesn't blow over on top of you, stupid. Girls," he said in disgust.

"Mom—"

"C'mon, Carly. We'll sit over here on this old log and watch."

"I want to cut down a tree."

"When you're older," Ellie promised, knowing better than to say no, and let loose a flood of tears and recriminations.

"I want— Hey, what's that?" Carly said. "Do you hear a dog barking?"

Ellie nodded absently, most of her attention focused on Matt and Tim, now prone on the ground beneath the fir as the little boy labored to cut a notch in the trunk so that the tree would fall in the direction they chose.

"It's Riley," Carly squealed as the setter bounded into the clearing, head and tail erect as he surveyed the activity before him. "Hey, boy, come here. Hi, boy."

Riley was nearly ecstatic with joy at finding friends in the middle of nowhere. He raced circles around Tim and Matt, acting as though he hadn't seen the teenager in months, kicking up snow and thrusting his nose so close to the ax blade he was in danger of being mortally wounded.

Matt had just grabbed him by the collar to drag him away for the third time, when Ben appeared from among the trees with far less sound and fury, but with far greater effect on Ellie's nervous system. He was wearing a pair of snowshoes and, if it hadn't been for Riley's advance warning, she would never have known he was there.

"Riley. Sit," Ben ordered as he shuffled toward them. "Whew," he said, "this is work." He wasn't wearing a snowsuit, just the dark blue parka, half-open over a green-plaid flannel shirt and dazzling white T-shirt. The fabric of his faded jeans stretched tight across his muscled thighs as he rested his hands on his legs to catch his breath.

"Hi, Ben," Carly said, dropping to her knees in the snow to give Riley a hug.

"Hi, Carly. What is this? A Christmas tree–cutting party?"

"Yes." Carly laughed. "We're going to get the most perfectest tree there is."

"Looks like Tim and Matt have already found it. Hello, Ellie." He straightened to his full height.

"Hello, Ben." Ellie reached over to scratch Riley behind the ears to keep her eyes from clinging to Ben's. "You should have opted for the snow machine. It's faster and easier."

"Yeah, but you don't very often run off the road into a tree on these babies."

"An excellent point," Ellie conceded, risking another look at him. Their eyes caught and held for a brace of heartbeats and then she looked away again. It had been nearly a week since she'd seen him, since the awful moment Lonny had burst into the cottage with the kids and made her feel as if she were doing something wrong by having Ben in her house.

"Besides," Ben continued as though nothing had happened, "I didn't have much choice. Matt's become permanently attached to the seat of the snowmobile since we got it up and running."

"You're doing a good job with him, Ben. I can see a lot of improvement."

He turned his head to watch Matt and Tim. "We have our good days. And our not so good days. Sometimes I feel like it's one step forward and two steps back."

"I think part of that comes with the territory."

He turned his head, a slightly puzzled look on his face.

Ellie risked a smile, hoping he'd return one. "You're raising a teenager," she reminded him.

The smile she craved came and went in an instant, but with all the emotional devastation of the explosion of the sun. "The uncharted universe." Ben sat down beside her. Ellie's pulse sped up. He didn't have to say or do anything in particular to throw her off balance. Just his being there, so close she could feel the warmth and heat of him was enough to do the trick. She sat quietly with nothing more to say, wanting and needing what she could never have.

It was Carly who broke the silence stretching between them.

"My daddy was going to bring us to cut a tree but he had to go to work," she informed Ben just as Riley reached over, snatched the mitten she was dangling from her fingers and raced away. "Riley," she screeched loud enough to startle a couple of crows from their perch at the top of a white birch, and gave chase.

"Oh, dear," Ellie said, struggling up from the fallen log. "I'd better go after her." The crows, in turn, had startled a small gray squirrel. It ran back and forth in the branches above her head, scolding the intruders loud and long.

"Sit down. She'll be fine." Ben closed his fingers around her wrist. He tugged her back, her momentary resistance reminding him forcefully just how deceptive her apparent fragility really was. Ellie Lawrence was a fighter. She'd had to be, he supposed, to keep her little family intact. "They won't go far. Riley only runs in circles. They'll be back in a minute."

She nodded, relaxing only fractionally, leaning back on her hands, straining the fabric of her coat over the swelling mound of her belly. He watched her for a moment from the corner of his eye and saw no movement. Perhaps she was wearing too many layers of clothes for the baby's gymnastics to be visible. Perhaps the child was asleep. He wondered how she would react if he asked her those questions, and knew from the tension in her posture, the taut line of her jaw, that it would not be the response he craved. A funny little pain arced through his heart and made him wince.

"I haven't had a chance to apologize for what I said the other night. About buying the Santa figure."

"Oh, Ben. Please, don't mention it again. It isn't you who should apologize. I . . . I overreacted." Her gaze skated away a moment, then returned to meet his. "And I want to apologize for Lonny's behavior toward Matt. I don't think he made a very good first impression."

He sure as hell hadn't.

But Lonny Lawrence's boorish behavior wasn't what bothered him. It was Ellie herself. She had been holding him at arm's length ever since her ex-husband had roared back into town. And that probably meant one thing. She was going to take the bastard back. Why else would she make excuses for him, allow him to move into her house? Anyone—except a lovesick fool—would put two and two together and come up with four, bow out and get the hell on with his life.

Except that was the last thing he felt like doing. What he wanted to do was beat the tar out of Lonny Lawrence and send him packing back to his oil rig in the Gulf of Mexico. Ben wasn't going to do that, of course. He wasn't going to do anything that would hurt Ellie or her kids if he could help it.

Being noble was hell.

"The tree's about ready to fall," Ellie said just before the silence between them became really noticeable. She'd obviously been waiting for him to say something, but he couldn't for the life of him think of anything neutral and high-minded to say. She leaned forward, her elbows on her knees, as though reading his thoughts and shielding herself and her precious burden from his gaze. "I'm glad Matt was willing to help Tim cut it down. Tim's still so little, and it could be dangerous. Even such a little tree. He needs a man—" She stopped, chewed on her bottom lip, didn't say anything more.

He didn't want to talk about her ex-husband. "C'mon," he said. "We have to be there to yell, 'Timber.'"

She hesitated a moment, then gave him her hands with a little smile that did crazy things to his breathing and his blood pressure. "I'd like to say I can do this myself, but the truth is, I don't think I can."

He pulled her upright. He hadn't been this close to her for a week, hadn't been able to smell the lemon and wildflower sweetness of her hair, hear her throaty laughter, brush his lips over the honey sweetness of hers.

At the last moment, he rocked back half a step so that her belly didn't bump against him, so that he wouldn't be tempted to take her completely into his arms. "Glad to be of service, ma'am," he said, trying to keep his tone light and unconcerned.

She looked at him for a long moment. He felt her green-gold gaze sear through him like heat lightning through a night sky. He wondered just how deeply into the murky shadows of his soul she could see with that clear, steady regard. What kind of fool was he to let her get as close as he had? There was no future for him with her. She wasn't a married woman. But she wasn't heart-whole and fancy-free, either, that much was clear.

She tugged her hands free of his grip. "Ben, I...we need—"

"Riley, wait. Don't run so fast." The wild-eyed setter erupted into the clearing, Carly at his heels.

"Carly, come here, sweetie. The tree's ready to fall." Relief was evident in Ellie's voice and smile. She half turned from Ben, focused on her young Paul Bunyan.

"Here we go! Mom! Ben! Are you watching this?" Tim, on his hands and knees, gave the trunk of the small tree one more whack with the hatchet. Matt was standing behind him, watchful. When the little fir began to shudder and rock, he grabbed Tim by his coat collar and hauled him backward, out of harm's way.

"Timber!" Tim shouted at the top of his lungs. Obligingly, the little tree toppled to the ground exactly as planned, the snow around it cushioning the impact.

"Yay!" Carly sang out, jumping up and down, clapping her hands in glee. "Let's get it home and start decorating."

"We have to get it on the sled first, munchkin," Matt cautioned. "You lift the top. Tim and I will get the trunk."

"Wasn't it awesome, Mom? Didn't I—" Tim glanced up at Matt with a grin. "Didn't we do good?"

"You did great." Ellie smiled, applauding the feat as unreservedly as Carly. "You are both incredible woodsmen."

Matt made a deep theatrical bow. "Thank you, ma'am."

"I wish I'd brought the camera," Ellie said to Ben while nodding graciously in return.

"I imagine your husband will be sorry he missed this."

Her mouth tightened, and she colored slightly. She looked down at her hands as though she didn't know quite what to do with them. Then, as she so often did, she folded them over her distended abdomen. Her chin came up fractionally. She looked directly at him. Her changeable eyes had darkened, now more brown than green, and unreadable. "He's always sorry when he disappoints the kids. Actually, I wanted the pictures for my parents in Florida. They miss seeing their grandchildren."

"My mistake." He knelt to refasten the straps on his snowshoes. He pulled off his gloves. The damn clumsy things were more trouble than they were worth. He stood up. Ellie hadn't moved an inch.

"Ben...I...I want to explain about my ex-husband," she said, rushing her words.

"Ellie, you don't owe me—"

Her eyes lifted then. She studied him for a long, charged moment. "No," she said quietly. A little sadly? Or was he only imagining it? "I guess there isn't any reason for me to explain about Lonny."

She was right. They'd shared little things. A raging house fire, a desperate, knife-wielding teenager, a couple of earthshaking, continent-shifting kisses. Nothing more than that. No reason she should tell him her secrets, her hopes and dreams for the future.

She stepped away from him, and Ben felt a chill, which had nothing to do with the temperature, strike deep into his bones, tighten the overly sensitive scar tissue on his cheek and temple. "Tim, don't tie the tree down so tightly. You'll break some of the branches and that will spoil the shape." She moved toward the loading operation without looking back. "Carly and I will pull the sled out to the road. That will be our contribution."

"Hey, Matt, will you give me a ride on the snowmobile before we go back to town?" Tim asked.

"Sure." He shifted his gaze to Ellie's face. "That is, if it's all right with your mom."

"Just a short one, Matt. It's getting late. We need to be heading back home."

Back to her home? Ben wondered in frustration. *Or back to the man she still loved?*

CHAPTER TWELVE

"GOOD NIGHT, Tim," Ellie said, sticking her head around the bedroom door. He was just slipping under the covers of his narrow cot, his clothes draped over the back of a straight chair underneath the window, his schoolbooks and bag on the seat.

"G'night, Mom."

"All ready for school tomorrow?" she asked.

"I hate school," he said, wrinkling his nose. "I can't wait until Christmas vacation starts."

"Only three more days," Ellie reminded him. "Then you're free as a bird for two whole weeks."

"Except for that science paper and a book report," he groused. "It's almost 2001. Didn't anyone tell Mrs. LeSatz no one does book reports anymore?"

"We did book reports in Mrs. LeSatz's class when I was your age and you'll do them now," Ellie said, laughing. "She's too scary a lady to cross."

"You're telling me." He snuggled down under the covers then raised up on his elbows. "Did you get the lights on the tree to work again?"

"All fixed. Just a broken bulb, that's all."

"Good," he said. "I knew Dad was wrong when he said the lights were all no good and we should throw them away."

Ellie stifled a sigh.

"Those were new lights. We couldn't afford to trash them and buy new ones."

"You're right. And they're working fine now, so there's no need to worry about it."

"Okay, Mom. G'night."

"Good night, Tim. Pleasant dreams."

"Mom, the tree does look good, doesn't it?"

"It's the most perfect tree we've ever had." She closed the door softly behind her and peeked her head around her own bedroom door to check on her daughter.

Carly was sleeping peacefully in the faint glow of the bedside lamp. Ellie closed the door carefully, so the rusty hinges didn't squeak and wake the little girl. She massaged the dull ache in her lower back that had grown stronger with each passing day. She suspected her doctor would tell her the backache was nothing more than the baby beginning to move into the birth canal. Then he'd tell her to come in for her regular appointment on Wednesday, and not to worry.

But she did worry. She couldn't remember feeling this washed-out, edgy and uncomfortable before Tim or Carly was born. Of course, she'd been much younger then—and she hadn't had the strain of being a single mother with an ex-husband back under her roof.

"Ellie, honey, come here. Sit down beside me and take a load off," Lonny invited expansively, his stocking feet up on the coffee table, a beer can in his hand. "The tree looks great. You and the kids did a good job on it."

"It's a pretty little tree," she agreed, smiling at Carly's white paper snowflakes and the strings of multicolored lights that Tim had wound carefully around each and every branch. For the top, her mother had sent the angel that had graced her own tree for almost twenty years, a little reminder of times past, since all of Ellie's Christmas decorations had been lost in the fire.

"Let's talk," Lonny urged, patting the sofa again. "We haven't had fifteen minutes alone together since I came home."

Ellie sat down, but at the other end of the sofa. She didn't look at the tree again, because along with the paper snowflakes and the lights and the angels, she also thought of Ben and Matt being there when they'd cut it down. And as usual, once she started thinking about Ben MacAllister, it was hard to stop.

"You aren't going to give an inch, are you?" Lonny asked, looking down at his beer can, not at her.

Ellie turned her head in his direction, not pretending to misunderstand his meaning. "No, Lonny," she said quietly but firmly.

He held out his hand, smiling his wonderful crooked smile. "I've missed you so damned much. I'm still missing you, living like a stranger here in our own house."

"It's not your house, Lonny," she said, fighting the sudden sting of tears in her throat.

"Yeah, you're right. It's not my house." He laid his hand along the back of the sofa, his fingertips brushing her hair, tucking it behind her ear, the way he always used to do. Ellie didn't brush off his caress, but didn't return it. "This isn't your house, either," he said. "It isn't a home."

"It's home for me. And for the children."

"Come back to Louisiana with me, Ellie. When the rig is up and pumping again, I'll be making enough money to buy us a real nice house down there. You'll like it. It's always warm. And it never snows."

"I like snow," Ellie whispered.

"We could be a family again," he said, leaning a little closer.

She shook her head. "I...I..."

The crooked smile disappeared. He shifted his gaze to her left ear, reached up, wrapped a stand of hair around his finger. "Ellie, what are we going to do about this new baby?"

She jerked away, dislodging her hair from his grasp. The question surprised her. It wasn't the obvious prelude to a seduction. "What do you mean?"

"I mean, what are we going to do about the baby?"

The baby? Her stomach muscles tightened with anxiety. "I don't understand."

"It's this way, El, honey. I'm doing pretty good now working on the rigs. But it's a boom-or-bust kind of job. You know I'll do my share moneywise to help raise Carly and Tim, but..."

Ellie sat up a little straighter. The baby was moving now, small agitated thumps against her tummy. "This is your baby, too," she reminded him. Conceived in an act of sorrow and loss, true, but their child, nonetheless, just as Carly and Tim were.

"A baby we can't afford," Lonny replied. He took a last long swallow of beer, then began twirling the empty can between his hands, still not looking her in the eye.

Ellie opened her mouth but no words came out. An unbidden, unwanted thought crossed her mind. *Ben MacAllister would never, ever tell the mother of his child that they could not afford the baby she was carrying. She knew that as well as she knew her own name.* Before she could speak, she had to clear her throat of the huge dry lump that had lodged there. "What are you getting at, Lawrence Edward Lawrence?"

"We're real lucky to have two such great kids, El. There...there are a lot of people out there who don't have no kids at all. Who would give anything in the world to have a baby to call their own."

She splayed her hand across her stomach, moving instinctively, automatically to shield her baby from what she feared was coming. "My God, Lonny, are you telling me you think we should give our child up for adoption?"

"Not adoption, El. Not turning him over to the state for strangers to raise, nothing like that. A private arrangement is what I was getting at. All legal and aboveboard, of course. My boss and his wife..."

Ellie sucked her bottom lip between her teeth, biting down hard to keep from screaming. "You've discussed selling our...*my*...baby with your boss?"

"Not selling, El," he said. "I mean, they'd pay all your expenses, of course, maybe put some money away in the bank for Carly and Tim...something like that—"

"No." She struggled to her feet.

"They're rich people, El. They could give the little tyke everything we can't." Lonny stood. "He'd live the life of Riley, and Carly and Tim would have a nest egg for college or whatever they want to do when they grow up."

Ellie covered her ears with her hands. "No! Never! Not if I have to peel potatoes and wash dishes and scrub floors at the Jack Pine until the day I die." Her voice came out in a hiss.

Lonny took a step backward, holding out his hands as though to ward off a blow. "It was just a suggestion, El."

"Don't ever mention such a thing again, do you hear?"

He shook his head. "Take a little time to think it over. I want to do right by our kids. I just don't think I can handle making any more support payments. I didn't like the idea. I just told my boss I'd talk to you about it, that's all." He sat down with a thump, put his head between his hands. His voice came out muffled and broken. "I didn't mean any harm, Ellie."

"Yes," she said wearily, "I know you didn't mean any harm. You never do."

Lonny lifted his head, his eyes suspiciously moist, smiling a sad, apologetic version of that thousand-watt smile that had always won her over in the past. "Ellie, I'm sorry, hon. We'll forget I even mentioned it, okay? We'll keep the baby. We'll never talk about this again."

She didn't even acknowledge the smile, had a little harder time ignoring the sheen of tears in his eyes. Lonny wasn't a bad man, she told herself for the ten-thousandth time, just a weak one. "We won't talk of it again," she agreed. But it couldn't end there, not this time. This time he had gone too far. "But I think you should leave North Star as soon as possible."

"I don't have to report back to work until after the middle of January. I thought I'd hang around till the baby was born." He obviously realized his mistake as soon as the words left his mouth. "I didn't mean that the way it sounded. I mean, I want to be here for you and Carly and Tim, El."

Ellie held up her hand to stop the flow of words. She was too tired and drained to argue any longer. The surge of adrenaline through her veins left her feeling dizzy and weak in the knees. It couldn't be good for the baby, her feeling like this. "I know what you meant. But I still think you should leave before then, Lonny."

"Leave before the baby's born?"

She nodded. "Yes," she said. "If you want to spend Christmas with Tim and Carly, that's fine. But I'd like you to find somewhere else to stay. And I'd like you out of North Star before the baby is born."

A COUPLE OF HOURS LATER, it still hurt. How could Lonny suggest *selling* their child? She was only glad his mother was not alive to learn about it.

Ellie sniffed back a tear. She wasn't going to cry. She couldn't. Tears would ruin her cinnamon rolls. She sprinkled more flour on her hands from the old-fashioned metal shaker and returned to kneading the fragrant dough, losing herself in the rhythmic, calming task.

A light tap on the window glass of the outside door startled her. She glanced at the big round clock on the wall. Just a few minutes before midnight. Who would have business in the Jack Pine kitchen this late at night?

"Who's there?" she called, hoping it wasn't Lonny coming over to renew their argument about the baby's future.

The door opened. Ben stuck his head inside. "You ought to keep this door locked," he said, shaking snow off the hood of his parka, pushing it back, onto his shoulders.

"I thought it was locked," Ellie said. "I guess I forgot."

"What are you doing here this late at night?" he asked, pulling off his gloves and sticking them in his pocket.

"I might ask the same of you."

"I couldn't sleep," he said, "so I thought I'd take a drive."

The baby, quiet since she'd left the cottage, moved, stretching elbows and knees. She gave the dough one last punch then reached for the rolling pin and dusted it with flour. "Does Matt know where you are?"

"Matt's been shut up in his room since this afternoon." Ben's face darkened. "We had a hell of an argument."

"Want to tell me about it?" Ellie finished rolling the dough into a rectangle, before turning to the big black restaurant stove to retrieve the glass dish of melted butter warming there.

He leaned one slim hip against the counter. "Yeah," he said finally. "I would like to talk about it."

"What happened?"

"Riley dragged Matt's old coat in off the back porch and chewed a hole in the lining. A marijuana joint fell out."

"Oh no." Ellie closed her eyes against a dart of pain and disappointment. "He's been doing so well."

"I know. He swears the joint had been there since before he left Columbus. Swears he only carried it so the other kids wouldn't give him a hard time."

"I guess that's possible," Ellie said, clutching at the slim hope. She didn't want to see Matt complicate his life even more with drugs.

"Yeah. I think so, too. The joint was as old as the hills. In bad shape. But it threw me, Ellie. I . . . I guess I was harder on him than I should have been. He slammed off to his room and he hasn't come out since."

"You told him you believed him, didn't you? You didn't drive off and let him think you're still mad at him?"

"I told him. If you call hollering through an inch-thick wooden door talking." He raked his hand through his short brown hair. "God, I don't know how people do it. Raise teenagers, I mean."

"Trial and error. But in most cases you grow up along with your child, learn the give-and-take of parenting over the years, what works and what doesn't. And then you try like hell to keep ahead of the curve during their teenage years. Ben, you haven't had the benefit of that experience."

"Well, I'm sure doing great on the error part." He was silent a moment, unsnapping his parka, pushing his hands into the pockets of his jeans. "I'm taking him back to Columbus the day after Christmas," he said unexpectedly. She stopped brushing butter on the pastry dough and looked at him. There were dark circles under his eyes, and the lines of old pain and suffering etched from nose to chin had deepened, as prominent now, she realized, as they'd been when she first saw him the night of the fire.

"Why? You aren't giving up on him because of the marijuana?" She'd been so absorbed in her own problems since Lonny returned she'd paid only scant attention to the teenager. Had there been more incidents than the one with the marijuana? "You aren't returning him to the authorities, are you?"

Ben looked puzzled. "Of course not. His surgeon wants a final check of his leg. And his counselor wants to have a face-to-face interview." He leaned back against the counter where the thick, white, restaurant-style china was stored on shelves behind his head. "Legally, the Ohio authorities are still in charge. I can't put them off forever. I didn't mention finding the joint when I spoke to them. That's between Matt and me. We'll settle it ourselves. I thought this would be a good time to go. Before school starts again."

"Oh. I see." She began sprinkling sugar and cinnamon, nutmeg, cloves and allspice on top of the melted butter. "Yes. That makes sense. I'm glad you'll be here for Christmas. Will you be spending the holiday with Eldor and Martha?''

"Yes," he said. "Martha invited us this evening. Ham and sweet potatoes and all the fixings. Including Martha's famous sugar cookies for dessert."

Ellie managed a laugh. She would be spending the day with Lonny and the children. A few days ago she had been looking forward to the holiday, if not with great excitement, at least with thoughts of a pleasant day together. But two hours ago that had all changed. Now she would have to eat Christmas dinner across the table from the man who had matter-of-factly suggested they *sell* their child.

"Ellie?"

She looked up, unseeing, focusing on Ben's face with difficulty as she tried to hold back the tears that threatened to spill over onto her cheeks. "Yes?"

"I think you have enough cinnamon on your rolls."

She looked down. The dough was covered with a thick, dark layer of the aromatic spice. "Oh, dear," she said. She grabbed a dry pastry brush and whisked the excess cinnamon into a bowl. "I'll sprinkle it on top," she said, knowing she was babbling, but unable to stop the flow of words.

"Ellie, what's wrong? Why are you over here at this hour of the night baking cinnamon rolls? You should be in bed. Or at least relaxing on the couch with your feet up."

"I'm not sleepy," she said too loudly, too vehemently. She could manage her end of the conversation if they were talking about the weather, or about Matt Westrick, but not about herself. She began rolling the dough into a tight log. "I thought cinnamon rolls would be good for breakfast tomorrow. It's supposed to snow. Warm cinnamon rolls always taste so good on a snowy morning." She began cutting off inch-thick slices of dough, setting them on their sides in the buttered pan, her thoughts spinning in tight spirals like the swirls of spice and sugar inside the pastry.

Ben reached over the table and circled her wrists with his hands. "Hey, be careful. You're going to cut yourself."

Instinctively, she tried to free herself from his grasp. He tightened his grip. "Ellie. What's wrong?" he repeated.

"Nothing. Please. Let go of me. I have to get these covered and onto the warming shelf or they won't be raised enough to bake first thing in the morning."

He didn't do as she asked, not right away. She didn't dare look at him. She knew her misery was plain to read on her face. She couldn't tell him about what had just happened with Lonny. She didn't want Ben MacAllister to know what a lousy judge of men she was. She didn't want him to know that the father of her children was... *the kind of man who would suggest selling his own flesh and blood.*

"If I let go, will you stop brandishing that butcher knife like a club?"

She nodded, managing to raise her eyes as high as the second button on his shirt. It was blue chambray, much-washed and faded to the soft hue of a spring sky after a rain. *God, how she longed to rest her head there, be comforted by the warmth of his embrace, soothed by the slow, steady beat of his heart.* She swallowed a sigh. "Please. Let me finish my work."

"C'mon. You just listened to my problem with Matt. Now it's your turn to tell me what's wrong."

"Nothing's wrong, Ben. It's just... hormones, the baby. Christmas." She tried for a bright little laugh and failed miserably. She tugged at the manacles of his fingers, and he relaxed his grip, setting her free.

The image of herself in his arms had changed, darkened, grown more heated, more elemental. *She always started trembling when Ben touched her.* Ellie laid the knife on the counter. Her hands were shaking too hard to continue. She squeezed her eyes tight shut to blot out the sight of his hands, his strong brown wrists.

She curled her own hands into fists to keep from reaching out and running her fingers over the scars that he no longer tried to hide from her. She didn't dare touch him. If she did, the desire and need for him she kept bottled up inside would break free and she would no longer be able to pretend there was nothing more than friendship between them.

She forced herself to concentrate on the cinnamon rolls, got the last ones in the pan, covered them with plastic wrap and set them on the stove. "There. All finished. Time to lock up and go home." Her voice almost broke on the last word, but she covered it with a little cough.

"I'm not going anywhere until you tell me why you're so upset. Let me help, Ellie—"

No. That would be the last straw. She'd never have the strength to stand on her own again if she gave in to the clamoring need she felt to unburden herself to him. She whirled on him, as quickly as her ungainly figure would allow. She couldn't and wouldn't confide in him. She couldn't trust herself around him. He was too close to being everything she wanted in life. And he was too much of a man to turn away from a woman in distress. He would take her in his arms and hold her and comfort her. He would do all the right things, say all the right things. For all the wrong reasons. Pity and compassion were poor substitutes for desire—*and love.*

"There's nothing wrong with me, Ben MacAllister. I'm tired and cranky. My feet are swollen and my back hurts like hell, that's all." She looked at him defiantly, refusing to recognize the hurt and bewilderment in his cloud gray gaze. "And I want to go home to my family."

"Home," he said, looking down at his hands, still planted on the stainless-steel worktable. "Of course. I'm sorry to keep you."

"Ben—" The baby's movements were more agitated now, little thumps and bumps. She tried to ignore them but couldn't. She felt equally jittery and off balance.

"I'll walk you home." The words were polite, the tone even and cordial, but the look in his eyes, the sudden impenetrable darkness there, made Ellie shiver as if she'd been shoved naked into the icy waters of the lake.

Home was a distance of perhaps fifty yards, a tiny fraction of the emotional distance that now separated them. She knew she'd upset him, but she didn't have the strength, the ability to shield herself from greater pain if she told him about Lonny's betrayal, so she took the coward's way out. "That's not necessary. I have to clean up here first. Eldor will be closing the bar soon. He'll make sure I get home safely."

"All right." Ben pulled on his gloves and headed for the door. He didn't look back, and Ellie couldn't look away, although the tears she'd refused to let fall stung her eyes and clogged her throat. At the door, he stopped before turning the handle. "If I don't see you again... Merry Christmas, Ellie Lawrence."

Then he was gone, and she was alone with her misery.

THE OLD LIGHT KEEPER'S house was a spooky place when you were there alone at midnight. It moaned and whistled in the wind, and every step you took made something creak or groan. Not that he was superstitious or believed in ghosts or anything like that. Matt shivered. Well, maybe he did believe in ghosts. Eric's ghost, at least. Although, fool that he was, he'd almost started hoping, believing that Eric's ghost had gone away, since things were going pretty good for him and Ben.

At least, he'd thought things were going pretty good until this afternoon. Ben had practically blown up in his face when Riley chewed through his old coat and that damned joint he'd forgotten all about rolled onto the floor. Matt had never seen Ben lose his temper that way.

Matt thought for a minute Ben was going to call the county sheriff and have him hauled away then and there. Matt had never talked so fast in his life, trying to explain. But Ben had just stood there, not saying a word while Matt babbled on. He still didn't know if Ben believed him, *really* believed he'd carried the joint around for almost a year, just so the other dudes would leave him alone. Sure he'd tried pot before, once or twice. But he didn't like it. It made him feel stupid and slow, not high and cool. But you didn't tell the other guys that. They'd think you were weird. They'd beat the hell out of you. So he carried the joint around inside the lining of his coat, but he always made excuses not to light it up.

Ben's face had been dark as a thundercloud. He'd looked like some kind of devil—like Freddy Kruger on a bad day—and finally Matt had let his fear get the best of him and stomped off to his room, locking the door behind him.

A little while later, Ben had knocked on the door. He'd apologized for flying off the handle. But Matt had been bawling, just like a little kid, because he'd blown it. Ben was a cop and cops didn't keep kids who did drugs in their house, not for very long, at least. Matt didn't want Ben seeing him that way, hearing in his voice the tears that clogged his throat, so he'd ignored the apology and eventually Ben had gone away.

Later, Matt had decided to come out of his room. Hiding wasn't making it look as if he was telling the truth. And he *was* telling the truth. But it was too late. Ben was on the phone when Matt padded down the hall in his stocking feet. He was talking to the caseworker back in Columbus. He was making plans to take Matt back there. The day after Christmas.

Ben had turned around and seen him then. He was a cool dude, Matt had to give him that. He hadn't slammed down the phone, hadn't lied about who he was talking to. He'd told Matt straight out that they were going back to Columbus. That they were going to see his doctor and his caseworker. It was all routine, he said. He wouldn't mention the marijuana, Matt didn't have to worry about that. They'd only be gone a couple of days.

But Matt wasn't fooled. He knew there wasn't going to be any "after we get back." Ben intended to leave him in Ohio. He was going to take him back there and turn him over to the juvenile people, no matter what excuses Ben made about doctor's appointments and his caseworker signing off for good. He knew it in his bones—felt it in the stone-cold lump in the middle of his stomach. He'd screwed up again.

God, his life was a mess, he thought now as he blew on the glass of his bedroom window, rubbing a circle with the cuff of his shirtsleeve. The shirt was an old flannel one of Ben's and he was wearing it over a T-shirt and the long-sleeved, waffle-weave thermal underwear Ben had bought him. And he was still cold.

He blew on the window again, and rubbed the circle a little bigger. It was darker than the underside of hell tonight, the wind sighing through the pine trees, and around the corner of the lighthouse. Maybe if Riley wasn't sleeping like a tree stump beside the woodstove in the kitchen, he really would start to think this drafty old place was haunted. But dogs were supposed to sense things like that. And Riley was snoring away like a chain saw. Maybe it was just Matt's thoughts that were haunted.

There wasn't any moon, and the stars were too high and far away to give any light. Only the pale glimmer of snow on the ground and in the branches of the fir trees made it possible to see anything at all. Except there was nothing to see. Ben was gone, out driving around someplace, probably cursing the day he'd let Matt into his house. And Matt was alone with his thoughts.

He turned away from the window and dropped into the hard-bottomed chair by the bed.

God, what a sucker he was to think he had a future here. Such a sucker that when he'd ridden into the Soo with Kevin and some other guys the night before last, he'd bought some lights and glass balls to decorate a tree for him and Ben. He'd been planning to bring them out from under his bed tonight and see if Ben wanted to help him decorate. But that had been before Riley had found the joint in his coat.

"What a jerk," he said, jumping out of the chair to slam his fist into the wall. "What a dumb-ass jerk." He'd actually suckered himself into believing there was a future at Chippewa Point. A place for him with Ben. Maybe even a family someday. He saw the way Ben and Ellie Lawrence looked at each other, touched when they thought no one was looking. They were falling in love with each other. Even a sorry loser like Matt could tell that.

God must be laughing Himself silly. There wasn't going to be a family or a future here. Ben was a cop. A man of honor and principle like all the heroes he used to read about when he was a kid and still liked going to school. He wasn't going to make room in his life for a loser like Matt. But he wouldn't just kick him out in the snow, either. He wasn't like that. He'd do it by the book. Make sure all the t's were crossed and the i's dotted. In the end, Matt would be back where he'd started from. Alone. At the mercy of the juvenile authorities of the state of Ohio.

Not if he had anything to say about it, he'd decided. He'd have to stick it out, though, play the game, until the day after Christmas. He'd have a little money then and North Star was still pretty near the back of beyond if you didn't have a set of wheels. But as soon as he and Ben hit the city limits of Columbus, he was history. Gone. And once he headed out on his own, he was going so far and so fast no one would ever catch up with him again.

CHAPTER THIRTEEN

A KNOT OF PEOPLE milled around the double glass doors leading out of the Baptist church fellowship hall. No one seemed in a hurry to leave the building. The organist was still playing, people were humming "Joy To The World," discussing plans for Christmas dinner, talking about the weather.

"Hey, what's holding things up?" Eldor Mac-Allister demanded from directly behind Ellie. "I've got to get back to the Jack Pine. I haven't got all night to stand around here chewing the fat."

"Eldor, hush. You're in the Lord's house," Martha reminded him.

"It's not the Lord's house. Not exactly. It's the fellowship hall and I've got to get back to my business. Some of us have better things to do than complain about the weather," Ellie heard him mutter under his breath as the scarf-gathering, glove-hunting pageant goers postponed moving out into the arctic cold of the December evening. Eldor sidestepped Ellie with an agility at odds with his rotund size and shape, and began elbowing his way to the door. "Merry Christmas! Great play! Coming through! 'Scuse me."

"It was a good play," Martha said, sending a minatory glance toward the back of her rapidly disappearing spouse. "The kids were great. Carly, you made an adorable shepherd. And Spock acted as if she were born to the part."

"Maybe we should get Spock an agent." Ellie laughed, shifting her weight to offset Carly, still in her costume a chenille bathrobe and white cotton headdress—who was pulling Ellie in the opposite direction. She frowned, and caught her breath as a quick, sharp pain almost caused her to stumble. She'd been having contractions all day, irregular and uncomfortable. False labor, she supposed. After all, she was due in less than two weeks. But the baby hadn't dropped, as least as far as she could tell, so she wasn't going to worry about it. Except that the last couple of contractions had been hard enough to get her attention—and keep it.

"Spock tried to herd everybody," Carly told the older woman. "Even the pig." Danelda had included live animals in the production this year, a bold innovation that had had the town buzzing with speculation, and the minister on pins and needles over the fate of the altar carpet.

"Where are Spock and Tim?" Martha asked, craning her neck to see past the slowly dissipating crowd around the door.

"Tim took Spock outside. She doesn't like crowds."

"I see Lonny's missing, too." Martha MacAllister was never one to mince words.

"He was the first one out the door," Ellie admitted. At least he had shown up for the nativity pageant. It was more than he'd managed in the past. She'd been a little surprised to see him. They'd barely exchanged a dozen words since he'd moved into the Safe Harbor Motel the night he'd suggested they give the baby up for adoption. She'd made herself believe that was what he meant. *Give the baby up for adoption.* She had to be civil to him for the kids' sake and if she allowed her mind to form the words *sell their baby* she wouldn't be able to do even that.

"Spock tried to bite the pig," Carly offered, swinging from the end of Ellie's arm.

"She did not," Ellie said.

"Did too. Remember, she bit me on the bu—"

"Carly, not again."

"She bit the pig," Carly insisted.

"She growled at the pig," Ellie corrected, wishing Carly would stop jumping around. It made the dull ache in her back that much worse.

"Pigs don't like to be herded," Carly observed, having the last word.

"Finally," Martha said approvingly as someone propped open the big doors and the crowd surged into the frigid December night. "Goodness, it's freezing out here. The temperature must have dropped ten degrees while we were inside."

Ellie looked around the parking lot for Tim. She spotted him and Spock beneath a security light. He was still wearing his crown and Wiseman's robe beneath his coat. She bid Martha good-night and Merry Christmas and walked toward her son.

"I didn't see Ben or Matt at the play," Carly said, swiveling her head from side to side, scanning the rapidly diminishing crowd on the church steps and in the parking lot.

"I don't think they were here." She hadn't expected to see Ben again after the way she'd acted in the Jack Pine kitchen. And she'd been relieved that he'd stayed away. She wasn't ready to face him. It was too hard to treat him as a friend. And it hurt too much to treat him as a lover. A lover she could never have.

"It's snowing," Tim announced as she reached him.

"I don't like this kind of snow," Carly muttered. "It's sharp."

"How can snow be sharp?" Tim asked, sounding disgusted.

"It's like hard little balls. Not snowflakes. That's how it can be sharp." Carly pulled her white headdress forward to shield her face.

"Let's go home," Ellie urged. "It's getting late. I'm tired."

Tim looked down at his new watch, a gift from her parents that had arrived the day before and had to be opened immediately. "It's not late. It's not even eight o'clock."

"Let's go to Ben's lighthouse," Carly piped up. "I want to give Ben and Matt their presents."

"No, Carly. Not tonight."

"Yes, tonight," Carly insisted. "Tomorrow's Christmas Eve. It will be too late if we don't take their presents out tonight."

"You can give them their gifts when they come to Eldor and Martha's for Christmas dinner," Ellie suggested without much hope.

"No!" Carly's big dark eyes filled with quick tears. "I made snowflakes for their Christmas tree, too, remember? Christmas Day is too late to give someone decorations for their tree. I want to do it tonight.''

"It won't take very long, Mom," Tim said, twisting Spock's leash between his hands. "I...I *would* like to see what Matt thinks of his bear cub."

Ellie felt herself begin to waver. Tim asked for very little these days. She knew he picked up on the tension between her and his father more acutely than Carly did. Carly had accepted her explanation that Lonny had moved to the Safe Harbor because the rickety cot in Tim's room was too uncomfortable. Tim hadn't challenged the story but his skepticism was obvious. She knew he worried about their financial situation, and how things would be different when the baby came. But until that moment she hadn't realized, hadn't allowed herself to realize, how much Ben and Matt's approval meant to him.

And she decided she owed Ben an apology for her behavior the last time they were together. "All right," she said. "We'll stop by the cottage and pick up the gifts." *Including the oak Santa. That would say she was sorry more clearly than words.* "But we can't stay more than a few minutes. And if they aren't home, we'll just have to leave the presents on the doorstep."

But there were lights in the windows of the light keeper's house when they drove up, and both Ben's pickup and the snowmobile were parked in the side yard.

"They're here," Carly said. "Good."

"We can't stay more than a few minutes," Ellie reminded the excited little girl. "It's still snowing and it doesn't look as if it intends to let up anytime soon."

Sometime in the twenty minutes since they'd left the cottage, the hard pellets of snow had turned to ice. Ellie looked around with a frown as they hurried up the sidewalk. Although the roads had been clear, there was already a thin glazing of ice on the roof of her car and the windshield of Ben's truck.

She hadn't listened to the weather report on the six o'clock news because she'd been busy making last-minute alterations in Carly's costume, and helping Tim track down Spock's leash. Was this half snow, half sleet combination an ice storm coming up from the south, or only a slight shift in the wind that would blow itself out before morning?

She probably shouldn't have let the kids talk her into coming out here tonight. Her brain allowed her that delusion, but in her heart of hearts she knew she wanted to see Ben even more badly than the children did.

After what seemed like an eternity, Ben opened the door to her knock. He stood there for a moment, not saying anything, his face in shadow, his expression unreadable. He looked past her, over her head, then confirmed her worst fears. "What are you three doing out on a night like this? Don't you know there's one heck of an ice storm on the way?" His black flannel shirt was unbuttoned over a dazzling white T-shirt. His jeans were soft and faded and clung to his thighs like a second skin. Ellie couldn't take her eyes off him, but she couldn't quite meet his gaze straight on, either.

"Oh, dear," was the only thing she could think of to say. Tim was looking up at her with worried eyes.

She attempted a smile. "We've been at the Sunday school pageant. We...we didn't hear the weather report."

"They put the warning out about an hour ago." He hadn't moved out of the doorway, hadn't invited them inside.

"The roads aren't too bad, yet."

"They will be," he said flatly.

This was worse than she'd imagined. Ellie slid her hand into her coat pocket, curling her fingers around the tissue-wrapped Santa figure. "Kids, maybe we should go back."

"No," Carly wailed. She held out the presents she'd wrapped with such care and anticipation. The bows were crooked. She'd used half a spool of tape, but she offered them to Ben as if they were diamonds wrapped in cloth of gold. "We came to bring you a Christmas present. And Matt, too. Where is he?"

Ben looked down at the little girl. The hardness left his mouth, softened his gaze. "Matt's watching TV in the kitchen, Carly. Come in, it's too cold to stand out here."

"We...we can't stay," Ellie said hesitantly.

Ben lifted his eyes, looked out into the winter storm once more. "Maybe you should wait till the plows have put down sand. Then, if you're careful, you should have an easier time getting back to town." He opened the door wider. "Come in."

Ellie looked over her shoulder. He was right. It would be safer driving after the snowplows had made their run. She looked at Ben. "Thank you," she said. She might as well have been talking to the stone walls of the light tower. Without saying another word, he stepped back into the deeper shadows of the doorway so she could walk past him.

The kitchen was warm and light. There were dirty dishes in the sink and a bowl of popcorn on the table. Matt was sitting on the old leather couch watching TV with Riley sleeping beside him. The dog woke up, barked a greeting and started wagging his tail, banging it against the back of the couch like a whip.

"Riley, settle down," Matt commanded. He stood up when he saw them, but didn't say anything. Ellie glanced at the screen. It was a rerun of the old Jimmy Stewart classic *It's a Wonderful Life*. She had the impression Matt wasn't paying much attention to what was going on in Bedford Falls.

"Let me take your coats," Ben offered. They shrugged out of coats, hats and gloves. Tim had changed, but Carly had insisted on remaining in her shepherd's costume. Her headdress was askew so Ellie straightened it for her.

"I was a shepherd in the play," she told Ben, twirling in a circle. "Why didn't you come to see me?"

"I...we forgot," Ben said, dumping their coats over the back of a kitchen chair. "I'm sorry."

"That's okay. You can watch the video."

"I'd like that."

Once more the darkness had left his face. He smiled at Carly and Ellie's heart turned over. *He would be a wonderful father.*

Agitated by the thought, Ellie smoothed her hand over her plum-colored sweater, then caught Matt looking at her stomach. She felt as big as a house. She was growing impatient for this baby to be born. He had been quiet the last day or two, unusually so. Probably saving his strength for the ordeal of being thrust into this big cold world. Or maybe just napping so that he could keep her awake with his antics all night.

"It's only two days till Christmas," Carly said to Matt, grinning shyly. "Here's your present." She held out the package. "Merry Christmas."

Matt didn't make any move to take his gift. Carly and Tim exchanged quick looks. Carly shifted a little closer to Ellie's leg, clearly bewildered by the teenager's apparent uninterest. Ellie hurried into speech to cover the awkward moment. "We've interrupted your movie. I'm sorry. It's one of my favorites, too."

Matt darted a glance at the screen. "Nah, I wasn't watching that old thing."

"I hate black-and-white movies," Tim said, "but that one isn't too bad. Did you notice the cop and the taxi driver are named Bert and Ernie? Like in 'Sesame Street'?"

"Hey, yeah, they are."

Tim looked pleased to have been the one to point that out to the older boy. "My mom figured it out first," he added conscientiously.

"I think Jim Henson was way ahead of all of us," Ellie said with a smile.

"Here, Matt," Carly tried again. "Merry Christmas." She thrust the package into Matt's hands.

He sat down with a thump. He turned the little package over and over in his hands. "Thanks, Carly. I...I didn't get you anything."

For a moment, she looked disappointed, then quickly recovered. "That's okay. Christmas is for giving presents, not getting them. Right, Mom?"

"Yes, Carly," Ellie agreed, swallowing a tiny lump that had lodged in her throat. "Christmas is for giving."

"I have one for you, too, Ben."

"Thanks, Carly." He held out his hand, his left hand, the scarred hand that he had kept hidden from them for so long, and she placed the small gift on his palm.

The lump in Ellie's throat got bigger.

Tim was standing stiff as a poker at her side, waiting for the packages to be unwrapped, waiting for Ben's and Matt's reaction to his handiwork.

"Hey, it's a beaver. Thanks." Matt held the small figure on his palm. Riley was eating the ribbon.

Ben held his gift up for Matt's inspection. His hands were shaking slightly. "A bear cub."

"Wow. Rad."

"Thank you, Carly. It's a great present."

"I carved them," Tim said, unable to hold back any longer. "I carved them all by myself."

"You carved them?" Ben sounded suitably impressed. "You did a great job."

"Mom taught me how."

"Then you had a great teacher, too," Ben said. Ellie smiled her thanks, but he still wasn't looking at her.

"Extremely rad. Thanks, bro," Matt seconded.

"Where are you going to put them?" Carly demanded, dancing up and down, her headdress falling over one eye. She straightened the white scarf and braided band that held it precariously in place. She scanned the room. "Hey. You don't have a Christmas tree. I brought you decorations." She pushed aside the skirt of the old bathrobe, dug her hand in her pants pocket and pulled out a handful of creased, folded, paper snowflakes. "See. Snowflakes for your tree."

"Yeah. Where's your tree?" Both children looked first at Matt, then shifted their shocked gazes to Ben.

"We...we haven't—"

"You haven't got a Christmas tree?" Carly's tone was incredulous.

"I've got a little one in my bedroom," Matt told her. Ben looked away from Carly's scandalized, disapproving expression, a frown carving a deep line between his eyebrows.

"Want to see it?" Matt's stare was defiant. Ellie found the tension between the man and boy impossible to ignore. Obviously the incident with the marijuana wasn't fully resolved. "C'mon," Matt added.

Tim and Carly, oblivious to the emotional undercurrents swirling around them, followed Matt down the uncarpeted hallway. Riley jumped down off the couch and trailed after the trio, red ribbon dangling from his mouth.

"You don't have a tree," Ellie observed. "Why?" Except for the bright splash of color made by the ribbons and the red-and-green, Frosty-the-Snowman paper Carly had wrapped the carvings in, there was no evidence of Christmas in the room at all.

"Matt didn't seem interested in putting one up, and I didn't get around to it." Ben leaned forward and placed the bear cub in the center of the Formica tabletop. "Not much of Christmas, is it?"

"No." Ellie had decided not to be evasive around him anymore, to speak her mind, but she couldn't find the right words to comfort a man who felt he didn't deserve to celebrate the holiday. "Are you and Matt still at odds over the drugs you found?"

"It hasn't been exactly sunshine and roses around here," Ben admitted. "I can't figure out what's wrong. I've told him more than once that it's over and done, but..." He shrugged.

He shoved his hands into the pockets of his jeans and leaned his hip against the edge of the table. "He hasn't said half a dozen sentences to me in the last week."

"I'm sorry."

"He just tunes me out. Spends all his time in his room, or in front of the TV."

"Maybe his counselor will have some suggestions."

"I hope so. I'm beginning to think I might have made a mistake keeping him with me."

The words shocked Ellie. "Ben, you can't give up on him now."

"Maybe he would be better off back in the group home, with kids his own age, people who are trained to get inside his head, get him to talk about what's really eating at him." Ben looked past her, down the hallway where Carly's tinkling laugh could be heard.

Ellie reached out and touched his arm. "Don't ever think that, Ben. You saved his life. And now you've given him a second chance."

"Maybe," he said, bringing his dark gaze back to hers. "And maybe I'm just fooling myself."

She didn't have an answer for that one. She had no resources left. She had to concentrate all her energy on her children, both Carly and Tim and the unborn baby. She couldn't take on Ben MacAllister's problems, too.

Instead, she reached into her coat pocket and pulled out her own Christmas offering. She handed him the tissue-wrapped parcel. "Merry Christmas, Ben. And along with my best wishes, I hope you'll accept my apologies—again."

He closed his long, strong fingers around the Santa figure. The paper fell away. The gentle features of the Santa came into view. "Ellie, you didn't have to do this."

"I wanted to." She knew the children would be gone only a few more seconds, and she wanted to apologize to Ben for the other night. "It's hard getting the hang of this single-mother thing."

"Single-mother thing."

"Yes," she said firmly. "Single mother. I'm sorry you keep getting hit with the fallout."

He looked down at the Santa, then into her eyes. "It was Lonny who upset you the other night, wasn't it?"

"Yes. But I can handle him."

"I don't mind the fallout, Ellie. I—"

"Ben—"

He was going to ask her to marry him.

She didn't know how she knew it, she just did. And she couldn't let it happen. She couldn't let him be the knight in shining armor, riding to her rescue. Saying all the right things for all the wrong reasons. Panic made her voice rough and too high. "Ben, don't say anything more, please."

He ignored her. "Ellie, marry me. Let me take care of you and your kids."

"No!" Her throat closed on the denial and no further sound came out. She didn't want to be his penance, his restitution to a dead comrade and a dead boy. An attempt to right the wrongs of the past. But for a moment she was tempted—tempted to gamble on his learning to love her as she had learned to love him. But she was scared. She didn't want to be hurt by a love gone wrong again. Not "poor Ellie." *Never, ever again.*

"Thank you for asking. But I can't. I won't...I won't be any man's wife. Ever again. I...we have to go." He reached out, closed his fingers around her wrist. His eyes were bleak, as cold and as black as lake ice under a December moon. She knew she had hurt him again and she was sorry, but she was hurting, too.

"Don't run away, Ellie. It's all right. We won't speak of it again."

She shook her head, grabbing her coat, the kids' coats, scooping up hats and mittens and gloves. "No, you're right. We won't speak of it again." She looked up but she couldn't see anything, blinded by the tears she didn't dare let fall. "Thank you, Ben. Thank you for...everything. But I don't think we should see each other again."

Afterward, Ellie wasn't sure how she got the children into their hats and coats and out of Ben's house. She must have said all the right things, given the right mittens to the right child, said goodbye and Merry Christmas and looked and sounded as if her heart hadn't shattered into a thousand pieces inside her chest.

It had stopped snowing, or sleeting, or whatever it was that it had been doing, but there was a much thicker layer of ice coating the sidewalk, making every step treacherous. Matt stood in the doorway. Ben followed her halfway to the car. "Let me drive you into town."

"No," she said. "We'll be fine. I'll be extra careful. Now, please, go back inside. You don't have a coat on. You'll catch cold and it's too close to Christmas to be sick." *God, she sounded like somebody's mother. But that's what she was. A mother.* She had to keep reminding herself of that. She had to be a mother first, now, always. Not a lover. Not a wife.

She was careful. Very, very careful. She scraped the ice off the windshield. She got herself and the kids into the car, fastened her seat belt, made sure the kids were buckled into theirs, backed slowly onto the driveway and headed out toward the road. She never looked back, although she knew Ben was still standing there, still watching her.

She swiped her hand across her eyes, set her mind against the turmoil in her heart, and another contraction, stronger than all the rest. She drove slowly. Ben's road was gravel. The traction wasn't too bad, but she'd have to be careful when she turned onto the highway.

"Ben liked my gifts," Carly said. She was sitting in the front seat beside Ellie. "And Matt put my snowflakes on his tree. It was so little. They looked great big. Why did we have to leave so soon?''

"I told Matt I'd teach him how to carve," Tim offered. "He said, 'Yeah, that would be great.' But first he has to go back where he came from.''

"Just for a while," Carly said. "Just for a few days. But he sounded funny when he said it. Didn't he, Tim?''

"Yeah, sort of weird. Like he didn't really mean it, you know, Mom?''

"Why wouldn't he want to come back here? Erika Shurmansky said her brother told her Matt's going to try out for football next year. If his leg's all right." Carly tugged on her seat belt and scooted around on her seat so that she could see her brother's face. The shepherd's headdress caught on the headrest, slipped down over her eyes and she squealed in alarm.

Ellie glanced over to see what the commotion was about and that was when it happened. Three white-tailed deer, a doe and two yearling fawns, burst out of the trees on the far side of the road and froze in the glare of her headlights.

The deer were already bounding away as Ellie touched her foot to the brake pedal. She knew enough not to slam on the brakes, but it made no difference. The back end of the car fishtailed, bounced off a wall of snow pushed up by Ben's plow, then swerved drunkenly across the road, and ended up nose first in a six-foot drift.

That was when she started to cry.

"You shouldn't have let her get away, man." It took Ben a moment to disentangle Matt's angry words from his own churning thoughts. He turned around to look at the boy who was standing legs spread, hands balled into fists in the brightness of the naked bulb above the door. Riley was beside him, his tail still for once, his head tipped attentively to one side, as though, he, too, was waiting for Ben to defend himself.

"You could have had something great going with her." The kid's voice cracked in the middle of the sentence. A dark stain of embarrassment spread up his throat, but he didn't back off.

"Drop it, Matt." Ben shoved his hands into his pockets. The cold from the snow and wind off the lake cut through his skin to meet the deathly cold at the center of his soul.

"You're a fool not to want a woman like that, even if she has got another man's baby inside her."

Ben wasn't in the mood for an inquisition, but he couldn't seem to stop himself from responding, "I do want her," he growled.

"Then what did you do to make her run off like that?" Matt was still blocking the doorway.

"I asked her to marry me," Ben said through clenched teeth. "You saw what happened. She couldn't get out of here fast enough." The icy wind made the scar tissue on his hands and face burn with a fire of their own. He was in pain inside and out, and all he wanted was to be left alone to nurse his wounds.

"You must have said the wrong thing."

A grunt of laughter escaped him. "Yeah. I said the wrong thing. She doesn't want me. Is that clear enough for you, Matt?" He started forward. He wasn't about to spill his guts to a not-yet-sixteen-year-old who hadn't spoken a civil word to him in the last six days. "Now get out of my way. I'm freezing my ass off out here."

"You must—"

He had started up the steps, now he turned back, listening. He held up his hand to halt Matt's words. It was deathly quiet, the sighing of the wind a frosty breath of sound, the icy branches of the trees a tinkling undercurrent to the silence of the winter night.

It was too quiet. He should have been able to here the rough-running engine of Ellie's beat-up old car for a long time after it turned onto the county highway. But there was nothing. Just ordinary night sounds. Or *was* there something, just at the edge of his consciousness, in that part of his mind and reflexes where he was still a cop?

Riley's ears came up. He trotted a few yards down the sidewalk, then stopped, whining, looking first at Ben, then up at Matt.

"Ben! Matt!"

Riley was off down the driveway in a single bound.

"It's Tim," Matt said as the wavering beam of a flashlight and the small figure who carried it came into view. "Something must be wrong."

"Hey, Tim. It's me, man. What's up?" Matt shouted, sprinting down the icy sidewalk only a step or two behind Riley, the slight unevenness in his gait slowing him only a little.

An image of Matt as he had looked a month ago, the night he came into Ben's life, flashed across his mind's eye. The difference in the boy, physically, was like night and day. Ben had that one good mark, at least, to help balance his life's ledger.

"Matt." Tim came huffing and sliding up the driveway, his coat hanging open, his breath a smoky wreath around his head. It was hard to be certain in the hazy, distorting glow of the security light, but Tim didn't appear to be injured. And there was certainly nothing wrong with his lungs.

"What happened, man?" Matt was on his knees in the snow beside the boy, both hands on his shoulders. "Where's Carly? Where's your mom?"

"The car. A deer. Three of them." Tim bent over, hands on knees, trying to catch his breath.

"Slow him down," Ben ordered, coming up behind Matt. "Get the details."

Matt held up his hand to show he understood. "Okay, man. Take it slow. Did something happen to the car?"

Tim nodded vehemently. "Deer," he said, straightening to his full height. "Three deer jumped in front of the car. My mom tried to stop, but the car slid one way. Then the other. Now it's stuck in a snowdrift and we can't get it out."

God, an accident with that rattletrap car. But Ellie always wore her seat belt. And Tim was unharmed. She and Carly must be okay, too.

"Where are your mother and sister?" he snapped.

Tim's head came up. His eyes were big as saucers. "In the car."

Ben softened his tone, hunkered down beside Matt and the boy. He forced his emotions into a steel-walled cell in his mind, shut them away, stepped outside of himself, let his cop instincts and training take over. "Is Carly okay?"

Tim nodded.

"And your mother? Is she hurt?"

"I...I don't think so." His lip trembled. He sucked in a deep breath. "She's just sitting there. And she's crying." He grabbed Matt's hand and tried to pull him to his feet. "Come on. We have to get back there. It's really cold. And Carly's afraid of the dark." Tim dropped Matt's hand and skipped sideways back down the driveway. "C'mon. Hurry." He took off running.

"Tim, wait." Ben was on his feet in an instant. Matt was struggling to rise, his injured leg clearly not quite up to the strain. Ben held out his hand and pulled Matt to his feet. "Can you catch up with him?"

"Yeah. In about ten seconds."

"Good. Go ahead. I have to go inside and get the keys. Tell Ellie I'm right behind you in the truck."

CHAPTER FOURTEEN

"MAMA, please. Don't cry anymore." Carly was shaking her shoulder, getting ready to cry herself. She was sitting on her knees, hanging on to the door handle, watching for her brother.

Ellie rubbed her hand across her eyes and leaned her head against the headrest. "It's all right, honey. I'm not going to cry anymore, I promise." The beams from the headlights were pointed up into the trees, but at least they were working. And she had managed to back the car out of the snowdrift, but the tires had lost their traction almost immediately and the car had spun around again. Now the back wheels were mired up to the bumper. They were stuck. Big time.

Until that last sickening lurch when the rear end of the car slid into the soft sandy muck beneath the snow, Ellie had hoped against hope she might get out of this predicament with some shred of dignity intact. But when she opened her eyes and saw her headlights illuminating the tip of a twenty-foot pine on the other side of the road, she had to admit defeat.

She was going to have to sit and wait for Tim to come back with Ben. Then she was going to have to accept help from the man whose proposal of marriage she'd just thrown in his face.

"A wolf is going to come and eat us," Carly wailed. "I don't want a wolf to come and eat me. She sniffed and started to cry in earnest.

Ellie had to do something to distract the child. "Come on, honey," she cajoled. "Don't cry. Help Mommy out of the seat, okay? I can't get my door open."

Carly twisted her head around. "Why not?"

Ellie managed a laugh. "Because we are stuck in a really big snowdrift, silly. Here, give me a hand."

She unfastened her seat belt, trying to decide whether it would be easier to climb through the open window into the snowdrift, as Tim had done, rather than work her way across the crazily tilted seat to wrestle with the passenger door. She looked out the window. The snow was glazed with a thick layer of ice and looked hard and unforgiving. She didn't like to think what might happen if she should slip and fall under the car. In the end, the door seemed the safer way to exit.

It was easier said than done. Carly was still wearing the long bathrobe. It was tangled around her legs. Ellie had to reach past her and push with all her might to force the door open. Carly's boots dug into her thigh as the little girl maneuvered to swing her legs out of the car. Ellie grunted in pain, dragged herself out from behind the wheel and across the seat. It was an ungainly and undignified exercise, but finally she had her feet on the ground.

She was leaning on the fender trying to catch her breath and ascertain how deep the wheels were buried in the snow, when a contraction far harder than the ones she'd experienced earlier in the evening rippled across her belly.

Ellie sucked in her breath, stifling a moan. The contractions had been absent for the past hour. Now they were back, stronger than ever. A dart of panic pierced her chest. What if the baby had been harmed by their accident? She hadn't experienced any pain as they slid into the snowdrift, but the seat belt had been stretched tight across her middle—and anything was possible.

The contraction had been swift and hard, but it didn't last long. She straightened slowly, wary that the pain might return. It didn't. She took a deep breath, then held out her hand to Carly. "We'd better start walking, honey. We'll catch up with Tim." He was only a little boy. She didn't like him being alone. There might not be wolves, but there were coyotes and stray dogs, and it was slippery and very, very cold.

"I wish Tim had left us the flashlight." Carly's grip was so tight Ellie winced.

"We'll walk slowly and be really careful."

Carly peered down the narrow, tree-lined road. "It's sure dark tonight."

"Your eyes will adjust in a few minutes," Ellie promised. "Hang on tight. It's slippery."

"Hey, it's snowing." Carly held out her mittened hand, palm up to catch a flake. It *was* snowing again. Real snow this time, not the icy pellets from earlier in the evening. In a couple of hours it would be Christmas Eve.

"Maybe if we sing a Christmas carol, the wolves will hear us and stay away," Carly said.

"Okay. What would you like to sing?" A gnawing ache was building in her lower back. Ellie did her best to ignore it.

"'O Little Town of Bethlehem,'" Carly decided. "That's my favorite.

They had taken about ten steps and made it to "thy deep and dreamless sleep," when the second hard contraction hit. Carly sang on alone for a moment then noticed Ellie's silence. "What's the matter, Mama? Did you forget the words?"

"No, honey. I'm...I just had a pain in my tummy." Suddenly, she didn't want to walk any farther into the darkness on the icy road. She turned herself and Carly around and stumbled back to the car. She sat down on the bumper, fighting to get her breath. The contraction peaked and died away. Ellie was trembling when it was over. She drew in a long, cleansing breath, tried to rearrange her pain-scattered thoughts in a coherent pattern.

This wasn't a tummyache, or false labor. This was the real thing.

She was less than two weeks from her due date. It was ten o'clock at night. Ten degrees below freezing. And she was marooned in a snowdrift forty miles from the nearest hospital. "It can't be," she said, unaware she'd spoken the words aloud until Carly reached up and touched her cheek with the tip of her mitten.

"What's the matter, Mama?"

"Nothing," she said hastily. "I...I was just thinking how much work it will be to get the car out of the snowdrift."

"Ben will do it. He can do anything," Carly said with all the confidence in the world. "What's that?" In the blink of an eye, she had scrambled onto the bumper. "I hear a wolf!"

Ellie heard the barking, too, and it was definitely coming closer. "It's not a wolf." Unconvinced, Carly had buried her face in Ellie's coat sleeve. "Look, Carly. It's Riley. Don't be afraid." The setter skidded to a halt in front of them, tail wagging, still barking delightedly.

"Quiet, boy," Ellie said. Riley jumped up, front paws on the bumper, and proceeded to thump his tail against Ellie's legs. "Ouch," she said. "Stop that." Then, "ouch," again because the gnawing pain in her back had returned and was working its way around her abdomen, strengthening as it progressed.

It was too dark to see her watch, but surely it had only been a couple of minutes since the last contraction. For the first time, Ellie began to be afraid.

"Mom! Carly! I'm back." It was Tim's voice. And he wasn't alone. Ellie said a little prayer of thanksgiving. Then she recognized the male figure accompanying her son. It was Matt Westrick, not Ben, and some of the fear returned. Where was Ben? Had she hurt him so badly he refused to come along to help her and the children? How could she expect a fifteen-year-old boy to deal with a stuck car and a woman who was about to give birth?

"Hey," Matt said, jogging to a halt next to Ellie. "Got yourself stuck real good, don't you?"

Ellie nodded. The pain was ebbing. She knew she was going to have to get her breathing and her emotions mastered soon, or it would be too late. She had to stay in control, not allow herself to be carried along on the waves of pain.

Matt motioned Tim to hand over the flashlight then bent down, shining the small beam under the car. Carly slipped off the bumper to drop onto her hands and knees at his side.

"We are *really* stuck," she announced with an air of authority. "Will we have to get a tow truck to pull us out?"

"Looks like it."

"How long will that take?"

"A while," Tim informed her.

Carly jumped up and came back to Ellie. "I have to go potty," she said in a penetrating whisper.

"Oh, dear." Ellie didn't know whether to laugh or cry. "You'll have to wait, honey," she said gently. "Help will be here soon."

"Ben's on his way with the truck," Matt told her. "Tim wouldn't wait around for him to get the keys so we hiked back here. Maybe he can pull you free and we won't have to wait for a tow."

Ben was coming.

Ellie couldn't hear anything over the rush of blood in her ears, but she held on to the comfort of those three little words with both hands.

"I have to go potty real bad," Carly said with emphasis.

Ellie stood up, slowly, a little gingerly, but the pain didn't return. "I'll get the flashlight. We'll walk a little way down the road."

"It's too cold to pee outside," Carly wailed. "I want to go back to Ben's lighthouse. I can use his *bathroom.*"

"What's the matter?" Matt inquired, standing, brushing snow off the knees of his jeans.

Carly wasn't shy about telling him. "I have to go to the bathroom. Now!"

"Uh-oh." Just then, headlights raked the trees along the side of the road. Snowflakes shimmered in the light beams as the pickup come closer. "Hey, good. Here comes Ben. Hang on a couple of minutes, munchkin, and he'll take you back to the house to use the bathroom."

"Not very long," Carly urged, jiggling up and down. "I can't wait very long."

The third contraction hit without warning, doubling Ellie over. She dropped to her knees in the hard, ice-glazed snow, rocked back on her heels, fighting for breath against the tightening agony. Matt was beside her in a flash. "What's wrong? Did you step in a hole? Sprain your ankle?"

"No." The single word took all the breath she could spare. She shivered. She'd worn a long woolen jumper and turtleneck sweater over leggings and boots to the Sunday school pageant. The outfit was comfortable and warm enough for wearing outside, but not for sitting in the snow. She shivered violently again.

"Did you hurt yourself when the car went off the road?" Matt's voice was coming from a long way away.

She managed to shake her head. "I'm not hurt." She looked up into his face, bathed red by the taillights of the car. His eyes were as big as saucers. "But I don't think I can wait very long to get back to the lighthouse, either, Matt."

"Mama? Mama!" Carly was hanging on her arm, crying. Tim was pushing at Matt's shoulder, trying to get past him, trying to get to her. Matt held him back.

"Jeez. Is something wrong with the baby?" he asked, his voice cracking.

"Baby." It was taking all her concentration to ride out the contraction. So fast and so hard. Neither of her other labors had been like this. It had taken seventeen hours for Tim to be born. And six hours of hard labor for Carly after almost a whole day of on-and-off contractions. She'd thought she would have plenty of time. Plenty of time.

A door slammed. Riley barked a welcome and a familiar voice silenced him. "What happened?" It was Ben, using his cop's voice, taking control. Ellie didn't answer, couldn't answer. She was concentrating on her breathing, counting each breath, riding out the pain. Matt scooted out of Ben's way. He hunkered down in front of her. "Ellie, are you in labor?"

She managed a smile, for the children's sakes. She'd never been so glad to see anyone in her life. Ben would help. Ben would make everything right. She fought back tears. "Yes," she said, amazed to find her voice almost normal, but the contraction had eased and she could think again. It wasn't Ben's place to be with her. She had to remember that. It was Lonny's place—but she didn't want him here. This was her baby now. This time it was up to her. Her alone.

"How long have you been having contractions?"

"Not very long." She looked up and her eyes met his. He didn't look away, didn't hide behind a bank of impenetrable storm-dark clouds. Even in the uncertain light, she felt his strength, his determination, his courage, and took what she needed of it for herself.

He finished the sentence for her. "But they're hard."

"And they last forever," she said, trying for a small joke, and missing. Her hands were clenched hard on her thighs, she uncurled them, trying to relax, trying to work through her options before the next wave of pain broke her concentration.

"We need to get you to the hospital. It'll save time if I take you to North Star in the truck. We'll call the emergency squad from your place."

"Who'll drive my car?"

"Your car's not going anywhere. We'll leave it here."

"What about the kids?" The ache was growing again. She began breathing in rhythm. Martha MacAllister was on the emergency squad. She'd promised to be Ellie's labor coach, but she wasn't here to keep her focused, help her relax. *She had to do it on her own.*

"They can walk back to the lighthouse with Matt. It's not far."

"No," Tim said. "I'm not leaving my mom."

"Me, neither," Carly said sobbing. "And I have to pee."

The pain was growing, their voices running together, becoming jumbled and meaningless. She shivered, her teeth were chattering. "How long has it been?" She kept breathing, kept her eyes on Ben's.

He looked at his watch. "Not quite four minutes."

"Oh, boy," she said. "This is going to be close."

He didn't look away. "We'll make it." The contraction eased. "Can you stand?" She nodded. "Everybody in the truck," he ordered. "Matt, you and Tim and the dog will have to ride in the back. Carly, up front with your mother."

Matt didn't say a word, just picked Tim up under the arms and hoisted him aboard. He didn't even take the time to put the tailgate down for Riley, but picked up the setter and dumped him over the side, put his foot on the bumper and dropped beside them. Ben took Ellie by the hands and led her to the truck. She managed to get her foot on the running board and hoist herself onto the bench seat. When Carly saw her standing and walking on her own, she stopped crying and let Ben lift her into the truck from the driver's side. She snuggled up to Ellie and tucked her small, mittened fingers into hers.

"It's okay, honey," Ellie soothed as Ben jockeyed the truck around on the narrow road and headed toward the lighthouse. "It's just the baby wanting to be born. Remember, I told you it hurt a little. But it's a good kind of hurting. Don't cry. It will all be fine." Ellie knew they were less than half a mile from the lighthouse, but she wasn't certain they would make it before another contraction tore through her.

"I don't like it," Carly said. "But I want the new baby."

"We all do."

"I don't want to stay out here with Matt. Take me with you," Carly whispered as they drove.

"Carly," Ben said, "we'll call Eldor from the lighthouse. He or Jackson Tall Trees can drive out and pick you guys up, and take the three of you into North Star."

"Yes," Ellie said, grateful he'd given voice to what she'd been thinking. "And Lonny," she said because she didn't want him to find out from a stranger that she was on her way to the hospital. She couldn't humiliate him that way. "Someone needs to tell him."

"Of course," Ben said.

"I'm glad you thought of calling Eldor," she told him. "I don't want the kids riding all the way to town in the back of the truck."

"Neither do I." Ben drove into the yard, pulling to a halt directly in front of the door. Matt and Tim scrambled over the side as Ben lifted Carly out of the truck and set her on her feet. Riley hit the ground running, barking at the top of his lungs.

Ben circled the pickup in the blink of an eye and opened the door. Ellie didn't move a muscle. She couldn't. *This one was a doozy*. She bit her lip to keep from screaming.

"Matt, take Carly inside and show her where the bathroom is. Tim, shut Riley in the shed over there. I'll help your mother inside." The kids scrambled to do as they were told.

"Stay in the truck. I'll go call 911, tell them to meet us," Matt called over his shoulder.

"No," Ellie said, remembering the frightened look on Tim's face, Carly's tears. "I'm okay. I'll come inside. It'll be simpler if I'm there to answer their questions, don't you think?''

Ben didn't look convinced, but didn't argue with her. "Can you walk?"

"I think so. They say walking is good for women in early labor. She slid off the seat, but her rubbery legs refused to hold her. She felt Ben's arms come around her, slide behind her knees, lift her high into his arms. The trouble was, she wasn't in early labor, not anymore. Panic beat at the edges of her consciousness, but she pushed it away.

In less than an hour, she'd be at the hospital. Surely her labor wouldn't progress that quickly. She just needed to stay calm, to remember her breathing exercises, to stay focused.

Tim caught up with them as Ben carried her into the cold, dark hallway. "Are you okay, Mom?"

"I'm fine. Put me down, Ben. I can stand." But just barely. He kept his arm around her shoulders and Ellie leaned against him.

"I'll go see how Carly is, okay?"

"Okay."

Matt appeared in the hallway with a portable phone in his hand. "I've got 911," he said. His face was deathly pale, his eyes didn't quite meet Ellie's. Instead, he shifted his gaze to Ben. "The dispatcher wants to know how close together the pains...the contractions are."

Ben noticed the odd note in his voice before Ellie did.

"Less than three minutes. Why?"

Matt handed him the phone. "She says the North Star unit is out on a run. Some guy crashed his snowmobile into a tree. They had to take him all the way to Marquette where there's a plastic surgeon." He lowered his voice to a whisper, maybe hoping that Ellie couldn't hear his next words. "She says it will take at least an hour for the Newberry unit to get here and then another forty minutes to the Soo."

Ellie stifled a moan. She wrapped her hands around Ben's arm as pain licked along her nerve endings.

"Another one?" His hand covered hers. She reached out blindly, and his fingers closed around hers, warm, strong. She held on for dear life.

"Another one." She panted, waiting out the contraction but the pain seemed to go on forever. Finally, it receded and she dropped her head back against his shoulder. "It hasn't been four minutes, has it?"

"Two minutes, thirty seconds. Who's your obstetrician?"

"Dr. Makowski." A family practitioner came to the clinic in North Star two days a week, but he didn't deliver babies. Ellie's obstetrician practiced in the Soo. "Oh, God."

He relayed the information on the contractions to the dispatcher, along with detailed directions for reaching the lighthouse. "Get them here as quick as you can," he said, and handed the phone back to Matt. "Ellie, I think it's best if we stay here. It's too risky to be out on the road."

Ellie closed her eyes against the nightmare image of her baby being born in the front seat of Ben's truck. "Okay. Let's stay here."

"Move the truck out of the way, will you, Matt? I'm going to let Ellie lie down on my bed until the ambulance gets here." She must have moved, made some sound she wasn't aware of. "It's okay, Ellie. You'll be on your way to the hospital in no time, I promise."

"I don't think I'm going to take that bet," she said, opening her eyes, searching for his. Her fingers bunched on his coat sleeve. "Have you ever delivered a baby, Ben MacAllister?"

"I know the drill." His eyes narrowed, his dark eyebrows pulled together in a quick frown, but his voice was as even and calm as before.

"So do I. Maybe I can talk you through it." She tried to smile, didn't quite succeed. "Help me, Ben," she whispered, fighting to stay focused, calm. "My water just broke."

CHAPTER FIFTEEN

"MATT, would you go sit with Ellie? There are things I have to get ready." Ben had his cop face on. If the thought of delivering Ellie's baby by himself scared him, it surely didn't show.

Matt wished he could hide his feelings like that. Right now, he guessed he looked exactly the way he felt—scared. A pain hit him just below his heart. Before he'd figured out Ben didn't want him and was going to try to send him back to Columbus, he would have asked Ben how he managed it. How he did the things he had to do even though he was scared to death. Matt guessed what he was really wanting to know was how to be a man. But he couldn't ask that now. Couldn't ask Ben anything. And there was no use thinking about what might have been, either.

Matt glanced at the TV in the far corner of the room. Tim was watching an Indiana Jones movie Matt had put in the VCR, and Carly was sitting on the couch, her arms wrapped around Riley's neck. The dog wouldn't stop howling after Tim penned him up in the shed. Matt had finally got tired of listening to the noise, and had let him back in the house. "If I sit with Ellie, who'll watch the kids?"

"I'll keep an eye on them." Ben took the biggest pan they had from under the sink and filled it with water. He caught Matt watching him as he turned to the stove.

"What's the pan for?" Matt asked, stalling for time to get his nerve up. He could baby-sit okay. But he didn't know about actually being alone in a room with a woman who was getting ready to have a baby.

"Hot water."

"You mean . . ."

One corner of Ben's mouth kicked up for just a second. "Yeah, that line from all the old movies is true. You do need to boil water. Lots of it."

"Do you really know how to deliver a baby?"

The smile disappeared. "I've had some training in emergency-medical situations."

"What does that mean?"

Ben set the heavy metal pan on the stove with a thud. "It means I've observed two deliveries in a Columbus hospital."

Matt's heart started pounding so hard he could feel it clear up in his throat. He swallowed around the lump it made. "You mean, you've never actually done this?"

The burner under the pan caught fire with a pop. "No."

"Oh, damn," Matt said.

"You owe me a buck."

"Huh?" Matt shot him a look.

"You owe me a buck for cussing."

He was smiling again. Matt blinked. "Yeah. Sure." Matt tried a smile, too. "I owe you a buck."

Ben's smile disappeared. He nodded in the direction of his bedroom. "Go on. I don't like Ellie being alone, and I have to find the other things I'll need."

Matt's stomach did a flip-flop. *Like something to tie off the cord and cut it. And something to put the afterbirth in.* He'd paid that much attention in biology class. He'd seen lots of babies born on TV. But this wasn't TV. This was real. And in real life women sometimes died having babies. The lump in his throat got bigger. He swallowed again. "Maybe the paramedics will get here in time." Matt wasn't much for praying, but all of a sudden he wished he was.

"Maybe." Ben didn't sound as if he thought that was going to happen. "Now, go talk to Ellie."

Ellie was in Ben's bedroom, lying on Ben's bed. The only light came from a lamp on the bedside table. The room wasn't very big. Or very warm, but Matt was sweating and the cool air felt good. He stuck his head around the door, his eyes focused on the ceiling. "Hey, Ellie. How ya doing? Ben sent me. Can I come in?"

"Hi." Her voice was a little funny-sounding, but not too much. "Come on in. I'm decent. Or mostly." She was sitting half propped up by pillows against the head of the bed, with her knees drawn up. When he was inside the room, she asked, "Are the kids okay?"

"Yeah. They're watching TV. Are you okay?" He was glad to see she was wearing her clothes. Or most of them. There was a blanket over her legs. That was good. He wasn't an idiot. He knew you couldn't have a baby without taking your clothes off, but he didn't think he was cool enough to actually have to watch the process.

"I'm okay." She didn't look okay. There were big, dark circles under her eyes, and lines along both sides of her mouth that he'd never seen before.

"You want a drink of water or something?"

"No." She managed a smile. "I don't think I could keep it down."

"Oh."

The smile disappeared. He saw her hands tense on the sheet, then deliberately relax. She began to breathe funny, making little panting sounds. Pretty soon he was breathing that way, too, and his stomach was beginning to heave again. Beneath her bunched-up skirt, he saw her big belly harden and flatten out with the force of the contraction. She lifted her hand in a helpless gesture and without thinking he held his out for her to grasp.

Ellie held on to him so tightly he thought she'd crush his fingers. He bit his tongue to keep from yelping in pain. He didn't know how long the contraction lasted, but it seemed endless. She kept on breathing in that funny whooshing way, and once or twice she moaned, odd little sounds that worked their way right into his heart.

The baby inside was tearing her apart trying to get out, and that was the only noise she made. He'd be howling at the moon if it were him. "Jeez, Ellie. If it hurts that bad, go ahead and holler."

She shook her head, gasping for breath as the pain seemed to ease, at least a little bit. "I can't. I...I don't want the kids to hear. It...it'll scare them. But God...Matt...it's hard." The death grip on his fingers relaxed a fraction. Her head dropped back against the pillows. A tear rolled out of the corner of her eye and across her temple into her hair. "It's... hard."

"I'll think of something to do with the kids," Matt said, forcing himself not to shake his numbed fingers to get the circulation going again.

Her head moved restlessly from side to side. "There's no place else for them to go." She was right. There was no place in the light keeper's house where they would be far enough away not to hear her if she screamed, or even yelled pretty loudly.

"I'll think of something," he said. But what? Ellie moaned again, her breathing changed, she started making those panting sounds. *Jeez, another one so soon.*

She pushed away from the pillows, her face contorted with pain and effort. *Pushed.* Pushing. That meant the baby was coming soon. Maybe now. She grabbed a corner of the blanket covering her legs and shoved it into her mouth. The muffled sounds coming out of her throat weren't quite human.

Think, idiot. That's the only thing she's asked of you, find someplace safe and out of earshot and take care of her kids. *Think of something.* But the only thought he could grasp at the moment was that if every guy he'd ever heard bragging about getting a girl pregnant had to be sitting where he was right then, they'd all run like hell for the nearest monastery. He couldn't watch Ellie suffer anymore. He stared out the window at the black bulk of the light tower ten feet away.

The light tower. That was it. He'd take the kids up into the tower... to watch for the red and blue flashing lights of the ambulance.

The contraction passed, but Ellie didn't relax and he figured there was another one coming right behind it. He rushed to get the words out of his mouth. "I'll take the kids up in the tower. I'll tell them we're going to be the lookouts for the ambulance."

She nodded, gasping for breath. "Be careful."

"Don't worry. I'll watch them like a hawk. I'll take blankets. I'll make a game out of it for them."

"Thanks." He didn't know if she said it out loud, or only formed the word with her lips.

"I'll go as soon as Ben—"

"I'm here, Matt."

He was carrying a tray covered by a cloth, balanced on what looked like every towel they had in the house. *There would be blood.* He'd known that in the back of his mind because there was plastic underneath the blanket Ellie was lying on. It crinkled and rustled every time she moved. But he'd tried not to think about that, either. He averted his eyes.

"The tower's a good idea," Ben said. "There's a lantern by the back door. Be careful, the steps might be slippery. And Matt." Ben's tone held a command. Matt's eyes snapped to his. "Thanks. Your being in charge of the kids will take a load off Ellie's mind. And mine."

His heart started beating even faster than before. "Yeah. Sure. I'll take good care of them. Good luck, Ellie." He gave her hand a last squeeze and all but ran out of the room.

He ducked into his own cold, dark bedroom and grabbed the quilt and blanket off the bed. Ellie was moaning again. He could hear her through the closed door of Ben's room. His feet barely touched the hallway floor. He skidded into the kitchen two seconds later. Indiana Jones was getting ready to fall into the snake pit. Matt felt as though he were already there.

"Hey, guys. I've got an idea. Let's climb up into the light tower and watch for the ambulance to come. What do you say?"

"I don't want to leave my mom," Carly said with a sniff. Her nose was red from crying. She still had her arms around Riley, who was sitting quietly by her side, obviously taking his job as a source of comfort very seriously.

Jeez, now he was going to have to argue with Carly. He didn't have time for this. "It was your mom's idea," he told her. "It will be a help to her if we can tell her when the ambulance is coming."

"Well." Carly was wavering. Matt held out his hand.

Tim looked more interested. "We can watch for the ambulance and for Eldor's car," he said. Matt didn't tell him Eldor wouldn't be coming for them until he could clear the customers out of the Jack Pine. Mrs. Eldor was on her way to Marquette with the injured snowmobiler and it was Jackson Tall Trees's night off.

The bad guys had just dropped the big stone cover and sealed Indy in the snake pit. Matt decided to take a page from Ben's book. He snapped off the TV. "C'mon, Carly. Have you ever been to the top of the tower? It's rad up there. There's a ledge all the way around the inside. You can see forever up there.''

"Can Riley come, too?"

"Sure, why not." Matt smiled and held out his hand. "I brought blankets. We'll pretend we're camping out."

"Okay," she said, frowning as she looked over her shoulder toward the bedrooms. "If my mom says it's all right."

"It's all right."

Thirty seconds later, they were out of the house. Just in time. Matt had heard Ellie's bitten-off scream as the door slammed shut behind them, but he was pretty sure the kids hadn't.

"Okay. Be careful," he warned as they started up the winding staircase. "We've all got snow on our boots. It'll be slippery."

Riley went first, his toenails clicking on the iron treads. The lantern light bounced off the walls, which were coated with a thin layer of ice. Their breath was like white smoke in the cold, still air.

"This is weird," Tim said, his voice hushed.

"I don't like it," Carly said.

"It'll be great when we get to the top," Matt assured them.

"Hey, Matt." Tim sounded excited and a little breathless from the climb. "I just had a great idea. Wouldn't it be neat if we could decorate this old thing? You know, put lights up here and everything. I bet people would come from all over to see it."

Carly stopped dead in her tracks. "Oh, I'd like that. Wouldn't you like that, Matt?"

"Yeah. It would be neat."

"We'd have to get one of those humongous long extension cords." Tim giggled. "There's no electricity up here."

"Mr. Larson probably has one at the hardware store," Carly said.

"I wonder how much they cost?"

"I don't know," Matt said. "We'll have to check it out." *He wouldn't be here next Christmas.* That didn't matter now. Keep them talking. Keep them moving. So far, so good.

"But it's already Christmas Eve. Or almost," Carly said with a sigh. "Too late this year."

"Next year," Tim said just before he disappeared into the darkness of the catwalk surrounding the platform where the light had rested all those years ago. "We'll save all our allowances and we can do it next year. Right, Matt?"

"Sure. Next year." Matt wondered where he'd be this time next year. Probably the same place he'd have been last Christmas if Eric hadn't invited him to his house—someplace with a bunch of other losers.

Except right now he wasn't a loser. He was doing what he could to help Ellie Lawrence. He was keeping her kids safe and entertained so she didn't have to worry about them while she worked to bring her new baby into the world. Maybe it wasn't much. Maybe it didn't make up for Eric being dead, but it was something. Something real and worthwhile. And no one else could do it but him.

"I bet we can see the Star of Bethlehem," Carly said after he had wrapped her in the quilt and turned down the Coleman to a dot of light no brighter than a fire-fly. It had stopped snowing since they'd got back to the lighthouse, and the wind had blown holes in the cloud cover so that the stars shone through in bits and pieces.

"The Star of Bethlehem. Do you really think we can see it?" Tim asked as though it were the most natural thing in the world that Matt would know the answer.

"I'm sure we can." He didn't believe in the Star of Bethlehem. He didn't believe in miracles. But Tim did, and so did Carly, and he wasn't going to say or do anything to spoil this magical time of year for Ellie's kids. "But we'll have to turn off the lantern. You won't be afraid of the dark, will you?" Riley settled down with his head on Matt's lap. He scratched the setter behind the left ear, his favorite spot.

Then Carly said something that he'd never forget, something that went straight to his lonely heart and lodged there like a heat-seeking missile. She squeezed his hand between her two little ones and looked up at him and smiled. "I'm never afraid when I'm with you."

"BEN." She didn't have the breath or the extra energy to get more than his name past her dry lips.

"Right here, Ellie." His weight settled on the lumpy old mattress. His hand closed around hers. She looked up into his eyes, longed to lose herself in their gray depths. She clung to his hands, clung to his strength.

"I'm so sorry—"

He smiled that wonderful, transforming smile. "Now what are you apologizing for?"

"For putting you through this. For making you come to my rescue again." The pain was building once more, overwhelming her, consuming her. "I don't know how much longer I can take this." Tears of exhaustion and anxiety filled her eyes, threatened to slide down her cheeks.

"You're doing great, Ellie. You're almost there. The baby's crowning. It won't be long now." She'd felt the touch of cool air, felt him rearranging the blankets in the last short, blessed interval between contractions, but she was long past worrying about her modesty, worrying about anything but bringing this baby into the world alive, and not dying, herself.

"You sound as if you know what you're doing," she managed to say before another pain caught her up in its talons, drove every thought from her mind but the need to push, to rid herself of the burden she carried.

"You're the pro, Ellie. I'm just here for backup."

He was much more than that. He was her anchor, the voice of comfort and encouragement that kept her from spiraling into a panicky, pain-filled void. She listened to that voice now, calm, level. Listened and did her best to respond.

Push. Breathe. Push. Breathe.

"Good girl, Ellie. We're almost there. Good girl. The head's ready to be born."

An animal groan broke from her lips. She pushed as he told her, rested when he told her, held on to the thread of reality that was his strong, sure voice. And then the comforting flow of words stopped. "Ben?" Red and black dots swirled before her eyes. She couldn't see what was happening between her legs. She locked on to his face, tried to focus, tried to hang on. "Ben! What's wrong?"

"Shh, Ellie. You have to listen to me now, okay? Don't push. Not now. Wait."

She knotted her hands into fists on the blankets. "I...I can't." The pain was so intense. It didn't ebb and flow anymore, it was just there, a constant.

"Ellie, listen to me. You have to. The cord's around the baby's neck. We have to slow up just a little, do you understand, give me time to turn him around."

The sharp thrust of terror that sliced through her heart was more intense than the birth pangs. She tried to relax, tried to hold on to her courage and her sanity. She tried not to scream, but the cries were torn from her throat. Time seemed to stand still, and then through the dark, swirling fog of agony came Ben's voice, still quiet, still calm. "There. He's free. Push, Ellie. Push! Let's get this baby born."

One more agonizing contraction and the shoulders were born, and then she felt the baby slip free of her body, and she closed her eyes, sobbing in relief. She let her head drop back on the pillow, drawing breath into her lungs, enduring the final pain as her body discarded the afterbirth, waiting to feel the weight of her baby on her stomach, waiting to hear his first cry.

But there was no crying. The only sound she could hear in the little room was her own harsh breathing.

Ellie struggled to sit up, see what was happening. "Ben?"

"Come on, little one," Ben whispered. He'd already cut the cord, wrapped the baby in a towel. He was using a cotton swab to clean the tiny nose and mouth, but still there was no sound.

The cord's wrapped around his neck. Ellie closed her eyes, willing away what she saw, the tiny, dusky blue, lifeless body of her child. "Ben! Please. Why isn't he breathing?"

He ignored her, turning the baby over, so small in his big sure hands, rubbing his back, patting him gently. "Come on, little one. Breathe! Now!"

"Ben!" She was crying now. She held out her hands. She couldn't lie there helplessly while her child died.

"Hang on, Ellie. Hang on." Ben stood up, lay the baby on the dresser top, supporting the head, bald, Ellie noticed with a tiny detached portion of her brain, totally bald.

Ben bent over the immobile, towel-wrapped form, slid his hand under the head, covered the baby's nose and mouth with his, breathing life into the lungs. Ellie sat up, swung her legs over the side of the bed, so dizzy the room spun in slow circles around her. She tried to stand and couldn't. Sat back down, pressing her hand to her mouth to keep the screams inside.

As she watched, Ben lifted his mouth, pressed his thumb gently against the baby's chest, three, four, five times. Then lowered his head again, breathing for her son.

Once, twice more he repeated the slow, deliberate steps. And then the lifeless bundle began to move. Tiny arms and legs kicked feebly at the restraining covers. Ellie blinked the tears from her eyes, afraid to believe, afraid she was only imagining what she so desperately wanted to see. And then the movements were no longer faint or sporadic. Tiny mewling cries filled the room. Ben lifted his head, picked the baby up and began rubbing his back again.

"There we go, sweetie. Go on and cry." The wails were more emphatic now. The baby was cold. And he was mad. Suddenly, Ellie realized she was cold, too. She sagged against the headboard, trembling from head to foot.

Ben turned with the baby in his arms. The little one's mouth was open, his hands had worked free of the towel. He was screaming at the top of his lungs, his face red and distorted, and she had never, ever seen anything so beautiful in her life. She held out her hands.

Ben placed the baby in her arms. "Merry Christmas, Ellie. You have a daughter."

"A daughter?" Surely he was mistaken. She unwound the towel, checking for herself. The baby howled even more loudly at the touch of the cold air on her skin. "It is a girl. The doctor guessed wrong?"

"The doctor was wrong," Ben confirmed. "She's a beautiful little girl." Deftly he rewrapped the towel. His hands were trembling, Ellie noticed. She looked up into his face and what she saw there took her breath away. Longing, raw and naked. And love. She was sure of it. There were no barriers, his eyes were clear and gray.

"Ben . . . I . . ."

He lifted his scarred left hand and touched her cheek, touched the baby's cheek. "Ellie." A door slammed, pounding footsteps echoed through the back of the house. Ben glanced toward the window. Red and blue lights flashed in sequence on the far wall. "Damn—"

Quickly he stripped the soiled linens from the bed and bundled them out of sight. Then just as quickly, he took a clean, worn quilt from the chair beside the bed and wrapped her in it as gently as he had the baby.

"Ben?"

"It looks like the cavalry has finally arrived." The stoic mask, the cop's face, was back in place.

"The ambulance is here," Matt called from the hallway. "We saw them coming up the road from the tower. Is everything okay?" Ben crossed the room in two quick strides and opened the door. Matt was standing there with Carly hanging on to his hand and Tim peeking around his shoulder. In the background, Ellie heard someone pounding at the front door.

"Everything's fine. Come in and see your new sister."

"Sister!" Tim squawked. "It was supposed to be a boy."

The next fifteen minutes were pandemonium. The ambulance strobes played over the walls like disco lights. People crowded into the austere little room, talking and asking her questions that she was almost too tired to answer. She didn't want to go to the hospital, although she knew she must, for the baby's sake, if not her own.

She wanted them all to go away. She wanted to be alone with her children. She wanted to be alone with Ben. But nobody asked her what she wanted, and Ben was nowhere to be seen.

Mrs. Eldor showed up, explaining she had not gone with the injured snowmobiler to Marquette but had hitched a ride home from the Soo with Laura Shurmansky who worked second shift in Intensive Care. She'd headed for the lighthouse as soon as Eldor told her what was happening, she explained, and turned into the driveway right behind the Newberry unit. "I'll take the kids back to town with me," she declared as one of the emergency techs unwound the blood pressure cuff from Ellie's arm, while a second woman wrapped the baby more securely against the cold. Mrs. Eldor already had one child on each side of her. Tim looked dazed, Carly mutinous. Her *elder* daughter obviously didn't plan to go anywhere without her baby sister.

Another blue-jumpsuited tech appeared in the doorway. "It's going to be a tight squeeze getting the gurney in here," he announced with a frown. "We'll have to clear some people out of the way."

"To hell with the stretcher. I'll take care of it."

"Lonny?" His sheepskin coat and Stetson looked completely out of place among the jumpsuits and parkas.

"Stopped into the Jack Pine to have a beer. Eldor was shoving people out the door right and left. He told me what was going on. I got here as soon as I could, darlin'." He barely glanced at the baby. "What came over you to go and have this baby two weeks ahead of time? You've never done that before, eh?"

"Hey, you can't just come barging—"

Lonny brushed the paramedic aside, bent over and scooped Ellie into his arms before she could protest.

Over his shoulder she saw Ben standing in the hallway, standing in the shadows, alone, detached, farther from her, it seemed at that moment, than he had ever been. "Don't tell me what I can do. She's my wife."

"I WAS WONDERING..." Matt's voice was hesitant.

"What?"

Ben turned away from the kitchen window. He was holding a coffee mug between his hands, and he looked as if he'd been standing there a long time. He looked like hell, like maybe he hadn't gone to sleep at all last night. On the other hand, Matt had slept like...a baby. At least for a couple of hours. It had been long after midnight before everyone cleared out and left them alone.

"I said, I was wondering if you could drive me into the Soo this morning." The sun was just coming up over the far side of the bay, outlining Ben in red and gold. The reflection off the Jack Frost pattern of ice crystals on the glass nearly blinded Matt. He shifted his gaze a few degrees to the left. "It's Christmas Eve. I...I want to buy some presents for the kids before the mall closes. And for the new baby." He wanted to see the new baby, too, but he didn't quite have the guts to bring that up right now.

But he'd get around to it. He was going to get around to a lot of things this morning. He didn't have all the answers figured out yet, but something had happened to him last night, up there in that light tower with those two little kids to take care of. He couldn't exactly say what it was, but he did know he wasn't the same person he'd been before.

Maybe Ben didn't want him to stay with him, but even if he had to go back to Columbus, back to the group home or foster care, he wasn't going to let it get the best of him. He had his whole life ahead of him.

He was alive.

And Eric was dead.

And it wasn't his fault. Not the way he'd been blaming himself for the last nine months. It was hard to put into words, even in his own thoughts. He wasn't responsible for everything that happened in the world. He was only responsible for his own actions. He *was* responsible for putting the idea of taking the Badens' car into Eric's head that night. He'd carry that guilt all his life. But he was *not* responsible for Eric trying to outrun the cop car. He'd tried to get him to pull over, tried his damnedest, but Eric hadn't listened.

And it wasn't Ben's fault, either.

He couldn't have stopped the other trooper from pursuing them.

He couldn't have saved Eric or his buddy, even if he had managed to get them out of the burning cars. They were already dead.

He wasn't any more to blame than Matt was.

And it was time to tell him so.

"I want to do some shopping for Carly and Tim," he said again because he didn't know where else to start. "And I want to go to the hospital and see Ellie and the baby. I never even got to get a good look at her last night, what with everything that was going on around here. Are you sure it was a girl?" He could feel his face getting red. That was about the stupidest thing he'd ever said.

"It was a girl. A very pretty little girl," Ben assured him, setting his coffee mug down on the table. His hands were shaking a little bit, Matt noticed. And he did look like hell, with dark stubble on his chin and harsh lines carved from nose to mouth. He looked like a man who had just lost everything he wanted in the world. And when you thought about the way that Lonny Lawrence had waltzed in here last night and carried Ellie out in his arms, he probably thought he had. But Matt wasn't convinced of that. He didn't think Ellie wanted to go back with her ex-husband. He thought she was just as much in love with Ben as Ben was with her. He just wasn't sure he was brave enough to tell Ben what he thought.

"Well. I... I just thought it was supposed to be a boy."

"She fooled us all."

"Yeah." Matt nodded. Ben had moved away from the window. He bent to scratch Riley behind the ears, then opened the back door to let the setter out to run. A rush of air so cold and so sharp it stung Matt's nose blew into the room. The ice crust on the snow was strong enough to support Riley's weight. Matt watched him race past the kitchen window like a bat out of hell.

Matt spread his legs, stuffed his hands into the pockets of his jeans. There was no turning back. *This was the first day of the rest of his life.* Was that how that hokey old saying went? Ben had taught him to tell the truth. He'd shown him a real man did what he had to do. "I don't want to go back to Columbus on Thursday," Matt said, steeling himself for Ben's rejection.

"Why not?" Ben didn't turn around right away. He stood there in the open doorway with the frigid air pouring past him for a long few seconds before he turned around and shut the door. It didn't matter that the temperature in the room had just dropped ten degrees. Matt was sweating like a pig.

"I want to stay here." *It was now or never.* "With you. If you'll have me. I won't be any trouble. I'll go to school every day. I'll make my own money. I won't do dope or alcohol. You'll hardly know I'm here."

"That's not what I asked you."

Matt took a deep breath. This was harder than he thought, but he'd gone too far to back down now. "It's not what you're thinking. It's not because I can't face going back there. I can. I know that. I figured it out last night. It wasn't my fault Eric died in that crash. It wasn't your fault he died. Or your friend's, either. They were responsible for their own actions. We're responsible for ours. And maybe there's something else, too. Maybe we were both supposed to be here last night. Did you ever think of that?" He didn't know how to explain himself. Religion. God. All that kind of stuff wasn't something he'd had a lot of experience with. Maybe he was just dreaming all this. Maybe it was because he'd been watching that old Jimmy Stewart movie the other night. The one with that angel guy, Clarence, who didn't have any wings— and it was all about what the world might be like if you weren't in it.

"What if all that just didn't happen to us for no reason," Matt went on. "Maybe we were supposed to get together and figure this all out. And help Ellie to have her baby. And for you to save the baby's life." Matt stumbled to a halt. He was panting just like Riley after a run.

"You've been doing a lot of thinking."

Matt screwed up his eyes. He couldn't be sure, but he thought Ben was getting ready to smile. "Yeah, I have. But that doesn't change anything. I'm not going back to Columbus. I'll find someplace to stay if you don't want me here."

"What makes you think I don't want you?" This time Ben was really smiling, but Matt was too nervous to try to figure out what the smile meant.

"Are you trying to tell me this trip back to see the doctor and my caseworker isn't just an excuse to dump me off down there because I've been giving you a hard time and you found that damned old joint in my coat?"

Ben opened his mouth. Matt beat him to the punch. "I know. I know. I owe you a buck."

Ben's smile disappeared as quickly as it had come. He looked down at his hands where they rested on the table, then back up, straight into Matt's eyes.

Here it comes. Matt braced himself for the words.

"I've told you the truth all along, Matt. We're going back because your surgeon and your caseworker want to see you one more time, that's all. I'll never lie to you."

"Does that mean I can stay?"

"You're welcome to stay here as long as you like." Ben held out his hand. Matt took it, a big silly grin splitting his face from ear to ear.

"I...I want this to be my home."

"I think we'll be able to manage that. We'll start the ball rolling on a permanent arrangement when we see your caseworker in Columbus next week."

Permanent. He liked the sound of that. "Okay," he said. It was all he could manage without starting to bawl like a little kid.

"It's settled then." Ben gave his hand another pump, then let it go. "Matt, I might as well tell you. My medical leave of absence with the patrol will be up in a couple of months. I don't want to go back to Columbus any more than you do. I have some money saved up and it's pretty cheap rent living out here. But I don't exactly know where I'm going in my life right now."

"What about Ellie?" Matt blurted out. "You love her, don't you?" *God. What was he trying to do? Get himself kicked out of Ben's life for certain less than thirty seconds after he'd been invited into it?*

"What the hell?"

"I've got eyes in my head." Matt hoped he sounded a lot more sure of himself than he was. Ben was his family now. He was going to do what he thought was best for him. "I think..." *Bite the bullet, man!* "I know you love Ellie Lawrence and her kids. Don't you think it's time you let them know, too?"

CHAPTER SIXTEEN

ELLIE TOUCHED the baby-doll-size fist curled on her breast with the tip of her finger. Merry Christine Lawrence had been suckling greedily for ten minutes, her tiny red face screwed into an intense frown of concentration, and then between one breath and the next her daughter had fallen asleep at her breast.

Nine hours old and already eating like a little pig. Ellie closed her eyes on a prayer of thanksgiving. Surely that was a sign that the baby was as healthy and perfect as the doctor had assured her she was, despite the trauma of her birth.

Nine hours old. And except for Spock sleeping in front of the stove and Muffin curled on the bookshelf, they were finally alone together for the first time. Ellie unwrapped the fleecy blanket and drank her fill of her precious little girl. She was small, just a few ounces over six pounds. Carly and Tim had both weighed nearly eight. And she was bald as a billiard ball, as Eldor had so bluntly put it when he stopped by to invite Carly and Tim to the Jack Pine for a pancake breakfast a half hour ago.

She was bald, but Ellie didn't care. She had ten fingers and ten toes and she was beautiful when she looked up at you with intensely blue eyes that didn't look as if they were going to turn brown like her older brother's and sister's. Merry's eyes were the same blue as Patty Lawrence's, a legacy, a reminder of the friend she'd lost when Lonny's mother died.

Merry frowned in her sleep, clearly not happy to be exposed to the cool morning air. Ellie rewrapped her in the green-and-peach-striped blanket, glad she hadn't given in to the temptation to buy all blue things for the boy she'd been expecting, and rearranged her own clothes. Smiling as she buttoned her shirt, a real shirt, not an oversize maternity top. She was stiff and sore and very, very tired, a little dizzy, and light-headed, but that was as much from lack of sleep as the aftereffects of childbirth. And she was in her own home. When she felt like it she could lie down on her own bed, and that made up for all the physical discomfort in the world.

Dr. Makowski hadn't been pleased to release her immediately after he'd checked her and the baby out in the wee small hours of the morning, but she had been adamant. She didn't relish spending Christmas Eve and Christmas Day in a hospital room. And since he could find nothing wrong with Merry Christine, despite how long it had taken her to start breathing, he'd let them go, with the stipulation that they both be back in his office for a checkup on the day after Christmas—and that Ben MacAllister also stop by so he could congratulate him on a job well done.

Ellie had promised to pass along the obstetrician's message, but she wasn't altogether certain when she would see Ben again, herself. There was no mistaking the look she'd seen in his eyes when Lonny swept her into his arms and out the door last night.

Her heart squeezed tight with painful longing, with the need to go to him, to be with him.

"Hey, where do you keep the coffee, darlin'?"

Lonny came out of the kitchen. He was wearing a white T-shirt and jeans, and his impractical cowboy boots. She moved her legs and made room for him beside her on the couch.

"I thought I'd make some breakfast," he said.

"That's okay. I'm not really hungry."

"Good. I'm not much of a cook."

He looked out the window, but it was frosted over in an intricate pattern of whirls and spirals, and there was nothing to see but the brightness of sunlight reflected off ice and snow. "God, I hate winter." When Ellie didn't answer, he changed the subject. "Is she asleep?"

Ellie had turned the baby over on her stomach, supporting her with one hand on her chest, patting her on the back with the other to dislodge any air bubbles in her tummy. "Uh-huh. Sound asleep."

"You should be taking advantage of her nap. Get a little shut-eye, yourself."

"I'm too excited to sleep," Ellie said, brushing a strand of hair behind her ear. "It's Christmas Eve day."

"You always did get carried away with Christmas." He reached out and touched the baby's cheek with the tip of one callused finger.

Ellie smiled. "I love Christmas."

"Are you really going to name this little one Merry Christine?"

"Carly would be heartbroken if *I* didn't." His head came up. He had heard her slight emphasis on the word. "She's the one who picked out the name," she reminded him.

"I suppose it could be worse."

"Yes. At first she insisted on Merry Christmas." Ellie looked down at the sleeping infant. "Everyone will spell it wrong," she conceded. "It would be better to put Mary Christine on the birth certificate."

"Oh, hell, don't worry about what the fuddy-duddies will think. If you want to call her Merry, go ahead. Do it."

"Okay. I will." She looked up at him and smiled. "She's a beautiful baby, Lonny."

"You always do good work, El." He reached up and touched her cheek with the same callused finger that he had used to stroke Merry's. "It's all over between us, isn't it, El?"

"I'm sorry, Lonny—"

"Is it because..." He dropped his hand to stroke Merry's bald, pink head. "Is it because I suggested that we let my boss...adopt the baby?"

Buy our baby. A pang of swift, pure anger pierced Ellie's heart, but she ignored it as much as she could. He was Carly and Tim's father. He had been her first love. He had given her Merry, as well. She couldn't afford to indulge in a bout of righteous indignation, no matter how much she might want to.

She could forgive. But she didn't think she could ever forget.

"No, Lonny," she said, bending the truth only a little. "It was over long before that."

"This little darlin' was nothing but a mistake." He looked up at her, and she saw real regret in his dark brown eyes, eyes so like Tim's, a smile so like Carly's.

She covered his hand with hers. "Trying to make a go of our marriage again was a mistake. Merry's a miracle. A gift from God. Don't ever think otherwise."

The door opened and Carly and Tim tumbled into the cottage, stopping as soon as they were inside the door, shushing each other in loud theatrical whispers.

"Be quiet. Don't wake the baby."

"Don't tell me to be quiet, you be quiet."

"Mom!"

"Whiny girl!"

"Hush, you barbarians," Ellie said. "Can't you see your baby sister's asleep?"

In the blink of an eye, Tim and Carly were hanging over the back of the couch.

"Can I hold her?"

"She's asleep, stupid."

"Shh," Ellie warned. "Yes, you can hold her. A little later. How was breakfast?"

"Mrs. Eldor doesn't make pancakes as good as you do, Mom."

"My egg was hard. I couldn't dip my toast in it, but I ate it, anyway. But guess what? Ben and Matt are over there. Can we invite them to come and see the baby?"

Ellie couldn't help herself. Her eyes flew past her children's rapt faces to the door. Ben was here, in North Star, at the Jack Pine. Would he come to see her, or would he stay away, separate, as alone as he'd been that first night, when he came out of the darkness to save them from the fire?

"So that's the way it is."

Lonny's words brought her back to a sense of self and place. She felt color flood her cheeks, saw her own longing and need for another man reflected in her ex-husband's eyes.

"I...I don't know, Lonny," she said, but they both knew she was lying.

"Well, I'd better get packed up."

"Packed?" She'd expected him to stay for Christmas.

He nodded, scratching his right ear, his eyes not quite meeting hers.

"Where are you going, Daddy?" Carly didn't seem upset by his announcement.

"Yeah, where are you going, Dad?"

Ellie ached for the pain those offhand queries must have caused him, but Lonny didn't act as if he minded.

"Think I'll take off and spend Christmas with your uncle Mark in Ann Arbor. If I leave now, I'll be there in time to eat Christmas Eve supper with them."

"But what about my present?" Carly squealed, then flashed a sheepish look at Ellie. "I mean. You can't go until you've opened your present from me."

Lonny stood up, held out his hand. "I'll tell you what. You run get your gift for me. But Santa's got your present from me. I sent it on up to the North Pole a long time ago. Just in case I didn't get to come back here for Christmas.''

"Okay." Carly danced over to the little tree on the table and began rooting through the gaily wrapped presents beneath it. "Come here, Tim. Help me find Daddy's presents."

"Ellie," Lonny whispered, spreading his hands in a helpless gesture. "I...I meant to go shopping today."

She smiled and whispered back. "Don't worry. I know how you hate to shop, Lonny Lawrence. I bought presents for both of them for you."

"You're one hell of a woman, Ellie. Thanks for not making them hate me."

"I would never do that, Lonny. You're their father. There will always be a place for you in their hearts."

"Yeah, well, it's more than I deserve." He leaned over and brushed her cheek with his lips, touched the baby with his fingertip once last time. "I'll send money, El. As often as I can."

"I know you will."

"So long. Merry Christmas."

"Merry Christmas, Lonny. And goodbye."

BEN HAD DECIDED to leave Riley in Eldor's kennel while he drove Matt to the Soo. It had been colder than he'd thought when they'd started out this morning, and he didn't want to leave the setter out in the pickup for a couple of hours while Matt shopped. Riley was still howling as Ben stepped out of the garage and closed the door behind him.

"MacAllister." The contrast between the interior of the garage and the brilliant sunlit morning had left Ben temporarily blind. He hadn't seen Lonny Lawrence until the man was right in front of him. "Didn't expect to see you this soon."

"'Morning, Lawrence. I didn't expect to see you, either." He figured he would still be at the hospital with Ellie. "Is everything okay with Ellie and the baby?"

"Right as rain." Lonny narrowed his dark eyes against the dazzling reflection of the sun off the snow, and watched Ben closely. "I owe you a debt of thanks for what you did for her last night."

"Ellie accomplished the miracle. I was just there to back her up."

"That's not what she said. Or the doc, either. You're a damned hero, MacAllister." There was a bitter twist to his words.

Ben didn't answer. He just stood there wondering what Lonny Lawrence was getting at. He didn't look as if he was angling for a fight, but he wasn't just making small talk, either. The man had everything Ben had ever wanted, yet instead of being with his wife and children he was standing in the parking lot of a bar, with a worn canvas duffel bag slung over one shoulder, looking like an out-of-place rodeo rider.

"It seems like I owe you a hell of a lot," Lonny said. He looked over his shoulder in the direction of the little cottage.

"You don't owe me anything," Ben said sharply.

"Yeah, I do." Lonny exhaled through his mouth with a gusty sigh, his breath forming a smoky wreath around his head. "I'm no saint. But I'm not such a fool that I'm going to hang around here and watch you move in on my wife."

"I..."

"I don't want to hear you deny it, if you don't mind. I saw the look on her face when the kids came racing in the cabin to tell her you were over here at the Jack Pine."

"Ellie's here? She's not in the hospital?"

Lawrence's eyes narrowed once more and Ben realized he'd betrayed himself, as surely as if he'd declared his love for Ellie from the top of the Baptist church steeple.

"You've got a lot to learn about that woman. 'Course she's not in the hospital. Made the emergency squad people wait while Doc Makowski checked her and the little one out. Said she was not going to spend Christmas in a hospital room if she didn't have to."

Ben's heart was beating hard and fast. Ellie was here. In the cottage, only yards away.

"Ben!" Carly appeared in the cottage doorway, her honey brown ponytail swinging. "Are you finished with breakfast already?"

"I haven't been in the restaurant to order yet. I was putting Riley in the kennel."

"Well, hurry! My baby sister is awake. You have to see her." Her clear, lilting voice carried across the parking lot like sleigh bells. "She is the mostest adorable baby I've ever seen."

He lifted his hand. "In a minute, Carly." He didn't know the baby's name. He didn't know if she had one, but he was damned if he was going to ask the baby's father what it was.

"Where's Matt?" Carly demanded next.

"Eating breakfast."

"I have to get him. He hasn't even seen the baby at all yet." She raced across the parking lot, bare-headed, without her coat or gloves.

"Hey, missy. You get yourself a coat on," Lonny hollered. Two seconds later, Tim catapulted out of the doorway with Carly's coat in his hand.

"Girls," he grumbled, chasing across the parking lot after her.

"Well, I'd best be on my way."

Ben eyed the duffel once more. "You're leaving town?"

"Taking off as soon as I stop in and wish Eldor and Martha season's greetings, give my kids one more hug and kiss, and then I'm out of here. Spending Christmas with my brother and his family in Ann Arbor, then back to Louisiana."

"How many pancakes do you want, Ben? Mrs. Eldor wants to know. Matt says he's starving and to hurry up." Ben and Lonny both turned toward the sound of Carly's voice. This time she was standing in the Jack Pine kitchen doorway, yelling at the top of her lungs.

"Tell Mrs. Eldor to go ahead and fix Matt's breakfast," Ben told her. "I'll just have coffee."

"Well, okay. I'll tell her so Matt doesn't have to wait. But you need to eat a good breakfast, too, you know."

"I'll be damned, she sure is a handful. I think Carly's kind of sweet on that boy. She'll make his life miserable in ten years. She's going to be even prettier than her mama."

Lonny gave Ben one more long, hard stare, then made a sweeping gesture with his hand that took in the Jack Pine and the cottage, and for all Ben knew, included the whole of North Star and Lake Superior, as well. "If you can take on this crew and not go stark, roaring mad doing it, you have my blessing." Lonny held out his hand. Ben took it automatically. Lonny shook it once, then loosened his grip. "I guess this is where I say the best man won. But I'm sure as hell not that noble, damn it." Then he turned on his heel and walked away.

ELLIE CLOSED HER EYES and savored the moment of silence that followed the children's abrupt departure from the cottage. She was under no illusion that it would continue for long, but for now she was content to be alone with her baby daughter.

At peace with the world and with herself now that she had made her break with Lonny Lawrence. Content. As long as she didn't allow her thoughts to stray from the sweet-smelling infant in her arms to the man who had brought the child safely into the world.

Where was Ben?

She knew he was nearby, but why hadn't he come to see her and Merry Christine?

A soft knock on the door brought her musings to a quick end. Her eyes flew to the wooden panel as though she could see clear through to the man on the other side, gauge his mood and his intentions. Her pulse danced in her throat where Merry's velvet-soft nose nestled against her. She straightened the afghan over her knees, lifted her hand to her hair, dismayed to find flyaway tendrils escaping from the soft knot on top of her head.

"May I come in?"

Ben's voice, strong and low, cold-roughened. She smiled a little, chiding herself for her vanity. She dropped her hand from her hair. After all, he'd seen her looking far worse.

"The door's open, come on in."

"Hi."

"Hi." Merry stirred against her shoulder, her blue, blue eyes popping open, her small head turning instinctively to the sound of Ben's voice.

He stood stiffly at the far end of the sofa, his face shadowed, as it had been so often, by the deep hood of his parka. Ellie felt a small shiver of uneasiness skate down her spine, but ignored the unpleasant sensation. This was not the stranger who had come out of the darkness to save Spock from a burning building. This was not the man who kept himself locked away from life and loving, even if she had glimpsed those old ghosts staring out of his gray eyes last night.

This was Ben the caring, giving man who had brought her child safely into the world. Who had probably saved her life, as well. The man she had come to admire and respect. The man she had fallen in love with.

Maybe it was the familiar blue parka, the hood drawn up to shield the sensitive skin of his scarred cheek and temple from the bitter cold, that hid his features and his emotions just as effectively, that made her uneasy.

"Take off your coat," she said, the words tumbling out of her mouth before she could soften them.

Ben did as he was told, laying the heavy garment over the back of a chair. He didn't avoid her gaze, but his gray eyes were still shuttered, his emotions hidden away.

"How are you feeling, Ellie?"

"Sore and tired," she said, her tongue still working with a mind of its own. She felt color rise to her cheeks. "I mean, I'm fine. Just fine."

"You look sore and tired," he said, moving to stand beside her. With one smooth, controlled movement he dropped to his haunches, so that his face was level with hers. "You look like a woman who accomplished a miracle less than twelve hours ago."

"Thank you," she said, accepting his compliment. "You're right. I am tired and sore, but very, very happy."

"What did you name her?"

"Didn't anyone tell you her name?" A pang of regret squeezed Ellie's heart. "I'm sorry. I...don't know how that happened. It's just that there's been so much going on. I only called my parents an hour ago and—"

"Don't apologize, Ellie. You had other things on your mind."

She may have had other things on her mind, it was true, but Ben was never completely out of her thoughts day or night. And she knew in her heart that he never would be. "Ben MacAllister, meet Merry Christine Lawrence."

Ben repeated the baby's name, emphasizing the vowel. One dark eyebrow raised a fraction of an inch.

"Yes. Merry. M-E-R-R-Y," she said, spelling it out. "It was Carly's idea. I know it's going to cause confusion. Everyone will assume it's—"

"She's a Christmas baby. She deserves a special name." Ben reached out and touched Merry's cheek. She had been moving her head restlessly on Ellie's breast, but quieted suddenly, her unfocused blue eyes fixed on the sound of his voice.

"Yes. She is very special. Thank you, Ben. Thank you for everything you did last night."

"I was just—"

She reached up and pressed two fingers to his lips. "No," she said. "Don't try to deny it, or belittle it. I won't let you."

He met her gaze head-on. "You're welcome, Ellie Lawrence."

"I'm not Ellie Lawrence anymore." Once more a dark eyebrow raised a fraction of an inch. "I mean—" Her heart was beating high and fast in her throat, interfering with her breathing, with her thought processes. She took a deep breath and started over. Everything she wanted in life depended on what she said in the next few minutes. "What I meant to say is, Lonny's leaving town. For good. He's not coming back."

"I know."

"You know?" Merry was beginning to fuss again. Ellie jiggled her up and down, patting her back.

"He stopped me in the parking lot. Thanked me for helping you deliver Merry. Then he told me he was leaving town."

"Oh."

"Is that what you want from him, Ellie?" he asked.

"Yes." She was still breathing too fast, too lightly. She was getting dizzy. She took one, two, three slow deep breaths, felt her pulse rate slow and steady, inhaled the fragrance of baby powder, and Christmas tree, and the warm mixture of spice and soap and warm, male skin that was Ben's own heady scent.

"Are you sure?" He reached up to trace the curve of Merry's tiny fingers. His knuckle brushed Ellie's breast. She shivered with the sudden spark of heat that burned like fire through her veins. She felt him stiffen slightly and knew the sensual current had seared him, as well.

The knowledge gave her courage.

"Why are you asking me this?" she asked.

"Are you sure you're over him, Ellie?"

"I've been over him for a long time. But all of my past is tangled up with his. Some of my future will be, too, I can't get away from that. But he is just that, Ben. My past." Her hands were shaking. She suspected her voice was, too. She was in love with Ben MacAllister. She'd been falling in love with him little by little since the first time she saw him. But she'd been afraid of her own feelings, her own motivations. No more. She didn't need him to keep her safe, or rescue her from life's hard knocks. She needed him because he was the one man in the world for her. "I want something very different for my future."

"What is that?"

Ellie closed her eyes and stepped off into the void. "You," she said so softly the word was more sensation than sound.

"Ellie—"

"I want you, Ben MacAllister. But on my terms."

"Your terms?"

"My terms." She opened her eyes, looked deep into the thundercloud gray of his. "You asked me to marry you last night, Ben. Why?" She already knew the answer. Last night he had asked her to marry him to save her, to rescue her from her problems and her heartaches. She didn't want a white knight, a champion. She wanted all he had to give. She wanted the real man, body and soul, the bad with the good, and she wouldn't settle for anything less.

"Last night I asked you to marry me for all the wrong reasons."

"What?" It was as though he had read her mind. Ellie was patting Merry so hard the little one whimpered in distress. Ben reached up and laid his hand over hers and Merry quieted at once.

"I said, last night I asked you to marry me for all the wrong reasons. Today is a very different matter."

"Why is today so different?" She didn't dare let herself believe what she was seeing in his clear gray gaze.

"Today I'm a different man than I was last night."

"And you've changed your mind. You don't want to marry me."

"I've changed my mind."

Thirty seconds ago those words would have broken Ellie's heart, been a death knell to her hopes and dreams. But not now, not as long as she kept her eyes locked to his, not as long as she could once more see all the way to his soul.

"Why did you turn me down?" Ben's voice was gentle.

"Because you asked me for all the wrong reasons. And I wanted to say yes for all the wrong reasons. I wanted to change you, to heal you. But I knew deep down you could only do that for yourself. What happened, Ben?" She reached out and laid her fingers against his scarred cheek. "What took the darkness away?"

"You," he said simply, covering her hand with his. "Your courage and your determination. And Merry, this tiny Christmas miracle we brought into the world together." He smiled. "And a good hard talking-to from Matt."

"You and Matt?"

"He's going to stay with me, Ellie. We're both going to stay here, even though God only knows what I'm going to do with the rest of my life."

"You don't want to go back to being a law officer?"

He looked down at his hands, the scars that he would carry to his grave. Ellie knew the scars on his heart, on his soul, were every bit as deep. But faith and love could heal those scars, she believed that with all *her* heart and soul. "No, Ellie. I don't want to go back to the Patrol. But the truth is, I don't know what I want to do with my life."

"You'll find something, Ben. And whatever it is, you will be very, very good at doing it."

"You really believe that, don't you?"

"Of course I do."

He smiled then, and the full glory of it warmed Ellie like the heat from a thousand suns. "It's going to be a tight fit in the light keeper's house."

"Surely it's big enough for the two—"

"Not the two of us. The...let's see—" he began counting on his fingers "—the four, five, six of us." He touched Merry's hand and her lilliputian fingers curled tight around his. "Plus, Riley and Spock."

"And don't forget Muffin." Ellie tilted her head toward the bookcase where the cat was curled in a ball. *Later. Later she would get all the details. Learn what had passed between Ben and Matt. For now, it was enough to know the two had settled their differences, come to terms with the shared tragedy in their past.*

"And lots and lots of Santas. I'm asking you to marry me again, Ellie Lawrence. This time for all the right reasons. One—because I love your kids as if they were my own. Two—because I want us to grow old and gray together. Three and four and five and five thousand—because I love you more than life itself."

"And I love you, too."

She leaned into his embrace, and his kiss was warm and sweet and laced with a promise of passion that would last a lifetime.

"Merry Christmas, Ben," she said, and placed her daughter in his arms.

EPILOGUE

A year later...

"No, Matt. The tree's crooked. You have to go a little to the right," Carly directed from her perch on the back of the old leather sofa.

"That's your left hand, dummy." Tim emerged from beneath the seven-foot pine, with needles in his hair and a disgusted look on his face. "She means it needs to go to the left, Matt," he corrected, crawling back under the sweeping branches of the big tree. "Girls. They are like totally bogus."

"I am not. Mom!"

"Santa won't come if you're bad," Matt said, having perfected his role as big brother. "Elves are watching every move you make."

"They are not," Carly insisted.

"Want to take the chance?" Matt retorted.

Carly didn't have a reply to that one. She folded her arms over her chest and stuck out her lower lip far enough for an elf to perch on it.

Matt made adjustments to the trunk. "How's that, Carly?" he called, his voice muffled by pine boughs.

Her bad temper instantly forgotten, Carly bounced off the couch and studied the tree from all angles. "It's perfect," she declared. "It's just perfect."

The babble of voices in the big, combination kitchen–family room had registered only on the edges of Ben's consciousness. He flicked a wood shaving off the essay he was grading. *Grading term papers. Teaching.* Him, Ben MacAllister, a teacher. A year ago, he would have never thought it possible. But a year ago, nothing seemed possible. Since then, with Ellie's encompassing love and unwavering support, he'd banished most of his demons. Because of Ellie, he'd opened himself up to life, come to terms with the past and embraced the future.

It was Lars Larson who had suggested the possibility of a teaching position last summer. Lars sat on the board of the local community college and with the projected opening of two new prisons in the Upper Peninsula in the next five years, enrollment in the school's law enforcement and corrections programs had almost doubled. They needed someone to teach an introductory course on criminal justice and firearms, Lars had said. He wanted Ben to apply. Ben had been reluctant, but Ellie had urged him on. To his amazement, he'd been hired and, even more amazing, he found he was good at the job. And he liked it. In the spring, he'd be enrolling at Lake Superior State in Sault Ste. Marie as a student himself, to gather the extra credits he'd need to teach full-time.

It was going to be tough going, financially, for the next couple of years. But Ellie had been behind him one hundred percent. Her carvings were bringing in a surprising amount of money. She had outlets for her Santas in three states, and more orders than she could fill. Farley Tall Trees had returned from Florida with the spring thaw with his new wife, who was not as rich as people feared, and a great deal friendlier than anyone had hoped. Jackson Tall Trees had decided to see Florida for himself and Farley had reclaimed the cottage and his job in the Jack Pine kitchen. Ellie helped him part-time, as much for the chance to be out and about among her friends and neighbors as for the money.

They were buying the lighthouse from Eldor on a land contract, a sweetheart deal, Ellie called it, but Martha and Eldor, with no children of their own, wanted the property to stay in the family, and were well satisfied with the arrangements.

Over the summer, Ben and Matt had remodeled the two big, drafty upstairs rooms into three smaller bedrooms and a bathroom, rewired, added insulation and storm windows, and put in a propane furnace, although most of the time they still heated the place with the reliable old woodstove by the window.

Living in an eighty-year-old lighthouse had its drawbacks. The television reception was still lousy. It was a fifteen-minute drive, one way, into town if you ran out of bread or milk. The tourists and the black-flies were all over the place in the summer. But the view of the lake freighters slipping past the kitchen window as you drank your morning coffee, watching the northern lights from the top of the light tower, wrapped in thick blankets with a kid on either side, on cold March nights, long walks along the beach in the lingering twilight of an August afternoon, more than made up for all those inconveniences.

"Ben! Help! I swear I'm cursed. These lights are brand-new. I just took them out of the package, and I'm still all tangled up in them. Look at me."

Ben raised his head, surprised to find Ellie perched on the worn leather couch, laughing with embarrassment and frustration. The last time he'd looked, his wife had been sitting beside him at the kitchen table, carving. Now she was indeed in a bind, strings of tiny multicolored lights draped over her shoulders and arms and puddled at her feet. She held out her hands in a supplicating gesture. "Help!"

"Hmm? I didn't know you were into that kinky stuff."

"Ben!" She shot a quick glance in the direction of the tree-trimming trio, color rushing to her cheeks. "Don't be ridiculous."

"*Ridiculous* is not the word I was thinking of." He twirled the edges of an imaginary mustache. "It might be interesting to re-create this little scene later tonight. When we're alone."

She colored more deeply, but her glorious, green-gold eyes met his with a twinkling challenge. "On second thought, there might be possibilities in—"

The phone rang.

Merry Christine woke from her nap and began rattling the sides of her playpen.

Matt and Tim called for another string of lights and Carly tripped over Riley in her haste to supply their request. Riley howled in protest. Spock, wakened from a nap, barked her complaint. Only Muffin, above the fray, figuratively and literally, on top of the refrigerator, didn't even twitch a whisker.

A typical Saturday at Chippewa Point.

"I'll get Merry," Ben said, rising from the table.

"I'll get the phone," Matt hollered. "It's probably for me, anyway."

"It's always for you," Tim grumbled.

"Can I help it the chicks think I'm a stud?" Matt said, wiggling out from under the tree.

The teenager had matured over the last year. He'd settled down well and applied himself in school. It was even possible, he'd told Ben and Ellie the night before at the dinner table, that he was in danger of making the honor roll this quarter. He'd put on weight, and added another two inches in height. His hair was shorter, just touching his collar, in compliance with his football coach's edict. But so that no one got the idea that he was becoming too establishment, he now sported two earrings—in each ear.

"Stud. That's a good one," Tim scoffed.

"I'll untangle you from the lights, Mom," Carly offered, unwinding a loop from her mother's arm. "We need them for the tree."

Ben reached into the playpen and scooped Merry Christine into his arms. "Hi, sweetie. Did you have a good nap?" he asked the toddler. Her fine brown hair, what there was of it, stood up in wispy curls. Her blue eyes sparkled with intelligence and mischief.

"Da-Da."

Ben was convinced that was the most beautiful word in the language. He wrapped his arms around her sturdy little body and inhaled her sweet, milky fragrance. "Give Daddy a kiss, baby."

Merry obeyed with joyful enthusiasm then wiggled to be set free. "Down," she demanded. She'd started walking on Thanksgiving Day, and now there was no stopping her. She curled her fingers around Ben's thumb until she got her balance, then took off like a shot for the Christmas tree. Halfway across the room, she toddled to a halt, swaying a little on her feet. "Da-Da!" She swiveled her head to bring Ben into view. One chubby little finger pointed directly at Ellie. "Mama. Pretty." Then with lightning speed she headed toward the boxes of Christmas-tree ornaments sitting on the floor, arms outstretched. "Mine." She giggled at the top of her voice. "Mine."

"She just said every word she knows," Carly marveled. "All at once." She dropped the coils of lights she'd removed from Ellie's lap and sprinted off to intercept her sister.

"Ellie," Matt said. Ben had the suspicion it wasn't the first time he'd tried to get Ellie's attention. "The call's for you. It's Lonny. He's calling collect. From Mexico. Want me to accept the charges?"

Ellie rolled her eyes in Ben's direction. "Mexico!" She threw up her hands. "It's okay, Matt. Tell the operator we'll take the call." She draped the last of the serpentine light strings over the arm of the couch and held out her hand for the receiver. "Hello, Lonny. Thank you. Merry Christmas to you. And to Barbara Jo, too." Barbara Jo was the new woman in Lonny's life. But Mexico? Nothing had been mentioned about Lonny spending Christmas in Mexico. "Yes, the kids are here," Ellie went on. "Carly. It's your father. He wants to wish you a Merry Christmas."

Carly handed the baby to Tim who had just crawled out from under the tree. She began talking excitedly to her absent father about the absolutely beautiful doll that had arrived in the mail just the day before. "I couldn't wait to open it. She's gorgeous."

Ellie crossed the room to slip her arm around Ben's waist. "It's a good thing Lonny's caught up on his child support or I wouldn't have been nearly as gracious about accepting a collect call from Cancún, of all places."

Ben smiled at her. His days of being jealous of Lonny Lawrence were far in the past. "I imagine Barbara Jo had something to do with that."

Ellie laid her head on his shoulder. "Yes, and she probably bought the presents for the kids. I wonder how old she is?"

"Does it matter?"

She tilted her head so that their eyes met, then smiled a little sheepishly. "No, it doesn't matter. It's none of my business, but I'll bet she's much too young and skinny for him."

Ben dropped a kiss on the top of her head. "I like my women with a little meat on their bones."

"If by that you mean the five pounds I haven't lost from being pregnant with Merry, just give me time. I'll start a diet—"

"I said I like you just the way you are. End of subject."

"Thank you, kind sir," she said, and squeezed him tight.

Tim was talking to his father now, thanking him for the electronic football game he'd sent. Merry's gift was a stuffed pink elephant which frightened her and made her run crying into Ben's arms, so it had been relegated to a shelf in the closet until she was older.

Ben stood quietly, listening to Tim talk to his father, a man he hadn't seen for over a year, a man who was fifteen hundred miles away. Only Merry called him Daddy, it was true, but he didn't care. He was the one that Tim came to when he had problems with his math. He was the one that Carly baked cupcakes for, and colored pictures for that she signed, "Love and Kisses, Carly." Not Lonny Lawrence.

Ellie turned in his arms. "I think I'd better cut this short. If I don't, our phone bill will cost us as much as a Christmas trip to Cancún."

"Good idea," he whispered in her ear. "It's getting late and I want to get to bed. I can't get the idea of you all wrapped up in Christmas lights and nothing else out of my head."

"We can't go to bed until the tree is up."

"Then hurry up and say goodbye."

"I said goodbye to Lonny a long time ago. But I'll wish him a Merry Christmas and then we'll trim the tree." She smiled up into his eyes, that special smile she saved for him alone, the one that said. *I love you. When we're alone, I'll show you just how much.* Ben reached out to pull her back in his arms, seal that silent vow with a kiss—

"Ben! Help me. Merry's eating the tinsel," Carly squealed.

"Da-Da!"

"Go on," Ellie urged, giving him a quick kiss and a little push.

They would have the night. And all the nights for the rest of their lives. He could wait.

"Come to Daddy, sweetheart," he said, and swept their Christmas miracle into the safety of his arms.

FREE VALENTINE'S BROOCH!
$9.95 U.S. retail value

This Valentine's Day Harlequin brings you all the essentials—romance, chocolate and jewelry—in:

VALENTINE *Delights*

Matchmaking chocolate-shop owner Papa Valentine dispenses sinful desserts, mouth-watering chocolates...and advice to the lovelorn, in this collection of three delightfully romantic stories by Meryl Sawyer, Kate Hoffmann and Gina Wilkins.

As our special Valentine's Day gift to you, each copy of *Valentine Delights* will have a beautiful, filigreed, heart-shaped brooch attached to the cover.

Make this your most delicious Valentine's Day ever with *Valentine Delights!*

Available in February wherever Harlequin books are sold.

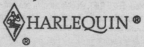

HARLEQUIN ®
®

Free Gift Offer

With a Free Gift proof-of-purchase
from any Harlequin® book, you can receive
a beautiful cubic zirconia pendant.

This stunning marquise-shaped stone is a genuine cubic
zirconia—accented by an 18" gold tone necklace.
(Approximate retail value $19.95)

Send for yours today...
compliments of ◆HARLEQUIN®

To receive your free gift, a cubic zirconia pendant, send us one original proof-of-purchase, photocopies not accepted, from the back of any Harlequin Romance®, Harlequin Presents®, Harlequin Temptation®, Harlequin Superromance®, Harlequin Intrigue®, Harlequin American Romance®, or Harlequin Historicals® title available in August, September or October at your favorite retail outlet, together with the Free Gift Certificate, plus a check or money order for $1.65 U.S./$2.15 CAN. (do not send cash) to cover postage and handling, payable to Harlequin Free Gift Offer. We will send you the specified gift. Allow 6 to 8 weeks for delivery. Offer good until December 31, 1996, or while quantities last. Offer valid in the U.S. and Canada only.

Free Gift Certificate

Name: _____

Address: _____

City: _____ State/Province: _____ Zip/Postal Code: _____

Mail this certificate, one proof-of-purchase and a check or money order for postage and handling to: HARLEQUIN FREE GIFT OFFER 1996. In the U.S.: 3010 Walden Avenue, P.O. Box 9071, Buffalo NY 14269-9057. In Canada: P.O. Box 604, Fort Erie, Ontario L2Z 5X3.

FREE GIFT OFFER   084-KMFR

ONE PROOF-OF-PURCHASE
To collect your fabulous FREE GIFT, a cubic zirconia pendant, you must include this original proof-of-purchase for each gift with the properly completed Free Gift Certificate.

084-KMFR

INSTANT WIN 4229 SWEEPSTAKES
OFFICIAL RULES

1. NO PURCHASE NECESSARY. YOU ARE DEFINITELY A WINNER. For eligibility, play your instant win ticket and claim your prize as per instructions contained thereon. If your "Instant Win" ticket is missing or you wish another, send a self-addressed, stamped envelope (WA residents need not affix return postage) to: Instant Win 4229 Ticket, P.O. Box 9045, Buffalo, NY 14269-9045 in the U.S., and in Canada, P.O. Box 609, Fort Erie, Ontario, L2A 5X3. Only one (1) "Instant Win" ticket will be sent per outer mailing envelope. Requests received after 12/30/96 will not be honored.

2. Prize claims received after 1/15/97 will be deemed ineligible and will not be fulfilled. The exact prize value of each Instant Win ticket will be determined by comparing returned tickets with a prize value distribution list that has been preselected at random by computer. Prizes are valued in U.S. currency. For each one million, or part thereof, tickets distributed, the following prizes will be made available: 1 at $2,500 cash; 1 at $1,000 cash; 3 at $250 cash each; 5 at $50 cash each; 10 at $25 cash each; 1,000 at $1 cash each; and the balance at 50¢ cash each. Unclaimed prizes will not be awarded.

3. Winner claims are subject to verification by D. L. Blair, Inc., an independent judging organization whose decisions on all matters relating to this sweepstakes are final. Any returned tickets that are mutilated, tampered with, illegible or contain printing or other errors will be deemed automatically void. No responsibility is assumed for lost, late, nondelivered or misdirected mail. Taxes are the sole responsibility of winners. Limit: One (1) prize to a family, household or organization.

4. Offer open only to residents of the U.S. and Canada, 18 years of age or older, except employees of Harlequin Enterprises Limited, D. L. Blair, Inc., their agents and members of their immediate families. All federal, state, provincial, municipal and local laws apply. Offer void in Puerto Rico, the province of Quebec and wherever prohibited by law. All winners will receive their prize by mail. Taxes and/or duties are the sole responsibility of the winners. No substitution for prizes permitted. Major prize winners may be asked to sign and return an Affidavit of Eligibility within 30 days of notification. Noncompliance within this time or return of affidavit as undeliverable may result in disqualification, and prize may never be awarded. By acceptance of a prize, winners consent to the use of their names, photographs or other likeness for purposes of advertising, trade and promotion on behalf of Harlequin Enterprises Limited, without further compensation, unless prohibited by law. In order to win a prize, residents of Canada will be required to correctly answer a time-limited arithmetical skill-testing question to be administered by mail.

5. For a list of major prize winners (available after 2/14/97), send a self-addressed, stamped envelope to: "Instant Win 4229 Sweepstakes" Major Prize Winners, P.O. Box 4200, Blair, NE 68009-4200, U.S.A.

MILLION DOLLAR SWEEPSTAKES
OFFICIAL RULES
NO PURCHASE NECESSARY TO ENTER

1. To enter, follow the directions published. Method of entry may vary. For eligibility, entries must be received no later than March 31, 1998. No liability is assumed for printing errors, lost, late, non-delivered or misdirected entries.

   To determine winners, the sweepstakes numbers assigned to submitted entries will be compared against a list of randomly, preselected prize winning numbers. In the event all prizes are not claimed via the return of prize winning numbers, random drawings will be held from among all other entries received to award unclaimed prizes.

2. Prize winners will be determined no later than June 30, 1998. Selection of winning numbers and random drawings are under the supervision of D. L. Blair, Inc., an independent judging organization whose decisions are final. Limit: one prize to a family or organization. No substitution will be made for any prize, except as offered. Taxes and duties on all prizes are the sole responsibility of winners. Winners will be notified by mail. Odds of winning are determined by the number of eligible entries distributed and received.

SWP-H12CFR

3. Sweepstakes open to residents of the U.S. (except Puerto Rico), Canada and Europe who are 18 years of age or older, except employees and immediate family members of Torstar Corp., D. L. Blair, Inc., their affiliates, subsidiaries, and all other agencies, entities, and persons connected with the use, marketing or conduct of this sweepstakes. All applicable laws and regulations apply. Sweepstakes offer void wherever prohibited by law. Any litigation within the province of Quebec respecting the conduct and awarding of a prize in this sweepstakes must be submitted to the Régie des alcools, des courses et des jeux. In order to win a prize, residents of Canada will be required to correctly answer a time-limited arithmetical skill-testing question to be administered by mail.

4. Winners of major prizes (Grand through Fourth) will be obligated to sign and return an Affidavit of Eligibility and Release of Liability within 30 days of notification. In the event of non-compliance within this time period or if a prize is returned as undeliverable, D. L. Blair, Inc. may at its sole discretion, award that prize to an alternate winner. By acceptance of their prize, winners consent to use of their names, photographs or other likeness for purposes of advertising, trade and promotion on behalf of Torstar Corp., its affiliates and subsidiaries, without further compensation unless prohibited by law. Torstar Corp. and D. L. Blair, Inc., their affiliates and subsidiaries are not responsible for errors in printing of sweepstakes and prize winning numbers. In the event a duplication of a prize winning number occurs, a random drawing will be held from among all entries received with that prize winning number to award that prize.

5. This sweepstakes is presented by Torstar Corp., its subsidiaries and affiliates in conjunction with book, merchandise and/or product offerings. The number of prizes to be awarded and their value are as follows: Grand Prize — $1,000,000 (payable at $33,333.33 a year for 30 years); First Prize — $50,000; Second Prize — $10,000; Third Prize — $5,000; 3 Fourth Prizes — $1,000 each; 10 Fifth Prizes — $250 each; 1,000 Sixth Prizes — $10 each. Values of all prizes are in U.S. currency. Prizes in each level will be presented in different creative executions, including various currencies, vehicles, merchandise and travel. Any presentation of a prize level in a currency other than U.S. currency represents an approximate equivalent to the U.S. currency price for that level, at that time. Prize winners will have the opportunity of selecting any prize offered for that level; however, the actual non U.S. currency equivalent prize if offered and selected, shall be awarded at the exchange rate existing at 3:00 P.M. New York time on March 31, 1998. A travel prize option, if offered and selected by winner, must be completed within 12 months of selection and is subject to: traveling companion(s) completing and returning of a Release of Liability prior to travel; and hotel and flight accommodations availability. For a current list of all prize options offered within prize levels, send a self-addressed, stamped envelope (WA residents need not affix postage) to: MILLION DOLLAR SWEEPSTAKES Prize Options, P.O. Box 4456, Blair, NE 68009-4456, USA.

6. For a list of prize winners (available after July 31, 1998) send a separate, stamped, self-addressed envelope to: MILLION DOLLAR SWEEPSTAKES Winners, P.O. Box 4459, Blair, NE 68009-4459, USA.

EXTRA BONUS PRIZE DRAWING
NO PURCHASE OR OBLIGATION NECESSARY TO ENTER

7. The Extra Bonus Prize will be awarded in a random drawing to be conducted no later than 5/30/98 from among all entries received. To qualify, entries must be received by 3/31/98 and comply with published directions. Prize ($50,000) is valued in U.S. currency. Prize will be presented in different creative expressions, including various currencies, vehicles, merchandise and travel. Any presentation in a currency other than U.S. currency represents an approximate equivalent to the U.S. currency value at that time. Prize winner will have the opportunity of selecting any prize offered in any presentation of the Extra Bonus Prize Drawing; however, the actual non U.S. currency equivalent prize, if offered and selected by winner, shall be awarded at the exchange rate existing at 3:00 P.M. New York time on March 31, 1998. For a current list of prize options offered, send a self-addressed, stamped envelope (WA residents need not affix postage) to: Extra Bonus Prize Options, P.O. Box 4462, Blair, NE 68009-4462, USA. All eligibility requirements and restrictions of the MILLION DOLLAR SWEEPSTAKES apply. Odds of winning are dependent upon number of eligible entries received. No substitution for prize except as offered. For the name of winner (available after 7/31/98), send a self-addressed, stamped envelope to: Extra Bonus Prize Winner, P.O. Box 4463, Blair, NE 68009-4463, USA.

Ring in the New Year with babies, families and romance!

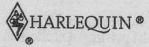

You're About to Become a *Privileged Woman*

Reap the rewards of fabulous free gifts and benefits with proofs-of-purchase from Harlequin and Silhouette books

Pages & Privileges™

It's our way of thanking you for buying our books at your favorite retail stores.

✂

```
┌─ ─ ─ ─ ─ ─ ─ ─ ─ ─ ─ ┐
   📖  PROOF OF    HS-PP20
          PURCHASE
   Offer expires March 31, 1997
└─ ─ ─ ─ ─ ─ ─ ─ ─ ─ ─ ┘
```

Harlequin and Silhouette—
the most privileged readers in the world!

For more information about Harlequin and Silhouette's PAGES & PRIVILEGES program call the Pages & Privileges Benefits Desk: 1-503-794-2499

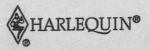

HARLEQUIN®

HS-PP20